THE ALPHA WOLF

The Alpha Wolf is an essential read for women who want to know if it is possible for their men to change from immature lads into mature men. As the book illustrates, it won't be a simple or easy journey, but it is worthwhile. The bumpy ride Roger makes from career orientated selfish user of humanity, to a caring and considerate human being is pertinent to us all. The skills he learns and shares along the way are relevant to both women and men. A funny and moving 'male tale' to accompany your 'chick lit'.
Alice Grist, author of *The High Heeled Guide to Enl*   *nment*

In his book *The Alpha Wolf*, Professor   sks a question of timeless importance: 'H   vith true masculinity and its essenti   ar that he has also lived the question   raordinary ways, making this more tha   ok, but a pure expression of the search for th   entic answer. You'll discover insights, reflections and a   wisdom on every page.
Anaiya Sophia, author of *Womb Wisdom* and *Sacred Sexual Union*

A funny, educational tale, and just what young and older men need to read to help them along their life journey. Full of instructive stories about the good and bad times. How men can have more by possessing less and by really being with other men.
Rose Rouse, Mother to a son, Writer, journalist, PR

The Alpha Wolf is the story of a man's awakening from being totally self-centred to growing in compassionate awareness. A journey of someone in rigid control of his life, a seeker after casual sex, a user and discarder of others, to the realization of an aching emptiness that was not being touched by his materialistic life. Nick Clements builds a picture that draws you in to the story and leads you on to find out what happens to this misogynistic, arrogant young man as he grows and matures. He crafts the tale well leading to the inevitable crack-up and the reassessment of his life. It is a strong story of the redemption of the worst type of 'masculinity.' In the final part of the book, Nick gives the tools for life reassessment, 'The Practice,' that he has used and taught for many years. These are wise words that ground the story in a useful and integrative practice for body, mind and spirit.

Revd Don MacGregor, Interfaith Officer, St David's Diocese, Fishguard

Nick Clements writes out of a natural knowing, born of years of experience of deep soul reality. He also has an ability to self-reflect that allows him to turn that experience into a story that concerns all of us and relates to where we are going at this time of change and transparency. He is in all senses a 'reliable narrator'.

Jay Ramsay, Poet, Psychotherapist and Healer

Nick has penned a real break-through book on masculinity. I love his style and verve, this is a must read for anyone investigating the role of masculinity in today's confusing world. It is not easy to find mentors such as Nick and I urge men and women to take the time to read the book.

Mel Carlile, CEO Mindbodyspirit Festival, London

The Alpha Wolf

A tale of the Modern Male

The Alpha
Wolf

A tale of the Modern Male

Nick Clements

Winchester, UK
Washington, USA

First published by Roundfire Books, 2013
Roundfire Books is an imprint of John Hunt Publishing Ltd., Laurel House, Station Approach,
Alresford, Hants, SO24 9JH, UK
office1@jhpbooks.net
www.johnhuntpublishing.com
www.roundfire-books.com

For distributor details and how to order please visit the 'Ordering' section on our website.

Text copyright: Nick Clements 2012

ISBN: 978 1 78099 504 5

A CIP catalogue record for this book is available from the British Library.

Design: Stuart Davies

Printed and bound by CPI Group (UK) Ltd, Croydon, CR0 4YY

We operate a distinctive and ethical publishing philosophy in all
areas of our business, from our global network of authors to
production and worldwide distribution.

CONTENTS

Acknowledgements

I owe a debt of gratitude to my father and mother. I acknowledge how much I have learnt from you and continue to learn from you even when you are not here. You remain with me at all times. Rob, my brother, thank you for teaching me how to observe nature, long may you watch birds and enjoy life. Tom and Anna, my two children. You have been my teachers since you were born, I have learnt so much from you. You make me so proud. Blessings to Vanessa for believing in me, loving me, and making my life so full of joy, you have helped me so much.

Thanks to Kevan Mainwaring for your help and assistance at the beginning of the crafting process. I'd like to honour the input of Steve Fedor for your advice and ideas about the characters. Thanks to Herewood, William, and Bear for supporting the principles and concepts, and for being my friends. Thanks to Chris Brooks for telling me the story of the bison, it has changed a little, but it is still very worthwhile. To Biddy, Nikki and Anna, thank you for your advice and guidance in the early stages. Special thanks to Sam Bloomfield for your vigilance and imagination in the creation of this work.

I owe a debt to Robert Light whose writings I have included, and who generously allowed me to include some details of his work and life. He can be contacted at: www.moonstone-therapies.co.uk

I owe a debt to all the men from the different men's groups I have worked with and known over the last 30 years. I admire you. I bless your diverse and wonderfully unique journeys.

I absolutely don't know what I'm doing, but I will try anyway.

The male path to maturation

'In the West you don't understand how a man can become mature. How it is to have depth. We know the pursuit of this is very important. It is our main priority in life. Instead, you spend your time chasing material goods that don't make you happy. This pursuit leaves you shallow. As a consequence you grow up either timid and fearful, or bullying and tyrannical. You are unstirred by responsibility and don't reach greatness. Here, in these lands, we observe our brothers and teachers, the wolf clan. Man's path to maturation follows that of a wolf very closely. Listen and you might learn something.'

Tsao Chinem Cllens

Chapter One

Begging for enlightenment

The score so far:
Roger: 22 years.   The world: 1992.

'What do you mean, you thought it looked better that way?'

The veins in Roger's neck bulged as he glared at his assistant.

'I thought the image was...more attractive.' Malcolm responded with eyes caste down.

'Malcolm, we don't pay you to think, we pay you to do.' Roger felt exasperated.

He continued, 'The campaign is retro, it's about feel-good, it's about ideal family values. Get with the programme.'

Roger turned away in disgust.

'I want that image in black and white on my desk in 30 minutes.'

Malcolm opened his mouth to speak.

'No excuses.'

Roger strode away from the desk, enjoying the feeling of power. He rode the wave of anger silently coming from Malcolm.

The score so far:
Roger: One   Malcolm: Nil

That night Roger towed his suitcase up the familiar Underground passageway, trying to get home as quickly as possible. He was wearing the Gieves No. 1 Saville Row, his best suit.

It was late, and the grimy tunnel reverberated to the sound of busy people going to busy places, mingled with loud laughter and jeers from a group of young men somewhere up ahead of him. The stained, grey ceramic-tiled walls, dimly lit, smelling of sweat and dust were just like so many other London Underground passageways. No one could want to loiter here, no one could call this home. For Roger home was just a few hundred yards away.

He strode purposefully, he was mentally checking his itinerary for the next day, he needed to arrive in good time, probably nine...

WALLOP.

As he hurriedly turned a corner he was sent flying.

Roger fell hard and sharp.

Pain rushed in from his hands and knees. He quickly looked up to see if anyone had noticed his embarrassment - far ahead the same gang of lads were singing to themselves, no one else was around.

He tried to compose himself, he tried to get up. Lying on the floor with him was a beggar, their two bodies now almost wrapped together in an embrace. Roger realized his nostrils were beginning to sting with the acrid smell of piss.

He saw up close the vacant, red-rimmed eyes, the puffy face, the drooling lips and dishevelled hair of this mumbling man. Roger felt humiliated to be on the same level as this noxious person. He tried to spring to his feet, but wobbled, staggered up, pains in his knees, palms scuffed.

'What...! Why the fuck did you do that?' He felt the blood rushing to his face, his anger rising.

The beggar looked up at him and said, 'I was trying to pick myself up, but seem to have brought you down, so sorry. It was not my intention...' The man's eloquence threw Roger momentarily.

'What?' Snapped Roger. 'What did you want to do? To get in the way, to trip people up?'

Roger picked up his suitcase.

The beggar was trying awkwardly, painfully, to lift himself

into a sitting position. 'No.' He replied looking up at Roger, then he added, 'What were you running from?'

'What am I running from?' Roger, felt his anger rising again. 'Oh, my God, flipping psychology from a pisshead, trying to be clever are you? Well, let's see. I'm not running from the social like you, not the police like you, not the benefit office like you, not the…not the other pissheads who think you're a wanker.'

By venting his anger so completely Roger felt more powerful, as if he was regaining control of the situation by being venomous.

He looked down contemptuously at the beggar. He saw his weak and feeble frame, his dirty, stained clothes, Roger compared them to his. He now felt fully in command of the situation again. The beggar mumbled, and Roger bent forward menacingly over him.

'What did you say?'

'Sorry to have hurt your feelings, many blessings to you and your family,' came the quietly slurred reply.

'Oh, fuck off, why don't you just get a job. Do something with your life, rather than pissing it away.'

Roger turned and started to walk quickly away, with purpose, with confidence. His rapid footsteps echoed down the passageway, they exclaimed his ascendancy, and he afforded himself a wry smile as he heard the vagrant call out.

'Blessings on your way.'

Oh, just sober up you smelly git, he thought.

Safely back at his flat, Roger folded and laid his clothes out for washing and cleaning. He stepped into the bathroom turned on the shower and glanced briefly at his reflection in the mirror. 'Not bad, brother,' he commented to himself as he held his stomach in and bulged his biceps. He was still upset about the incident in the tunnel. His knees throbbed as a reminder of his fall. He decided the best way to recover his equilibrium was to indulge himself.

He gathered the tools of the modern man.

The Biotherm Homme Aquapower Absolute Gel as a moisturizer.

The Lab Series Milf Foaming Face Wash for that gentle but tough rub.

His Perricone MD High Potency Eye Lift.

Then the Dermalogica Invigorating Shave Gel.

Finished off with their Post-Shave Gel.

He knew he'd feel good after that lot.

He set to. About three quarters of an hour later and he was warmly reflective and calm.

Now the final job.

He closely inspected his hairline in the mirror checking for any signs of thinning, and he was about halfway through this when the phone rang.

He saw it was Giselle, and quickly picked up the phone.

'Hi, how are you?' He cooed.

Her husky tantalising voice came over loud and clear. 'I'm in London. I'm at the station, meet now. I need sex, right away.'

The score so far:
Roger: One foaming bath   Beggar: Nil

Note to self:
Avoid falling over beggars in the underground, it can seriously hurt your knees.

Chapter Two

Conceiving and conniving

Giselle was a dark-haired Parisienne who worked as a rep for some of the largest fashion and perfume houses in Europe. She and Roger had 'come across each other' at trade fairs and corporate events.

He hadn't registered she was over ten years older than him. He'd just seen a beautiful, exotic and sexy woman who kept appearing in his life.

He didn't realize it, but she had been stalking him.

She'd made sure she'd attended the same conferences and trade fairs, she plotted their encounters. At first, she'd acted haughty and aloof, pretending to be mildly flattered by his attempts at seducing her, but then one night in Hannover, she let him have what he wanted.

They were sitting in the restaurant at a large table full of reps and fair officials. The throng was consumed with chatter and banter, fuelled by the free wine and buffet food perched on knees and table edges.

She'd known her monthly cycle was right.

She'd squeezed herself into her most revealing little black dress, worn her fertility-enhancing gold bracelet, and applied a liberal amount of Chanel No.5. She had ensured they sat together and her knee pressed against his thigh. They chatted about the day, bitched about other traders, and she kept paying him small compliments. Roger wasn't particularly aware of anything Giselle was saying, his whole mind was focused on her knee pressing against his leg. He adjusted his leg, ensuring their thighs and knees were now hard against each other.

She smiled a deeply seductive smile, she drew his eyes to hers, and at the same time, her hand gently rested on his thigh.

He could hear nothing but the pounding of his heart.

'Oooh, Roger, your legs, they are very athletic, no?' She squeezed his thigh. 'You must work out a lot?'

She pressed herself closer to him.

He could smell the warm musk of her body, his head began to spin, he was intoxicated by her.

'Yes, er, no, actually I don't.' He mumbled. 'Sorry, it is very loud in here…can't hear above the din.' He looked around at the milling people.

'Yes, very loud, why don't we go up to my room, there we can talk.'

She squeezed his thigh decisively, let her hand gently brush his torso whilst making sure he could catch a glimpse of her cleavage as she leant forward. She slowly rose from her chair, and waved him forward discreetly.

He didn't need a second invitation.

They consummated their lust together in a series of hotel rooms in major cities throughout Europe as they followed that years trade fairs and events.

This time she was in London.

When they made love, it was unlike anything he'd experienced before. He was taken to places he hadn't been before. The encounters with Giselle made Roger feel vulnerable and exposed. He felt such a rush of emotion whilst in her arms it was on occasions overwhelming. Twice he had cried after they made love, which disturbed him.

Roger was unsettled by such intensity. She stirred feelings in him he had never experienced before. He had little previous experienced of being with women, most were brief and uninspiring affairs.

This was something else.

He was used to being in control of his emotions, being able to stifle feelings. All his life he had learnt to suppress emotions and it came as a shock to him that they still lurked in his body. He thought he'd conquered his vulnerability.

He hadn't.

The next week Giselle disappeared from his life, didn't return calls and was unavailable. Roger was baffled, a little disappointed that it had ended so abruptly, but also relieved that he didn't have to be so emotional any more. He resolved to himself that he wouldn't be that way again with a woman, as it had distressed him. He would retain control in future. He would be in charge, as he felt it should be.

After two months he had resolved the affair in his head. He'd had a great time with Giselle, he'd enjoyed it, but it was now time to move on, to seek more conquests on his terms. He didn't need Giselle.

The score so far:

Roger: One   Giselle: Nil

Then she called.

'Roger, I have news for you.'

'Yes, what's that?' He thought it was something work related.

'I'm pregnant…it is your child.'

There was stunned silence, followed by a brief. 'What?'

'I will have a baby.'

There was an even longer and deeper pause.

Roger didn't know how to react, he was torn between feeling betrayed, maybe used, immediately frightened by the prospect of being a father, angry at the inconvenience this could cause, but deep down, also a little bit proud of himself.

They met a couple of weeks later. Giselle sat with her legs crossed at the bar of an expensive hotel. Her immaculate hair matching her beautiful black dress revealing stockinged legs which made Roger's mouth water.

He drooled internally, but then checked himself.

He was resolved to sort this out once and for all, and he opened his mouth to speak.

Before a word came from his mouth Giselle had intervened.

'I've used you, Roger.' She waved a hand indicating that he should sit next to her. 'I've been very, how you say, manipulative?'

He nodded his head.

She continued and it was clear Giselle had planned the event, she admitted as much.

'I feel it is time for me to become a mother, I am 37, always single, I have no prospect of a long-term partner, I have my work commitments.'

She explained she'd wanted to have a child, so she'd deliberately gone out and looked for a sperm donor. Roger had fitted the bill nicely, young, fit, handsome, intelligent, hard working. He was all she would have wanted in the father of her child, but she didn't have the time to build a relationship.

She then told him in no uncertain terms she didn't want him to have anything to do with the child, she was very capable of bringing up the child on her own, she was a lady of considerable means. She would bring up the child with her mother.

In this day and age, she argued, a daughter, for she hoped it was a girl, really didn't need a father. She uncrossed her legs to adjust her dress and Roger, his mouth still open as it had been throughout Giselle's tirade, was able to re-focus his attention.

'A mother can provide everything a girl needs throughout her life. I'm no feminist. I am much more pragmatic and sensible than that. I have always been in charge of my life, I want a child, so I have got one. This is how the world works, supply and demand. You have had fun, playing your part. I know you liked it. I thank you for that, but now I am in charge, and I will do as I like.'

She slid off the bar stool, straightened her dress, kissed Roger on both cheeks and left.

Roger watched as she departed, with some regret. He turned to the barman, thinking that this was the last time he'd ever see her 'Double scotch on the rocks, please.'

Giselle had it all planned out. She would buy her daughter lots of fashionable clothes, and the two of them would be the talk of the town. They'd go to international receptions and parties, wearing the same outfits. Her daughter would be just a sweet, lovely, mini-Giselle.

As Roger nursed his glass, he realized he hadn't uttered a word in their time together. A large part of him was hugely relieved by Giselle's news. He felt a sense of release. He felt as though he was back in control of his life again. He was free of the unknown responsibilities of being a parent, which had suddenly loomed over him. Children had never been part of his long-or short-term plan. He was again free to pursue his busy work life and commitment free lifestyle.

A little part of him which lurked in the darker recesses of his heart was upset and disappointed, but that was quickly suppressed. When he was home, he returned to his Game Boy, but he remained disturbed. That night he had a haunting dream about being in a pit full of snakes, which made him feel queasy.

The score so far:
Roger: Nil   Giselle: One

Note to self:
If you want to become a father, do it consciously, or not at all.

Chapter Three

Everything according to plan

The score so far:

Roger: 23 years.   The world: 1993.

Roger was eating his lunch outside a restaurant when his friend, Crispin, passed by with a woman in tow. Crispin had been at LSE with Roger, and worked in an executive law firm. He annoyed Roger intensely with his casual and sarcastic way, but Roger was in awe of him as he earned twice as much and he was 'in the city.'

'Hi, Roger, this is Harriett, works at Attic recruitment, very bespoke and boutique.' laughed Crispin. 'How's the advertising world, me old mate?'

Roger suppressed an angry look.

'As you well know, Crispin, I'm not in advertising, I'm in marketing,' he retorted.

'Yeah, all the same, old man, you and Harriett in the same game, pushing and shoving, trying to con people.'

'Oh, and you're a paragon of virtue and honesty?' laughed Roger.

'Yes, you know me.' replied Crispin with feigned indignation. 'Anyway, we must dash, good to see you, see you soon.'

'Bye.' Roger replied to the space which had been hurriedly vacated by the two of them. They'd spied someone else, more important than Roger, an executive from Coopers Lybrand.

They made time to chat to him, not Roger. He continued to eat his sandwich.

Roger had known from a very early age he wanted to be in marketing. His mother had not understood his interest and certainly couldn't fathom where it came from. He'd been a loner who studied hard and earnestly throughout school then went straight to the London School of Economics. He'd gained a First Class Honors degree in Economics and Politics. On graduating he'd been selected as a graduate trainee on Proctor and Gamble's Marketing and Development Programme. Within eighteen months he'd been promoted to marketing assistant, whilst qualifying for his Marketing Diploma from the Chartered Institute of Marketing.

He had set himself a series of targets, and had achieved the first of them within a very short period of time. He was a shooting star who had forged ahead of his same-aged contemporaries, and he knew where he was going.

The score so far:

Age 23:   Marketing assistant manager.   Job done.

The projected score to come:

Age 25:   Assistant brand manager.   Very likely.

Age 28:   Brand manager.   Achievable.

Age 31:   Category Director.   Yes please.

At Proctor and Gamble he had a very varied workload. No dull routine, each day being different. He'd be visiting clients and going to exhibitions one day, followed by research or overlooking production schedules the next.

He liked the precise nature of the market research and the attention to detail and accuracy which was vital in his field. He was fully committed to the job, and happily worked overtime and through the night if needed.

Such dedication meant he didn't have a wide circle of friends. He hadn't had many whilst at school, and his loner behaviour at work didn't attract them either. He thought it was a worthwhile sacrifice.

He wasn't interested in alcohol or drugs; happy to gain his

kicks from work.

He lived on his own, surrounding himself with the latest 'boy's toys' that kept him occupied for many hours in his limited leisure time. The games acted as a counterpoint to the arduous work, and he enjoyed the distraction they offered.

From an early age Roger had been taught how to compartmentalize his life, how to shut down and keep things separate. He specialized in being in control at all times. He didn't know when this behaviour started, he just knew he was very good at it.

If other people talked about their childhood memories, Roger listened with politely feigned interest, but was unable to participate or contribute.

He only had memories from the age of 11 onwards.

All memories of his earlier years had been erased by the momentous event of that year, 1981, the death of his father.

He presumed life was pretty normal before 'The Car Crash', and he only had three distinct memories from that year, but they were crucial to his survival after the event.

The first was at his home, with his mother.

She was sitting in the front room looking into a large wooden chest. Inside were some clothes, papers, a picture frame, other small personal articles.

She had looked up at Roger, smiled sadly and then said. 'This is your father's box, you need to help me put it in the attic.'

With that she closed the lid and fastened a small lock.

In Roger's recollection this was completed in slow motion.

He was thinking, 'This is it, this is all there is left of my father, a box with a lock on it'.

He couldn't remember putting the box in the attic, but knew it must still be there, securely locked.

The second memory was at the funeral.

There were many people gathered around the hole in the ground. These indeterminate people were dressed in black. There was an oppressive feeling. It was as if the sky was closing in on him. There was very little space between the sky and the earth.

Roger's heart was beating fast.

He felt a deep yearning to scream welling up inside, but it was being squashed. Suddenly his mother's face was up close to his.

She was pressing herself onto him, squeezing him downwards, as she did this she whispered, 'Big boys don't cry, big boys don't cry.'

She squeezed him tightly, one small choke of air was expelled, and then he was silent, breath held, still.

The third memory was at school.

Roger was in the playground and Nick the Stitch was baiting him.

He was circling around Roger chanting, 'Stinky Cologne, Stinky Cologne, 'asn't got a father, doesn't live at home.'

Nick was the school bully. He took great pleasure in tormenting the smaller, weaker kids, anyone more vulnerable than himself.

Roger slowly turned and watched as Nick chanted at him, and they were caught in a momentary dance.

Roger had initially been afraid. Then from within Roger's gut came a huge force. A deep-seated energy burst out of his body into his clenched fist and onto Nick's face.

The next instant Nick was lying on the floor, blood spurting from his nose, his hands desperately trying to staunch the flow.

Roger was now on top of Nick, his face pressed hard against the bully's.

Roger panted 'Yes, what did you say? What did you say?'

A look of fear was etched deep into Nicks' features

'Nothing...sorry,' he mumbled as he turned away.

From that point onwards Roger decided he would be in control and fix all aspects of his life. He would know where everything was and was meant to be. To do this he kept everything separate, in its own box.

He controlled how much time and effort he gave any aspect of his life. He also made sure that everything was fixed and secure, he'd tied everything down.

During the week, he worked hard, he was pressured, but it was worthwhile and satisfying. On the weekends, he had his games.

He went to visit his mother every first Saturday of the month, he did his duty.

He stuck to his routines.

Roger opened the door slowly and reverentially, looked up, smiled, and stepped once more into his favourite shop, Forbidden Planet.

He paused and looked around, breathing in the frusty smell of comic books, films, videos, and, his favourite, the games section. The store was full of the arcane and the extraordinary.

He sighed to himself, aah, this is my home.

He was warmly greeted by Gavin, his favourite assistant.

'Hi.'

Gavin and Roger bowed to each other.

'Sayonara, Roger, are you ready to play "Hoshi no Kabi"?'

Roger smiled back. 'Too right.'

It was the launch day for Kirby's Dream Land, and Roger had been waiting for months.

Gavin walked out from behind the counter and showed Roger where the Game Boy were stacked. Roger picked up the slim package and inspected it closely. The image on the front cover had a large white bubble figure and several smaller coloured features, as well as a wide mouthed tree creature.

Roger felt the tight covering of cellophane sealing the game, and he knew in a few hours he'd be home breaking the seal and then playing the game for the first time.

He felt content with the world.

The score so far:

Roger: Level 3 Bonus game   King Dedede: Nil

Note to self:

I am the king, I am the master of Game Boy.

Chapter Four

New Age Traveller

The score so far:

Roger: 24 years.   The world: 1994.

'Hey, Roger, what you doing next weekend?' asked Harvey, the marketing assistant for Lenor, as he passed Roger's desk.

'Oh, nothing much, the usual.'

'What watching footy on the tele? Why don't you come with me? I'm on a magical mystery tour, I'm doing a workshop which should be great fun.'

Roger liked Harvey, but he had a reputation for doing weird and wacky things.

He was a dabbler in the emerging New Age scene, he liked his crystals and meditation.

Roger had never done anything like that. He was cautious about such things, and went with the mainstream view that they were a bit strange.

'Go on, Roger, you know you want to.' goaded Harvey. 'A weekend of fun, relaxation, resting and peace, what more could you ask for?'

Roger thought about it.

The more he thought about it the more it appealed to have a restful and relaxing weekend of meditation. He hadn't been on holiday in years, and he could do with a break. Having very carefully read and re-read the flier advertising a weekend of meditation without finding any references to cults or weird rituals, he decided to join in.

What had he got to lose?

When Harvey told him that the majority of people on the workshops would be women, he decided he'd give it a go. A change of scenery and some women, why not?

They arrived late on a Friday night at a huge country manor in the depths of the lush English countryside.

It was only on the Saturday morning that Roger fully understood what was being offered. The participating group assembled in a big drawing room after a sumptuous vegetarian breakfast. Twenty-five 'punters' as he later called them.

He looked around the room, licked his lips, and realised he'd stepped into heaven.

He and Harvey were two of the four men present. The other two men looked like refugees from the 1960's, whilst he and Harvey stood out as shining, fresh, young and vibrant men. The rest of the punters, twenty-one women were all happy, open, keen and very much out to enjoy themselves for the weekend. Many were already seeking eye contact with him, and giving him full smiles. Roger smiled inwardly.

That weekend changed his life.

Harvey spent the time relaxing and transforming himself with meditation, he was genuinely interested in such activities.

Roger skipped through the meditation, but threw himself into other, more 'base chakra' activities, which he found equally transforming.

He'd never had so much fun before.

For the next few years he attended New Age events as and when he could. He'd found a new leisure time activity, and it was even more pleasurable than Game Boy.

He may have to work long hours and very diligently during the week, but on the weekends when he could, he transformed himself. For those weekends, much to his own amusement, he called himself "Roger the New Age Traveller". This didn't mean he dressed up as a Rasta man with a dog-on-a-string. No, no. It meant he frequented New Age Workshops up and down the country. Not just any old ones, the best, the latest and most prestigious.

He pursued spiritual enlightenment. Or so it seemed.

First he ditched Harvey. Then he attended Reiki, Working with Angels, Regressions, Soul Retrieval, EFT, Yoga in all it's forms, Shiatsu, Singing, African Drumming, Shamanic Trance Dance, Endorphins, he'd attended so many he couldn't remember them all.

For him to commit so much time, energy and money to such pursuits was out of character. Such "flaky enlightenment" workshops as he called them, enabled him to indulge in something else, much more personal and ego driven. They gave him access to riches, pleasures and delights. It was a world of unprecedented reward for him and he bestowed on himself 'king' status, he was the king of the New Age scene.

This had nothing to do with the pursuit of enlightenment - it was a pursuit of a different kind.

Sex.

The score so far:

Attendance: 7   Sex: 5   Success rate: 71%

Note to self:

Women punters, divide and conquer into three categories:

Nubiles

Features:

Late teens and early twenties.

Mostly second generation hippies.

Fresh-faced seekers of enlightenment.

They like asking questions.

They want to sit at the feet of the guru.

Hooking them in:
Talk fast and trashy to them.
Flirt straight away.
Benefits:
They can be up for it very quickly.
Lovely, fresh and innocent.
Peachy and firm.
Drawbacks:
Bit self-obsessed, want to talk about themselves all the time.

Passion mothers

Features:
About 30 to 45 years old.
Mostly mothers of small children, but some with quite old children as well.
Need to be more subtle.
They are getting away from the kids, and from the partner.
Want to have fun, yes please.
Hooking them in:
Need to be more subtle.
Need to listen to their stuff for a bit.
Benefits:
Can become very passionate, very keen.
Still lovely and firm, lots of energy.
Much more attentive to me, want to know my stuff.

Lesbians

All the women not interested in me.
And me not interested in them –
The lame
The fat
The ugly
Maybe even a few of them are actually lesbians – only joking
– or am I?

Supplementary note to self

Sub-division of women, particularly passion mothers.

(Important to identify early on)

Consolers

Features:

They use the weekends to deal with their issues.

At some point they break down into a pool of tears.

Benefits:

There, there, need a big hug, strong arms for comfort, which I am very happy to provide.

Lightbeings (Best of all)

Features:

At some point in the weekend they transform their lives, reach enlightenment.

Become full of love for everyone.

Benefits:

Wham bam, thank you ma'am.

I'm available to help them spread their love as widely as possible.

How kind am I.

Roger felt as though this smorgasbord of sex was served up on a regular basis in large country houses and hotels throughout Britain just for him.

What could be better? Turn up on Friday, have fun, then go home on Sunday. No questions asked, it was all in the process.

For Roger it was irrelevant which workshop he attended, none of it sank in. As far as he was concerned, the messages were for the punters, not for him.

He didn't need all that New Age stuff.

He had a good job and real prospects. He was there for his own basic needs, and in order to indulge himself on a regular basis, he needed a minimal tool kit.

'Oh, yes, I've got the lot.' He laughed as he turned his head to the right under the intense spotlight over his bathroom mirror.

The bathroom was full of steam from the hot bath he'd just had. He smiled at himself as his fingers edged along his hair-line, checking for loose and thin hairs to be plucked. He continued to talk to himself.

'Whilst those punters are practicing self love and positive affirmations in the mirror, I don't need to, 'cos I'm so well equipped.'

He turned his head to the left, looked himself in the eye and began to dance rhythmically to an imaginary tune. He sung to himself, using his hairbrush as a microphone.

'I need to look handsome, smart, young and virile. Oh, yes. Check.'

He twisted one way and then the other whilst still looking at himself.

'Need to pull a sincere face, need to "do" listening.' He put on his sincere face and looked keenly into the mirror.

'Be a listener. Oh, yes. Check.' He gave himself a big tick.

'Need to flirt without being too obvious. Flirty and dirty.' He wiggled his bottom and looked down at it in the mirror.

'Oh, yes. Check.'

As the king of the New Age workshop scene, he'd arrive in his black BMW Alpina B7, deliberately parking it out front. Then he'd woo the punters with his tales of the gurus he'd been to see, mostly repeating phrases and descriptions he'd heard others use, as he never was that interested in the message being promoted.

'Oh, yes, I went to see Neil Donald Walsh, such a great talker, and I love his back story so full of meaning.' He'd blurt out.

'I think Deepak Chopra has such a brilliant synthesis of spirituality and science.' He'd nod wisely.

'Ken Wilber? I love his spiral dynamics.' He'd concur.

'Louise Hay just so inspires me with her bravery.' He'd smile bravely.

'I'm trying to live in the now, like Eckhart Tolle.' He'd entreaty others.

'I love the endorphins effect which William Bloom talks about.' He'd smile. 'I'm trying to stimulate them as we speak.'

He was a regular at all the best and most expensive workshops.

The score so far:

Roger: 6 sages   Everybody else: Impressed

Note to self:

Welcoming and greeting new customers

Unlike at work, where a brisk handshake will do, the norm for such events is to give big hugs straight away, even to complete strangers.

A practice with which I thoroughly agree.

Must ensure that every woman gets a hug, whether they offer a handshake or not.

The initial hug can be a good gauge of what might follow.

Some typical greetings:-

The handshake - can often be given at beginning, but don't rule them out, they may just be shy.

The tent - hugs round the top, but keeps the genitals well away - she isn't interested, probably married.

Bean pole - hug with extra wrap round quality - good prospect.

The bear hug - all consuming, deep and warm - yes please.

Chapter Five

The New Age of the King

His favourite weekend had been in Stroud. A residential weekend at a rambling old country house, surrounded by deep green woods and lush grassy verges. The light grey building was full of creaking stairwells, wooden panels, dusty sofas and random armchairs. The smell of vegetarian cooking permeated the fabric of the place.

Roger was most interested in the upstairs, the rambling pile of small rooms tucked away on four floors, connected by corridors and small balconies. A hive of rooms filled with potential and possibilities.

His memory was of a blissful time spent singing in a choir. There had been about 8 men and 40 women punters. It was a good mix of nubiles and passion mothers all of whom he deemed keen and willing.

He was almost overwhelmed by the possible choices, but settled on a raven-haired nubile called Janie. A second-generation hippy, uninhibitedly wearing deep-cut revealing colourful silk tops and short tempting skirts showing off her tanned legs and bare feet.

The teacher organized the group outdoors all weekend in the dappled sun, and Roger had easily played along with Janie, drawing her to him, keeping her laughing and amused at all times.

They'd performed a little dance of attraction throughout Friday night and Saturday morning.

By Saturday afternoon he was confident about her, and indulged in a little flirting with Janie's attractive friend Summer, making sure Janie was jealous.

They'd all stayed up late on the Saturday night, and then he'd given both a deep longing hug (bear hugs) and kissed them on the lips as they all went to their separate rooms.

He'd cast a lingering look their way and said, 'My room is just up here, door always open if you're interested,' as he made his way up the wooden stairwell.

He'd waited in his room for about quarter of an hour until Janie had slipped lightly through the door and into his bed.

Ten minutes later Summer let herself into the room and joined them.

He didn't sleep at all that night, and the next morning his voice was a little croaky, but there was a huge grin on his face the whole day.

He'd not taken either of their phone numbers, he had a policy of never giving anyone his. This was one of his rules.

What happened at the weekends stayed securely locked away and finished. No exchange of numbers, always onto the next conquest.

The score so far:
Roger: Two nil in the lead! Wow.

Roger thrived on this pursuit of casual sexual encounters. He called them 'conquests without consequence.' He made sure none of them lasted longer than the weekend, as he was more addicted to the buzz of the conquest than the actual consummation.

For Roger there was no better fix than the chase. He loved wooing and charming people, he was good at it, after all, he was in marketing.

During the pursuit of a nubile or a passion mother he felt deliciously alive. His body became cat-like, he felt heady, all his senses alert. He became an expert watcher adept at observing body language, noticing what was going on. He used his considerable charm, gift of the gab, and handsome physique to ensure that his prey would eventually succumb to him.

He'd employ the glance. The touch of a hand, the brush of hair. The subtle and not so subtle comment. Each nuance of the chase lit up his life and made it all worthwhile.

He felt alive in those moments, vibrantly in pursuit. It really didn't matter if he was successful or not, it was the delicious anticipation that he enjoyed the most.

Often the sex was deflating. They'd be unfamiliar with each other, uncertain what to do next. It could become awkward and strained, not very satisfying. Uneasy fumblings and couplings during the night.

He was often disappointed in the moment of victory.

He would frequently quickly return to his own bed to sleep, or go for a walk in the early morning to separate himself from his conquest as quickly and decisively as possible.

The spark of lust didn't lead to the flower of love.

He didn't want to repeat the Giselle experience, when he had felt so out of control. He deliberately turned cold and frosty on the new conquest in order to ensure she didn't ask for his number, or want anything more.

The spurning of the conquest would lead to him seeking another. Always moving on. It became his addiction. The pursuit became the game, and it never fully satisfied him, so he continued. He lived for the chase, he was addicted to the ideal of the sexual encounter rather than the actuality. He was driven onwards.

A weekend in Autumn. Another successful pursuit.

The two of them were giggling.

Theatrically they tried and failed to keep quiet as they crept into her room.

The single room had a spartan wardrobe, chair, small table and single bed, very functional and simple. A musty smell of lavender and cleaning detergent pervaded the forlorn space. The fuzz of the street lights created an orange glow in the unlit room.

Roger pressed himself up against her responsive body as they stood together in the semi darkness. His hands searched around her back, rubbing her shoulders, squeezing her to him. She opened her mouth to speak.

He had thought this was an invitation to kiss and plunged his tongue in.

She spluttered but stayed open.

Her hands tentatively reached round him, they were calm and gentle. His were rough and grasping. Roger didn't noticed the difference in the quality of their touch, he had been thinking 'What is her name, Janet or Jane?' He couldn't remember which.

He pulled her towards him, almost lifting her off her feet, and she let out a giggle as their mouths came apart.

He unceremoniously laid her on the bed.

Once there he pulled off his shirt and started to un-belt his trousers.

He presuming she'd be undressing as well, but when he looked she just lay watching him.

He continued to undress quickly and then stood awkwardly hovering over the bed.

He was conscious of his nakedness, and not sure how to get into such a small space alongside her fully clothed form. He squeezed in, each of them shifting and moving to accommodate their bodies on the frame of the bed, as they did this little jig his hands fumbled to undress her.

'My, you're a quick worker, aren't you?'

'Yes.'

He reached to pull down her skirt, a determined look on his face. 'I'm very keen.'

He looked up and smiled at her.

She looked down with a slightly bemused expression and laughed

'I can see that.'

She helped him pull her skirt off, and decided to go with the flow. He was strong and determined.

He knew what he wanted, he thrust and pushed, he pulled and he nudged.

She tried to coax him towards gentle stroking, a softer touch, but each time she calmed him he would speed up again.

His actions were like the attentions a calf for their mother.

He prodded and poked, he gently but firmly shoved.

He insisted, and persisted, until he satiated himself, using her body as if suckling at a bovine teat.

Once he had finished, he settled. He lay still for a few minutes.

His mind already away, distracted, somewhere else entirely.

Janet or Jane lay next to him in the cramptness of the single bed. She was observing him.

Their bodies were pushed hard against each other to prevent either of them falling out. The crumpled single duvet partially clothing their naked bodies.

'So, where do you live, Roger?'

'Oh, London.' Came his terse reply.

'Wow, I live in London.' She answered keenly.

'Um.'

'Whereabouts?' She wanted to know.

'North.'

At that point he started to unlock himself from their embrace.

'Oh, sorry, my arm has gone to sleep, got cramp.'

He'd slid backwards out of the bed.

'Need to go to the toilet.'

He slipped his pants back on, picked up his trousers and shirt, before disappeared from the room and her life.

Janet watched as the door slowly pulled to, and then she lay for some time looking at the closed door.

Roger only pursued alpha women. The good looking, slim, mainly dark-haired ones.

His criteria for an alpha woman was purely on looks. He was seeking an ideal, but wasn't quite sure what she looked like. Certainly, he hadn't found her yet, and wasn't actually looking very hard for her. He was enjoying the selection process too much. He didn't mind whether she had big or small breasts, long or short hair, but there were certain minimum standards. He knew she couldn't be too fat, she needed a thin waist, she mustn't have bad breath, or be sweaty. She needed to be well-groomed.

Often Roger was pursued by what he called big fat passion mummas. Not just pursued but openly lusted after.

He found it disgusting.

They would come on so strong that everyone at the weekend knew what was being offered. This was not playing Roger's game. He couldn't understand how someone who was obviously not an alpha woman would have the nerve to even pursue an alpha man like him. They were just not in his league, and surely they should know their place.

At first Roger was a little cautious about committing himself to the 'fullness' of the activities on offer – really stretching his body in Hatha Yoga, or getting into a trance state. These were not the kind of activities his normally reticent and sensible self would choose to do. He liked to remain in control. But as he attended more and more events, his barriers were lowered, and he started to let himself go. Drumming until his hands bled on an African drumming workshop was as close to an ecstatic experience as he'd come. He started to really enjoy the silence of meditation, the burn of his inner thigh as he stretched into a yoga pose. He realised by participating fully he was attracting more attention from likely conquests. Skulking in corners was not an attractive look. Skulking in corners was what most other men punters did. He was pretty contemptuous of the other men at such events.

The score so far:
Attendance: 14 Sex: 9 Success rate: 64%

Note to self:
Men punters, categorize and define:

Lost souls

Harmless hippy folk.

Colourful clothes, wow, I've got bright red trousers!

Took too many drugs in the '60's. Spend their lives desperately wanting to get back there.

I was at Woodstock, I was Jimmy Hendrix's friend, blah, blah.

They haven't got a clue what is going on in the here and now, bless their little holey rainbow coloured woolly socks!

The dragged man

Attending because his partner has told him to come.

Much rather be down the pub.

Some are clever, can see they've sussed me and know what I'm up to.

They'd like to compete, they haven't got a chance, they're there with their partners.

That last dragged man kept a very beady eye on me, he didn't trust his woman, and he was right not to, she was desperate for it.

That made the chase that much more exciting.

It happened behind his back.

Oh yes.

Mother's Boy

'The wolf is born in a dark deep cave. He is blind, pink, hairless, totally helpless. At first he remains deep beneath the earth in the company of female wolves. Inside the cave he is taught the ways of the female wolves. They teach about close contact, intimacy, self knowledge, going inwards. During this time he has little or no interaction with his father or male wolves. He is what you call a Mother's Boy.'

Tsao Chinem Cllens

Chapter Six

Mummy's Boy

The score so far:
Roger: 25 years.   The world: 1995.

Roger's mother didn't live far away. She lived in St Albans, just on the outskirts of London, it was a drive of about an hour and a half. During that familiar drive he would revert back to being an eleven-year-old. By the time he pressed the doorbell, he was in deeply familiar territory.

His mother had never re-married, she had never seemed interested in moving on. It was all very familiar. The semi-detached house in the middle of the suburban street. The smells, the dust, the TV in the corner of the front room. His room, the same as when he lived there, on the front top landing, full of his paraphernalia.

The visits too had their routine.

'Hallo, love, how was your trip down? Would you like a cup of tea? Why don't you sit in the front room and I'll bring it through to you.'

His mother generated a flow of questions and statements to which he never really applied any answers.

'How's work then, love?'

'Yes, work's good, lots happening, big changes, they've been sacking quite a few people, early retirements, but I'm safe. They won't get rid of me.' He talked abstractly back to her.

'Uuum, there's a lot of that about, isn't there?'

The score so far:
Visits to mum's house: 32   Mum's visits to my house: 2

He'd lie on the sofa with the television remote on his chest and switch between channels all afternoon, dozing whilst watching bits of sport programmes and trashy films. At 6pm his mother would insist they should watch the news, 'to see what is happening in the world.' Once this was over it would be supper, she would invariably cook him his 'favourite' - a steak and kidney pie, with potatoes, some greens and thick gravy. After they washed and dried the plates and pans, she'd settle in front of the screen to watch the Lottery, then Ant and Dec on the other side, she liked how cheeky they looked. Roger would slope off up to his room, watch a film or play a game on his laptop.

He would rise early on Sunday, they'd have a cooked breakfast together, and then he'd be off. Sometimes, he'd bring his washing round, and she'd have cleaned and ironed all his clothes by the time he was ready to go.

Roger and his mother conspired together. They pretended everything was fine, that this was the way life should be. They pretended they were happy with this life.

They never talked about his father.

Roger would tell her brief bits about his work, but didn't expect her to take much notice. She told him stories about other family members, but didn't expect him to show much interest. They'd discuss celebrity lifestyle choices, and TV shows, but their own personal, emotional landscape was not to be visited.

They had a routine. It developed over the years, and neither of them wanted to upset it or each other.

Roger assumed his mother wanted him to behave like he did, lying on the sofa, giving her his washing, which she didn't.

His mother assumed he liked to behave in that manner, that he enjoyed steak and kidney pie, which he didn't.

One Sunday morning at his mother's he woke with a start from a very vivid dream. He waited whilst the familiar shapes and forms of his room took a solid rather than liquid state. He sat up in bed and looked at his alarm clock, it was 4.30 in the morning. He tried to remember what the dream had been about.

He recollected being in a very dirty and deserted cityscape. His mother was far ahead of him. He could see her walking alone on the pavement far in the distance. She had her head down and was walking with pace. He watched as she continued and then she very abruptly turned a corner and was gone. He was now alone on the street corner, and he crossed to the pavement on the side of the road she'd been and he started to walk after her. He walked and walked. No-one came, no cars passed, no birds sung, no noise was heard.

He felt alone, he felt uncomfortable. This stark loneliness started to disconcert him, and he looked around for familiar signs or people. There were none, he looked up and there was a road sign, pointing in the direction his mother had gone, it read: 'Lone Street'.

He walked on, and as he continued he become tired, fatigued, he felt slightly sick, queasy, and he slowed down. 'Hold on' he thought to himself, 'I'm not like my mum, I'm not alone, I've got a great job, I've got a great home. I've got prospects. I'm not following in her footsteps.' He tried to cross the road, but he couldn't, it was as if he was on a railway track. His feet were stuck in a rut and every time he tried to move forward or back he reverted to following his mother.

He started to panic. 'This isn't right, I want to go over there.' He pointed at the other side of the road.

At that moment he had woken. He dismissed the dream and the uncomfortable feeling he had been left with, and lay awake playing on the Game Boy in his bed until it was seven, then he went and made himself a cup of tea.

'Hey, Roger' It was Hugh. 'Can you show me how to do some animation on Powerpoint for my presentation? I know you're really good at it.' Roger smiled and came over, looking intently at the screen of the computer. Hugh showed him a graph he wanted to animate, and he clicked on the item to highlight it for Roger.

'Oh, uum, yup, I see what you want to do. It would look good. Unfortunately, I don't know how to do that I'm afraid, I can't help you with that, a bit beyond me.'

'Oh, shit, I needed it for this afternoon.' Hugh continued to look worriedly at the screen.

'Sorry, can't help you.'

Roger could have helped Hugh, he knew exactly how to do it, but he was not going to give him any help. Roger had a big Competitor Analysis presentation the next day. He was going to use all his animation knowledge in that display, and he didn't want Hugh showing off similar skills before his big turn.

The next day the sales and marketing team were assembled, including Hugh, and Roger showed the prices of the competitors and their promotional offers using the latest and most colourful animation. At the end of the presentation there was a reverential silence, the team had been impressed by Roger's presentation, all of them except Hugh, who scowled at Roger.

The score so far:
Roger: One brilliant presentation   Hugh: None
    Ha ha

Chapter Seven

The Buddha Beggar

Roger: 26 years.   The world: 1996.

'I want that report by 8 tomorrow morning. I've got to present it to Greg at 9. I want to know everything there is to know beforehand.'

Stuart was Roger's manager, and he'd just given Roger the responsibility to look through over 200 pages of financial reports, market research reports and projections. This was Roger's first real solo challenge as assistant marketing manager. Because he had done so well at his last presentation, he was being given the task to assess a product's impact on the British market over the last two months. His task was complicated by a major rival launching a similar product within the first week of their coming on the market, and they'd also offered it as a 3 for 2 offer at Tescos. In response Proctor and Gamble had cut the price, called it an introductory offer, but they now needed to see what share of the market their actions had attracted.

Roger felt elated to be given such a major task, and relished the challenge of producing the report to such a short deadline.

He worked on it all afternoon and evening.

He took it back to his house and worked through till midnight.

He set his alarm clock for 5 and continued working.

He analysed the statistics by creating bar charts, graphs and data analysis, making recommendations, all as a power point. He was very proud of the work, he knew how important the report was, and felt he'd done a very competent job.

By 8 he was into the first part of his presentation and mid-flow when Stuart interrupted him.

'Yes, yes, Roger, but where's the analysis of the first four days before the Tescos 3 for 2 offer?'

'What', Roger's heart sank.

'You've shown me all the records but there's no analysis of the first days before the offer which are vital to see if the longer term trend is to be trusted.' Stuart looked across angrily at him. 'Roger, I need those statistics NOW.'

Roger hadn't done them. He was dismissed.

He hurried back to his desk and frantically looked back through the reports and research to find the details. He felt humiliated that Stuart had reacted so abruptly, but also now realised he'd missed a hugely important component, which was his fault. Within the next half hour he brought in an additional report and placed it in front of Stuart.

'That's better.' Stuart smiled 'Now show me the power points.'

Roger put the memory stick in the computer, and the first slide was projected.

'No.' Shouted Stuart. 'All our products are shown in corporate colours, come on, Roger. White, red and blue for our products, rival products in grey.'

Stuart was furious. 'Roger, we've got twenty minutes, change them NOW.'

Roger flushed and rushed out to alter the work.

The score so far:

Roger: Nil   Stuart: Two

    Shit, shit, shit

Roger never mentioned what he did on the weekends at work, and his work colleagues never asked. Other people his age went to raves on the weekends, they drank and took drugs to deaden the pain, to forget the day job. Roger didn't feel that way about his job. He had commitment. He loved the fact that he had left college and gone straight into Proctor and Gamble, and he was still there. He felt he had a mutually respectful relationship with the company, he saw his future as being with them for a long time. He'd been approached on quite a number of occasions by other companies, offering more money, but he'd stayed loyal. His innate conservatism, linked to his mother's sensibilities were reflected in this harmonious and mutually respectful relationship, or at least he thought it was.

He was the job, and the job was him. As a reward for this dedication he had been made assistant marketing manager for Head and Shoulders, one of the companies top brands. This meant longer hours and stricter deadlines. The further up the ladder he climbed the more demands were being made on him. He accepted this. It was the way it should be. These were the demands made of all modern sophisticated businesspeople, he told himself. Besides, he had the best of both worlds. At both work and play he was the king.

At work he was sharp, tough and without compromise. He was delivering a service for the company and making his way upwards all the time.

On the weekend workshops he was also providing a service. All those needy women who hadn't been with a king before. He was allowing them to indulge themselves, he thought he was helping them.

He'd created a compartmentalized life in which he could be himself, indulge himself, without ever having to think too hard.

Most weekdays he took the tube early. Getting the 6.45 am train if he wasn't on a deadline, and returning on the 8.30 pm. As he strode through the underground passageway in the morning he'd often see the beggar, leaning against a smeared and dirty patch on the wall. He'd shudder at the recollection of their entwined bodies and speed up, making sure not to trip over him again. Because there were so few people about, the beggar was a feature of his journey in the mornings. The man often mumbled a greeting to Roger as he sped past. In the evenings Roger was tired, wanting to get home quickly and he wouldn't notice if the man was there or not.

One morning Roger was speeding, trotting, running to work, he was a little late and he dashed by the beggar. In the instant he passed he thought he saw the beggar sitting in the lotus position. Erect back, hands held loosely open on his thighs, eyes shut, a brief smile on his lips. By this time Roger was at the turnstile and through.

Surely not, he thought to himself. I've been to too many New Age workshops, I'm seeing smiling Buddha beggars now!

That evening he returned later than usual, and there sat the beggar propping himself against the wall. He noticed how straight the man's back was, how simply rested and calm his appearance.

As he strode past him, the beggar called out. 'Blessings to you Brother Wolf. How are you?' Roger flushed, blushed, looked at the floor and hurried past.

Once at home he chastised himself for feeling embarrassed by the beggar's greeting. He took some time to consider the beggar in more detail.

Roger hated everything about the man.

His greasy hair, the dirty and decayed teeth, the smelly greasy coat tied with string. He was needy, poor, probably addicted, probably scrounging all sorts of benefits.

He told himself the beggar would have no sense of duty, no discipline, no understanding of what was important.

The beggar was so ugly and dirty he had absolutely no hope of improving his life.

Roger thought, once a beggar, always a beggar.

He felt sick just thinking about him.

Roger said to himself:

'I am everything that man would like to be, and he will never become.'

The score so far:
Roger 151 creatures   The Pokedex: Nil

Note to self:
Pokemon Red and Green
Such a great game. Capture those Pokemon, battle those Pokemon, using all four moves is fantastic. Transfer those hit points into experience points. Realised you can throw the Poke Ball as well, the lower the target's HP and the stronger the Poke Ball the higher capture success rate. Brilliant!

'I'm good.' Roger shouted to himself as he sat on his sofa playing on the Game Boy. He'd completed all the tasks, reached all the levels.

He put the toy down and then looked around his flat. He hadn't pulled the curtains and he realised it had turned dark outside, he'd started playing in bright sunshine, been so absorbed that he'd lost track of time.

As he surveyed the room, he felt a shiver, a chill ran down his spine. He turned his head, and as he did so he thought he heard a voice say.

'Something is missing.'

It startled him. He was on his own in the flat and he checked around quickly to make sure he was alone.

His mouth was dry, he felt uncomfortable, his heart was pounding. He rubbed his arms to warm them and to stop the hairs from standing up.

'What's missing?' He said out loud.

'Nothing's missing, I've got the lot.' He added, not convinced, still a little afraid.

He looked around the room to see if anything or anyone was disagreeing. Nothing stirred. He felt relieved, but remained on edge.

He picked up the television remote and switched on. Soon he was absorbed by the flickering blue light. He was distracted, consoled and back in his comfort zone.

The next morning, Roger stood in the middle of his sitting room in bright sun light. He surveyed the room and all that was in it. He knew he had created a very desirable lifestyle, he had all anyone could want in terms of material goods and belongings. As he looked around, he became conscious of his having reached a pinnacle. He allowed himself to bask in this reflection. In his continued thoughts he concluded he'd played the game and won.

He was now an 'alpha boy'. Young, single, a leader, in charge. Desirable, living the life.

As he looked around his flat he saw that he had been very adequately rewarded for the long hours, determination and the self-motivation which had been necessary to become the alpha boy.

As this glow of self-satisfaction continued he strode into his living room. He looked around again.

This time, he saw gaps, flaws.

Despite being the alpha boy, there was always room for improvement. He thought about the furniture he wanted, the new large red sofa he'd seen the department store just a few days ago. The new gadgets he didn't own, but he desired. He looked into his kitchen and mused on the latest food processor he'd seen at Habitat.

He sat at his desk and wrote on a piece of paper:

'I'm good. I'm great.
I've done what I set out to do.
I'm here.
This is where I wanted to be.
I went out and I got it.

I'm not going to let any of this slip.

I'm going to continue upwards, outwards.

I want more. Much more. Much more of the same.

I'm not going to lose any of this. This is all mine.'

He finished his affirmation with a rueful smile and stuck it to the fridge, so he could see it each day. He smiled and rubbed his hands. He thought 'Uumh, what about that Expresso machine? Yes. Why not!'

Roger hadn't experienced disappointment in his working life, he'd always moved onwards and upwards, very quickly. He'd achieve a lot at work in a short period of time.

However, he still lacked emotional maturity or intelligence. He'd not experienced emotions or feelings on a deep level. He'd not allowed himself to behave that way, besides he didn't want serious relationships. He'd kept himself to himself, he led a solitary existence, he'd had a few encounters with women along the way, his conquests without consequence, but he'd always put work first.

Roger watched as Terry struggled to add the large sum on the flipchart. Roger came over feigning interest.

'Hey, Terry, do you need a hand?'

'Oh, yes…no.' Terry looked at the ground. He then looked up at Roger and admitted.

'Yes, I do, I've always struggled with maths. Never really got the hang of it.' Terry looked at him anxiously 'I'm not very good with figures, please don't tell anyone.'

'No trouble, mate.' Roger quickly used the marker pen to finish the calculation.

Two days later in a team meeting, Roger was delivering a quick message about the effects on the market of a rival companies' opening offers, and wanted to show the amount of profit they had made.

He looked across at Terry and in front of all the others, he asked 'Hey, Terry can you work out how much that would be in the first six months?'

He casually threw Terry the calculator, then he dramatically stopped and looked at Terry 'Oh, no, you're no good with figures are you.'

He took back the calculator and turned away from the red faced Terry. 'What about you Jason?'

Chapter Eight

Saskia

The score so far:
Roger: 27 years.   The world: 1997.

Roger received a phone call from Giselle.

She was staying in London, just round the corner from him, could they meet up? He'd not heard from her for four years, he hadn't given her any thought or consideration. She didn't mention a child, so he cautiously thought it would be good to meet up. He was guarded, maybe she hadn't had the child?

The phone call disturbed and intrigued him.They agreed to meet in a nearby park.

The small park was lined with trees and benches. In a wooded corner it had some children's play equipment. Roger walked along the path in the dappled sunlight coming through a row of large trees just about to bud and leaf. He wasn't in the mood to notice the coming of Spring. From a distance, he saw Giselle walking toward him holding the hand of a young girl. Roger felt sick.

He instantly thought about escape and wanted to run away.

His head was spinning…this was his daughter!

'Hi, Roger.' Giselle fixed a stare straight into his eyes.

She was not the sophisticated elegant and sexy woman he had met previously. She retained some of her poise and elegance, especially in her clothing, but she now looked her age.

'Meet your daughter, Saskia.'

The thin little girl looked up and fixed a similarly determined stare in his direction, shrugged her shoulders, then looked away.

'Er, hello, Saskia.' He mumbled.

This was not what he had wanted, he felt embarrassed and awkward.

'I think we need to talk, Roger, it is time for you to take some responsibility.' Giselle hissed, trying to remain calm, but inwardly boiling with emotion as they walked towards the play equipment.

Giselle's life had fallen apart, she was now at her wits end. She was a lone parent trying to care for a sick child. Saskia had been a poorly child from birth, she suffered from a wide range of allergies, which had caused her to have difficulty breathing, hives, stomach cramps and diarrhoea. She then had chicken pox, which had debilitated her considerably, followed by eczema, and finally she'd contracted Hepatitis B leading to jaundice and impetigo. Giselle's mother had not helped her, and was now diagnosed with cancer, living back in Paris. Her friends had one by one abandoned her. They had thought her baby cute for a few weeks, but soon disappeared when the sickness started.

The dream of a perfect baby and a quiet transition into motherhood had not occurred. Giselle was now seriously on the edge of a nervous breakdown. She hadn't slept for more than 3 hours at a time since her daughter was born and fatigue was taking its toll. At the end of her maternity leave she found her job description had changed, she was on a part-time contract, with little hope of gaining the status she had enjoyed previously.

'Saskia, go play on the swings.' She snapped at her daughter.

'But, Mammon…' Saskia curled her lip in distain.

'Do.' Hissed Giselle as she shooed her daughter towards the play equipment. Saskia reluctantly trudged into the play area and sat disconsolately on a swing.

The two adults walked a short distance away to be out of hearing.

Giselle looked at Roger fiercely. His heart rate increased dramatically, he cowered and looked at the ground as they walked. 'I am suffering. It is your child, you need to do something. You are responsible for this. This is not what I wanted, it is your fault!' She raged at him.

He was silent, in terror, he didn't know how to react.

He felt afraid of Giselle and the intensity of her emotions, he was under attack.

She berated him for being an absent father.

'You have done nothing. I have done all the work, I have been up all the nights, you have left me to do all the work.' As they walked she was looking far into the distance. Wiping tears from her face, she continued 'You didn't contact me, you haven't tried, you have been completely absent.'

'But you told me not to, you didn't want me as the father.' He blurted.

'Roger, Roger, I told you, you were the father. Doesn't that mean something to you? You should at least have tried to find out what was happening. You knew it was happening, you knew you were the father. You never called, you have ignored your daughter for years now.'

Roger was dumbstruck by this turn of events. He was completely bemused and unable to express anything, so he shut down. He was out of his comfort zone, and he went onto automatic pilot.

He said nothing and looked at the ground, hoping it would swallow him up.

He resented Giselle's words, and was particularly unhappy about how she had changed her mind about his level of involvement. As far as he was concerned she had not wanted him involved and had clearly said she never wanted him near the two of them. Four years later she had suddenly turned up demanding he become the father. He remembered her saying that her daughter didn't need a father, and now this.

This was irrational and maddening behaviour.

Women, women, he didn't understand them. He felt he was being wronged, and yet, something in Giselle's words had struck home.

Deep down he had known he was a father.

He realized he hadn't bothered to find out if it was true. He'd not bothered to find out how either of them were. He hadn't tried to contact Giselle,

He'd carried on. He'd just not thought about it and continued his carefree lifestyle.

He'd distracted himself from such thoughts or responsibilities.

The score so far:

Roger: Nil   Giselle: One daughter

Note to self:

I am a father.

I am the father.

What am I supposed to do?

How do I 'be a father.'

Who do I turn to for advice?

Where's the instruction manual?

What does a father do?

I don't know. I haven't got a father, I've never had a father, so how can I be a father? What have I done? What do I do?

Do I tell Giselle to fuck off? Do I just say to her, piss off. It was your choice to have the baby not mine.

That seems to be the best option.

I'll be crap as a dad. I didn't mean to become a father. I've never wanted to be one.

She's at fault, it's all her fault. I'll tell her, I don't want anything to do with her daughter, she can find someone else to look after her.

She's probably just trying to scam me.

She wants my money, and she's going to screw me over.

She's tricked me into getting her pregnant, now she's going to trick me into paying for her daughter.

Despite his anger and outrage at the way Giselle had treated him, Roger found himself unable to let her know how he felt. He never did tell her that day or the next time they met. In Giselle's presence he would crumble. The alpha boy would look at the floor, feel small, and do as he was told. He had never felt so powerless with anyone before. He was told to look after Saskia the next day for an afternoon so Giselle could do some shopping. She delivered a tidy and very smart Saskia at his door precisely at one o'clock, and said she'd be back in four hours.

Roger stood in the kitchen whilst Saskia scouted round his flat, looking into all the rooms, which rather unsettled him.

'Do you want a cup of tea?' He asked hopefully.

She came into the kitchen and silently scanned him from toe to head, finally looking up at him in a very wise way for such a young soul.

'You've not really thought this through have you?' She responded.

'What do you mean?' He asked defensively.

'Well, there are no games for girls, no dolls. All the gadgets and toys are for boys. It's far too tidy and neat in here for a four year old, where can I play?' She swept her hand round dramatically, and twirled so that her dress spun round her legs. 'I don't drink tea, how old do you think I am? Old people drink tea, I'm only four, have you got some squash or juice?'

'Er, no.' He shook his head.

This is going to be the longest four hours of my life, he thought.

He wrung his hands, and then his face brightened and he asked 'Are you hungry?'

'Yes.'

'Oh, good, then we can go to Luigi's, it's just on the corner.'

'Does he have a children's menu?' she looked at him inquisitively.

'Oh, I don't know.'

'Do they have a vegetarian option?' She addressed this questioned to the whole room, having given up on receiving a sensible answer from Roger. 'Not really thought this through.' She muttered under her breath.

At the restaurant Luigi was enchanted by Saskia, and she was instantly granted access to the kitchens. She was serving her own ice cream as well as ordering the staff around within an hour.

She barely sat at the table with Roger, just to eat, and then she was off again. Roger was taken aback, but also impressed. He'd enjoyed her company, and it had been a very funny and entertaining time.

They returned to his flat.

On the way they had to cross a road, as they stood at the curb, she looked up at him and said; 'Have you forgotten something?' She took his hand; 'You're supposed to hold my hand.'

As they sat waiting for Giselle to collect her, Saskia smiled at her father, and then asked; 'Have you got a piece of paper and a pen?'

Roger rummaged through drawers and found an A4 sheet and a biro, which he handed to her. 'Do you want to draw?' He asked.

'No, I want you to write down a list.' She replied as she took them from him.

'A list of what?'

'The things you're going to buy before my next visit.'

In the beginning of his parenting career Roger had taken Saskia on a hit-and-miss basis. Often Giselle phoned him imploring him to come over and take the child, sometimes this was convenient, and other times he'd be away or at work.

This ad-hoc approach infuriated Giselle and after a while she imposed a two weeks rule. He had her for a Sunday once every two weeks for at least four hours. At first she didn't allow Saskia to stay, she still wanted to control her daughter's relationship with her father. As a consequence Roger continued to have a spare room, but after a while it started to turn into Saskia's room. There was a shelf for Spice Girls toys, jackets and other clothing; below this a shelf of books and magazines; a William Bunnykins Plush Toy and Casper glow in the dark pillow on the sofa; and a special cushion for her Tamagotchis which she brought with her from home.

She would stay for the afternoon and during this time they would often visit Luigi's where she'd visit the kitchen, watch the preparation of the meals and then help with the service. The staff quickly got to know her and encouraged her to become involved behind the scenes. Roger was a little anxious at first with his daughter's eccentric behaviour, but he became used to it, and watched with glee as his daughter bossed them all around.

The score so far:

Roger: One daughter   Saskia: One father

Note to self:

How did that happen?

'You will not talk to me like that.' Shouted Giselle.

'Why not?' Saskia replied, standing her ground.

'It is disrespectful, it shows you don't have respect.' Spluttered Giselle in her anger.

'You need to earn respect, Mammon, you get respect when you deserve it.' Snapped Saskia.

'You can not talk like this, it is very bad.' Her mother was feeling confused and a little dazed.

'I will talk the way I want.' Saskia turned and slammed her door shut.

Giselle and Saskia had a high-octane and high-volume relationship.

From the start they had both spoken to each other in highly pitched voices. Saskia asking in her own inimitable way for cuddles, comfort and love. Giselle steadfastly wanting her daughter to be well-behaved, silent and passive. As both of them were very headstrong, wilful people, this clash of interests hadn't yet been resolved.

Giselle continued to shout loudly and shrilly at her daughter, and Saskia replied in kind.

Constant high-pitched conversations and arguments were the norm, and both had severe headaches, heartaches and emotional trauma from being in such an atmosphere.

Deep down Giselle resented her daughter, she had never really bonded with her. She felt betrayed by her daughters' tendency towards illness and frailty. Giselle had wanted a "Bebe Bonbon", and all she had was a "L'enfant terrible". Saskia couldn't understand her mothers' reluctance to be kind or compassionate, and had realized the only way to gain attention was to be equally pig-headed.

Roger brought the two plates through from the kitchen, and placed them on the small table at which Saskia sat. He'd cooked beans on toast for the two of them, and was rather proud of himself. Saskia looked down at the plate in front of her and laughed. Roger flashed a look of annoyance at her. She took her knife and fork and looked up at him.

'Well done, beans on toast and nothing burnt, Luigi would be proud of you. Well done Roger.' She smiled at him.

'Yes, thank you.' He replied, but with a continued frustrated look.

'Something bugging you, daddy?' Asked Saskia as she leant over the plate to eat.

'Well, yes…sort of.' He started.

She interrupted. 'Yes, it is me too. What do I call you, that's the question, isn't it?' Saskia nodded at him, he nodded in return.

'Yes.'

'Well, what do I call you, Roger?' She had a pensive yet smiling look on her face. 'Shall I call you father? A bit too formal I think, don't you, Dad? A bit too old fashioned for you isn't it? Daddy? Daddy-oh? Daddy-oh, daddy-oh?' She giggled as she sang to herself.

'Yes, enough.' He laughed. 'I think you're going to call me whatever you like, and I don't have much of a say in it.'

'Yes, you're learning fast, Daddy doodle.'

That year something momentous changed in Roger's life. He wasn't actually aware of it, and if you had asked him he wouldn't have acknowledged what you were talking about. However, without him trying, he became a father. The subtly of that shift was slow and deep, occurring internally, and changing his perception of himself. He didn't want to be a father at first, but he couldn't deny he had become one, and with this his mindset changed. A variety of factors had influenced him, all of them supporting and aggregating the change within himself.

The biggest of those influences was obviously his daughter. When they were together she commanded his attention, she 'bossed' him, told him what to do, and he loved and enjoyed being obedient. She had an innately cheeky, precocious nature that made him smile, and which he admired. She stood up to her mother, he was very impressed by that. On occasions she was vulnerable and needed him as a father, needed support, and he was only too happy to give it. He'd never considered other people's needs before. Saskia stimulated parts of his nature he'd never been aware of. She did this by showing him unconditional love.

She didn't know he didn't want to be her father. She didn't know the circumstances of her conception. She just knew her mother and father didn't live together. She had accepted him from day one, and remarkably and unfathomably for him, she liked everything he did.

By accepting him as her father, she had enabled him to become her father. This happened slowly and imperceptibly, but it happened.

This change was also influenced by Giselle. She was a very insistent and persistent person who nagged him into taking the child. Through her own personal circumstances changing she had been forced to ask for help, something she had never done before in her life. She didn't like to feel dependent on anyone, it made her feel weak. In order not to admit to this perceived weakness, she behaved the way she did. She nagged, she bullied, and she insisted. Roger, unfamiliar with being treated like that, just gave way. From the beginning he found it easier to accept guilt and blame even if he felt it was undeserved, rather than fight against it. He found himself in the victim role for the first time in his life.

He told himself he was the victim of Giselle's bad behaviour and tempers, and he felt comfortable there. He accepted the place of the victim. He believed he was innocent, and gave Giselle the role of domineer, the perpetrator. He told himself how wonderful he was to take on the child, and how generous he was in giving her time and energy.

He started to think of himself as a father, and, most importantly, he actually started to enjoy being a father. He liked telling people at work he was a father. It gave him status. It was similar to when he became a marketing assistant manager. He felt promoted and somehow made more important.

Paradoxically, it also increased his chances with women on the weekends. Many of the passion mothers liked to talk about children, and he could share his anecdotes of his daughter, stressing his caring and compassionate side.

Chapter Nine

Receding hairline

The score so far:
Roger: 28 years.   The world: 1998.

'Roger, what a shocker, disgusting!' Stuart came in looking very angry. 'What did you do this weekend? Go on a rally?'

Roger had spent a lovely time in a yoga class in Sussex chasing a nubile. 'Oh, nothing much', he mumbled.

'Your car is covered in mud, Roger. You know your car is your office, come on, come on, get it clean. I can't have you seeing a client in a tractor, can I?' Stuart's eyes were bulging with the effort of maintaining his anger. 'Come on, get it washed, now.'

Roger went out into the car park and saw there were a few flecks of mud on the bodywork near the front wheels.

Fussy bastard, he said to himself as he bent down to wipe the flecks off with a piece of cloth.

Roger turned 28. His hairline receded.

It seemed to have happened overnight on his birthday or at least within a week. Roger didn't like this at all. It came as a shock. He saw the loss of his hair as a sign of weakness. His hairline was in decline and he equated that with the rest of his life. He felt angry, but also powerless. He had known it was inevitable he would lose some hair, that was why he had checked so fastidiously.

He had never considered it would actually happen.

This event gave him a sense of his own mortality. He felt he was no longer indestructible and the all-conquering king. The alpha boy was in decline. This wasn't the only event to make him feel this way.

Recently he had found he was tired a lot of the time, he had been ill with the flu for over a week, which was very unlike him. He was starting to struggle at work.

He'd always wanted to be a marketing assistant, and now after three years in the job, he felt insecure, stressed, and pressurized. The job description had changed, his responsibilities and tasks had increased, and it felt like he was suddenly doing two people's jobs for less money. His bank overdraft told him so anyway.

Proctor and Gamble, who until that time had seemed like a benign and helpful mentor, were changing. A fifth of the staff were laid off, many made redundant.

Roger just made it through those cuts for which he was grateful, but it unsettled him, it made him feel uneasy about the future.

One day in December he was approached by Unilever to become the assistant brand manager for their soap, Dove. This was a step up for Roger, and he found it too tempting to turn down. He had some qualms about leaving Proctor and Gamble, but he knew it was an opportunity he'd regret if he didn't take it. Any loyalty he'd felt about his job and relationship to his employers had vanished in the last year or so anyway. He told himself it was how the modern world was, move or be moved. Onwards and upwards.

The job meant even longer hours, he expected that. He threw himself into the new tasks, monitoring the market trends, overseeing the production of TV adverts, and running campaigns in the press and magazines, as well as organising direct mail and email campaigns.

These were the tasks he'd always wanted to do. He felt slightly out of his depth at first, the pressure of responsibility weighed on him right from the start, but he convinced himself that everything was fine.

Deep down he knew things weren't fine. Even with the step up to assistant brand manager, he couldn't escape the feeling that something was missing in his life. He'd wanted this job so much, and now he had it, within months he felt empty and hollow.

He didn't sleep well. He took pills on a regular basis. The pills would knock him out, but in the last months he'd noticed he'd had to take more and more of them, and they were less effective. He would wake early in the morning and in those moments he had the sense of having missed out on something, despite all his success. This was an alien concept to him.

In those early hours of the day he would reassure himself. 'I have everything I've ever needed, the flat, the car, I am the king, I've got the lifestyle'.

He'd revisit his affirmation on the fridge when he got up. But the worries and insecurities continued. He wasn't sure where this unease came from or what it was about, he was just aware of it looming over him. He found it difficult to find the words to describe how he felt. He tried to name it, he called it, somewhat poetically for him, 'the hole in the core of my being'.

This feeling made him melancholic and he'd fill with self-pity as it came on. He noticed he'd started to feel lonely for the first time in his life, despite the fact he had been on his own for so long. He tried to avoid these feelings by playing games on his computer, or drinking alcohol, but increasingly these distractions failed, the worries grew stronger and the hole in his being grew larger.

Another change had occurred which added to this sense of depression. He could no longer be his independent carefree self. He had a daughter. She didn't live with him, but he felt the added responsibility.

When he was feeling down about the world he believed he had a sick and ill daughter who needed lots of attention and care, whom he had been forced to look after.

In his good moods, he found having a daughter a blessing, he really enjoyed her company and she always found ways to brighten his life. She was now able to stay overnight and had made herself at home in his spare room.

Things were changing on the weekends as well. He wasn't getting the girls any more. More men were attending the events, and he was no longer the king of the scene.

He went to Glastonbury for a dance event, he'd gone because he was certain he'd have success. Five rhythm dances were always good for him.

After a deep and full bear hug Roger asked 'Hi, who are you?'

'Oh, hi, I'm Kate. Are you Roger?'

She looked intently up at him as they stepped back from the embrace.

'Wow, yes, how did you know?' He asked with a happy smile on his face.

'Oh, you know, intuition, and my friend Amelia told me about you.' Came the reply. Roger wanted to press on with the conversation.

'So, how did Amelia…' He broke off as Kate was now looking away from him and moving towards a man who had just walked in the door.

'Hello, Toby, how lovely to see you, how fantastic that you're here.'

She broke into a big welcoming smile and hugged the newcomer, for a lot longer than she'd hugged Roger.

They kissed passionately on the lips.

Roger was left standing, watching.

He continued to watch as the embrace lengthened and lingered.

Roger realized he was staring, he turned and walked away.

That night he'd slept fully and deeply, alone in his room.

The next morning at breakfast he was about to sit next to Kate.

'Hi, did you sleep?' He enquired.

'Oh, not a lot!' Came her enthusiastic reply. 'Oh, sorry, could you not sit there, someone is already sitting there.' She turned away looking for someone. Toby he presumed.

The score today:
Roger: Nil   Toby: One

The overall score so far:
Attendance: 62   Sex: 28   Success rate: 45%

Note to self:
OMG. For the first time my success rate is below 50%.

This is the fault of all these new men. There's too many of them, not only are they clogging up the aisles, they're not all lost souls and dragged men.

It was all so much easier back then!

The new competition is coming in the following forms, identify and classify:

Male model look
Sunny skinned surfer boys with bouncy blond hair.
Special appeal to the Nubiles.
Have much in common with them, in other words, are all focused on self, self, self.

Hurt by father men
Oh, I was such a deprived child.
My dad beat me.
I had to go without.
All the passion mothers love it, they lap it up.
Oh, you poor dear, let me console you.

This new-found male competition on the weekends

reinforced his feelings of insecurity and loss. The male model men made him aware of the growing age gap between him and the nubiles. They strengthened his insecurity about his hairline with their flowing locks. The hurt by father men were able to gain and hold the attention of the passion mothers, who were no longer impressed by his car and long list of sages.

To compound his feelings of unease he became conscious that there were only a limited number of workshops and women. Wherever he went now he was coming across the same women time and time again. He didn't want familiarity or commitment, he wanted 'new' every time.

What also concerned him was finding his reputation going before him. That was fine when it had been as the good-looking king, but for some women he was.

'Roger the predator.' He had heard some murmurings, disquiet about him, at previous events. He didn't understand how these women felt that way about him. 'Remember girls, it's just conquests without consequence, a bit of fun,' he said to himself. He justified their discontent as anger against men in general, or as jealousy for his successful lifestyle.

At one workshop he was confronted by an irate woman, whom he'd seen at many an event and had catagorised as a passion mother. She strode up to him.

'Ah, you're Roger the predator.'

She was a red-haired small earnest woman, who was looking him straight in the eye and not moving.

'Do you remember my friend Lizzie? You met her at the Satish Kumar lecture in June.'

'Er, no.' He was on the defensive.

'Yes, I'm not surprised. All you did was sleep with her.'

She rose on her heels and looked even more intently into his face. 'Well, she was devastated for weeks after. You just slept with her and then cast her away. Threw her away'

'Yes, but, hold on...'

'Don't interrupt me. You slept with her when she was very vulnerable and feeling really down. You then refused to give her your number, you just cut her out of your life. That was so not what she needed, exactly not what was going to help her. She was vulnerable and you took advantage. You made her feel even worse about herself. You managed to lower her self-esteem even further. You just used her. You left her down and out, and couldn't give a toss. So long as you got what you wanted, that was all you were concerned about.'

'Yes, but, it was just a bit of fun.'

'A bit of fun? Do you think spending the next two weeks feeling like shit is fun, do you think being used by a man is fun, do you think being made a fool of is fun?'

'She didn't say anything at the time.'

'She didn't say anything at the time, because you didn't allow her the time.'

The woman turned away, and then looked back at him.

'You make me sick, grow up, you're a grown man, stop acting like a teenager.'

With this she stormed off and re-joined a group of women, who were alternately giving her admiring looks and staring angrily at him.

He tried to dismiss the conversation. 'She's probably just a lesbian. She doesn't know about these things. She's just jealous.' But what she said struck deeply into him, disturbed him, the conversation got through to him, into the core of his being. He added it to the long list of changes in his life over which he had little or no control. His mood continued to darken. He resolved not to go to any more New Age events. He wanted a rest from them, too much hassle, he wasn't enjoying them any more.

He needed a different strategy, he decided he could meet women at clubs. This didn't inspire him, or fill him with confidence, but he could think of nothing better. That night he felt the hole in the core of his being grow just a bit bigger.

He decided he'd go to America and do a sweat lodge. He'd heard about the rituals and wanted to know more.

He thought to himself; 'the change of scenery will do me good as well. If I get away from the UK I'll get away from my critics. I can become a new person, not be judged.'

Chapter Ten

Grandfather in the lodge

Roger travelled a great distance. He'd been without sleep and through time zones.

A group of four people from England, Roger, another man and two women from Bagshot had made the journey. Roger had known the two women, Carol and Claire, for some time. They'd come close to being conquests, but they'd eluded him. He told himself he hadn't tried that hard. They agreed to no romance on the trip, and that made Roger feel relieved.

The group traveled by plane, bus and Land Rover and this left them jet-lagged and weary. They had thought the journey ended in the red heat of a very small dusty village, but they had been shaken and stirred in the back of a truck for another half an hour, to finally arrive truly in the middle of nowhere.

Mountains, scrub bush, scorched earth.

The end of the road.

They'd come to the Badlands, to the Black Hills of Dakota to sweat with 'the teacher'. He sat before them, this famous man...smoking Red Stripes and sipping Coca Cola! Fancy cowboy hat set at a jaunty angle. He was well over six feet tall, braided hair, dusty jeans and cloth waistcoat. Grandfather's wrinkled face looking out over the 40 or so people who were assembling. Roger too scanned the group. Out of habit noting the potential nubiles and passion mothers, and then rested on one of the rickety old chairs provided.

The teacher had four helpers with him, younger men and a woman, they were making tea for people from a rusty kettle a charcoal-filled fire. The teacher was smiling, wait just hanging. The helpers had informed them the happen today, but it may take some time. They careful to tell all the women to make sure they didn't find themselves alone with the teacher, if they did, 'He might take advantage of you, seeing as you're a white woman.'

Sat next to Roger were two insistent American men, who were constantly nagging and arguing with the assistants. They wanted to know, 'When are we going to start?' 'We can't wait all day.' 'We've got a meeting tomorrow morning which we need to go to.'

Roger sympathized with their need to have things happen when they were supposed to, but for some reason, he was also strangely unaffected. Normally, he too would be insisting on punctuality. Maybe it was the jetlag, but he was quite happy to sit on the rickety chair and look at the distant hills.

He immersed himself in the wild landscape, the dry smells and the feel of the teacher's company.

He was aware of the warmth of the sun on his skin and the faint touch of a gentle wind.

He didn't need to be anywhere else, or do anything else, he was content to sit.

The two men were getting more and more agitated, they kept hassling.

The assistants saying, 'It'll start soon.'

The teacher sat, smiling, nothing happening.

Then in the late afternoon something happened.

The two men left, jumped in their car and burst off in a cloud of dust and anger.

Once the dust from their wheels had settled, the teacher looked around, and said, 'Right, let's start.'

Later as the teacher and Roger sat surveying the bounteous spread of food, Roger broached the subject of the men.

'Oh, them two,' he replied 'I couldn't start anything till they'd gone, they weren't meant to be here.'

'But, how long were you going to wait, what if they hadn't

gone?' Roger asked.

The teacher chuckled to himself.

'Spirit needed to teach them a lesson, I don't do the teaching round here, I leave that to Spirit. All I knew was they were on "White People" time. I'm on "Red People" time - they're different, very different.' He cracked a smile to himself as he surveyed the array of mostly vegetarian food.

'Lots of rabbit food here,' he said. 'Nice food...but I prefer to eat the rabbit.'

He helped himself to a plateful and looked intently into Roger's eyes.

'So, where did you say you come from?'

'Britain.'

'That's part of London, right?'

'No, it's the country.'

'Oh, like England.'

'Yes, England is part of Britain' replied Roger with a little smile.

'Yes, that's right, it must be a good place,' the teacher continued.

'Why do you say that?' Roger asked.

'I like you and your people. You are more like Red People than the White People I normally get.'

'Wow, really,' Roger felt a blush, as he waited for some personal recognition from the teacher. 'Why do you say that?'

'Because the White People I normally do ritual with come with a lot of guilt and shame. You don't.' He paused, and then added. 'You're more ignorant and innocent, I like that.'

Roger was left trying to work out whether it was a compliment or not.

Grandfather addressed the whole group as they watched the sun slowly set.

'So, you have come here to learn about Inipi or sweat lodge.

You have come to sit at the feet of the teacher who knows the history of the Inipi. And I have to say to you, why did you come all this way?'

He looked out across the assembled keen and enthusiastic faces.

'I know the history of the Inipi, the true history of the ritual. These are the real stories, not the ones you were taught in your schools, I know more about our shared history than you can ever remember.'

He settled into his chair as he told his story.

'My people, the Red People, know how to remember important things, we don't write them down, we tell them as stories. That way you can retain the history in a pure form, without it being re-written. You came here and told us to read your book called the Bible. You told us that Jesus wrote it. It turns out Jesus didn't write it, and it has been re-written many, many times. That's not a true record of history.'

He pushed backwards in his chair and smiled at the silently enthralled audience.

'The stories I was told came from my grandfather, and from his grandfather, from his grandfather, and so on, we didn't write 'em down. We kept them as a secret from you, but also for you, because we knew sometime you might come over here and ask to hear the truth. So, what was I told? Inipi or Sweat Lodge is not a Red Person's ritual. We, the Red People, were taught the lodge by you lot a long time ago. The story goes that White People came through the North of our land, and brought the Inipi with them. It seems like you've come on a long journey, flying in your planes, travelling in your cars, to learn how to do something you already knew. Something your ancestors knew well, something you used to do for thousands of years. My job is to remind you of who you are. When you hear my voice you will be hearing the voice of your ancestors.'

By late evening the sweat lodge was built. They gathered round in the growing gloom of the sunset, and prepared to enter. Grandfather said they'd all smoke the pipe before entering, they knew this was an ancient pipe, hundreds of years old. The group fell to a reverential hush as the ceremonial pipe was unwrapped and assembled. The teacher was acutely aware of the reverential awe.

He fumbled for his tobacco; 'Where's the sacred flashlight when you need it?'

After the lodge the group sat round the fire and the teacher continued;

'Before your people came over here and changed the way we behave. We lived on the plains and in the mountains, and we relied on the buffalo. It supplied all our needs, and we had a sacred agreement with it.'

The teacher looked around as if trying to see if there were any buffalo out there.

'In those times there were so many buffalo that sometimes you couldn't see anything but buffalo from one part of the sky to the other. In that time we learnt to read their movements, we sought to know as much as we could about them. We became intimately linked because of our willingness to observe and interpret them. When you learn about another animal it is also a teaching for yourself, about your own nature.

We noticed most of the buffalo wanted to live in the middle of the herd. There they were very safe, they felt the company of others and were aware of all the stories and gossip. That was all very fine, but there were disadvantages as well. Those buffalo in the middle of the herd were often hit by others because it was so cramped. They had to move when the herd moved, and they lived with the dust of the plains in their nostrils all the time. To live this way meant you only ever ate trampled grass, not fresh or new grass.'

He looked down at the red raw soil under his feet and gently smiled to himself.

'Whilst observing the herds we saw that some of the buffalo chose not to live in the middle of the herd. These ones chose to live at the edges. They were more likely to be killed by the wolves, they ran a higher risk. But, they ate fresh and luscious grass, they could go at their own speed, they were not hurried by others, and they got to see the vista, the full magnificence of the wider and bigger picture.'

He stopped to let the story sink in.

'Some of you people who come from London and Britain, you live on a pretty small island, you could fit most of it on one farm here in the States. As a consequence, you people live in the middle of the herd. You have a lot of dust in your noses and lungs. But, every now and then you're going to come across someone who chooses to live on the edge of your herd. When you do, listen to them, they have seen the bigger picture, they eat the nice green grass, they can help you.'

Back home, Saskia's trips to stay with her father became isolated islands of bliss and calm for her. She enjoyed them as they were in stark contrast to her home life. Saskia and her mother continued to have conversations at a very high pitch and intensity. As a consequence Saskia still felt weak and ill on occasions, but not as often as before.

Roger occasionally used reflexology or massage to alleviate some of Saskia's pains and aches. The first attempts at help had been fumbled by him, he was unsure about what to do, but such attention was very enthusiastically welcomed by his daughter. The physical contact calmed her considerably. Over the years, he started to pay more and more attention to the workshops he attended - purely for his daughter's sake of course. He learnt new and effective techniques for pain relief. Eventually, he could see the benefits of all his weekend New Age activities. His daughter found relief in his passing them on.

He would massage her feet and practice reflexology. She would respond with a great big smile and curled toes.

He encouraged her to breathe deeply when in pain, and often they spent time meditating and practicing yoga.

His relationship with Saskia deepened as she grew. He really looked forward to their times together. He made himself available every second weekend, and insisted that Giselle ensure she came. Giselle was happy to comply. He was very proud of Saskia, he talked about her often at work. Becoming a father made him happy, and he enjoyed the changes it brought within himself. He was now able to consider others needs, he liked to be of service to his daughter, he took on responsibilities. He did on occasions miss the thrill of the pursuit and his conquests without consequence, but he shuddered when he thought of the confrontation with the red headed woman at the last workshop, he'd didn't want to go back to that.

With the weekend workshops being unavailable to him, he decided he'd try to meet a woman at 'Suzie's', a local bistro and bar. He took his time in the bathroom and bedroom, selecting and arranging. In the end, he put on a smart shirt, a classic from Farah Vintage, and some casual trousers, a designer pair from Mark Westwood. He had sprayed himself liberally with Michel Gemain 'sexual fresh' Pour Homme deodorant, then brushed and combed his hair to cover his thinning areas as best he could. 'Looking good' he waved himself goodbye in the mirror as he left his house.

Someone had told him it was a good place to pick up women. It was a smart and fashionable bar, full of people, loud music, lots of posing and watching going on.

He squeezed his way to the bar, ordered a drink, and then took his time perusing the large room. The red, white and black décor was highlighted by the glittering attire of several groups of women, who were laughing, chatting and glancing around. All the groups were at least six or seven strong, they were all very loud and dominating, he felt intimidated by their numbers. He continued to look and observe.

He settled his attention on a couple of women in a corner seat. They were chatting intimately and every now and again looking up and around. He thought they looked young, attractive, vaguely familiar, so he decided to focus on them. After about half an hour the blonde rose and made her way to the toilets. He didn't approach her, but he moved closer to the toilets, and awaited her return. As she came through the door he gave her his big welcoming smile.

'Hi, how you uum doing?' His greeting came out wrong, stumbled over his words, he felt hurried.

'Yes, I'm doing fine, thanks. How are you?' Came the embarrassed response. The woman was also awkward, she shuffled her feet, and then looked him in the face.

'Yes, sorry, fine.'

He struggled, he felt awkward, he didn't know what to do or say next. There was a pause before she responded.

'Look, hi, Roger, nice to see you. I'm over with Kensy in the corner, it's her birthday, we're about to go. Got to dash.' She was slowly backing away from him.

He was dazed, he didn't recognize her, desperately searching in his mind, he couldn't place her.

The woman realized this.

'I'm Lizzy, Lizzy from finance?' She was now feeling annoyed with Roger and flashed an angry look his way.

'Oh, yes, of course. Oh, well have a good evening, have a good time.'

He still didn't know who she was and starting to flush again.

She waved at him, turned, and rejoined Kensy.

'Just met Roger from Marketing, he's over there. Don't look, don't look, we don't want him coming over.' She whispered. 'He didn't even recognize me.'

'Oh, God, I know him, he's kind of cute in an older man sort of way.' Kensy answered.

'No way, Kensy, he's far too old for you. We're looking for a proper man for you tonight'

'Oh, alright then.'

Roger sat nursing a drink for the rest of the evening, he was feeling out of place and crest fallen.

Two men, late evening drunks, included him in their conversation about football and the state of the celebrity world. Eventually, they invited him to join them at a club round the corner for 'more of a good time'.

They edged down tight, dirty and ill-lit stairs, past the imposing bouncer, through the small door and into a starkly lit bar. Roger was greeted by the smell of stale beer, loud techno music pumping out a bass tune, and about twenty other punters. The three of them headed for the bar and paid exorbitant prices for minute shots. They turned and stood propping the bar, looking forlornly out over the empty dance floor.

'It always hots up after two.'

Shouted one of the drunks into Roger's left ear.

'Full of totty by two thirty this place.'

Shouted the other drunk into Roger's right ear.

Two thirty came and went and the bar continued to be deserted and desperate. Roger made his way to the toilets and then gave his two new friends the slip and went home.

The score so far:

Roger: Two bars   Success: Nil   Humiliation: A lot

Note to self:

Who are Lizzy and Kirsty?

It's better, easier, less humiliating to have a wank than to go out. Stick to porn.

Chapter Eleven

Out of the world and down to earth experiences

The score so far:

Roger: 29 years.   The world: 1999.

Roger had enjoyed the trip to America and the sweat lodge. He really liked the challenge of the heat and release of sitting in the lodge, and he wanted more. He sought out a teacher in Britain. He found one, and committed himself to attending the event regularly, they were every two months. At these lodges he found himself actually paying attention to the teacher, and committing himself to the process each time. He was now part of the group who were all committed to attending as often as possible, he wasn't there for conquests without consequence. He felt comfortable not having to make the effort of chasing someone each time.

His attitude to the other group members softened as he got to know them. He didn't treat the men with contempt as he had done at other events. He enjoyed the company of two men in particular, Richard and James. The three of them shared details of their lives and by doing so they were able to build trust. The other two had well-paid and responsible jobs, and Roger enjoyed being able to offload and share his concerns about the stresses and strains of work.

The sweat lodge teacher was a fierce, bearded, swarthy Mediterranean man in his late fifties. He had a huge belly, sharp temper, was very cutting on occasions, but also had a wonderfully inviting laugh. This was a huge troll of a man. He took the ceremonies very seriously, and insisted on focus and attention to detail, which appealed to Roger.

The group assembled once every two months in the middle of the deeply green, luscious fields and woods of northern Devon. The event was supervised by the teacher and his assistant, the fire-keeper. Each time they'd construct a low, circular, willow framework onto which they would pile blankets and tarpaulins. At a short distance from the lodge the fire-keeper would build a sturdy wooden pyre, holding many volcanic rocks in its' core. When both structures were completed they would light the pyre, which would consume a huge amount of wood in order to heat the rocks to red-hot. Once the rocks were hot enough the group entered the covered structure and sat in the darkness of the willow frame. The fire-keeper brought in some red-hot rocks on a shovel and placed them in a hole in the middle of the floor. He'd then shut the door and continue tending the fire. He would bring in the rocks four times, each time increasing the heat.

The teacher would chant, pray and pour water onto the rocks. The steam from the rocks intense and almost unbearable. In the pitch black of the lodge, each person would take it in turns to say prayers, offer their thanks, or to just sing or cry. The immense heat and the darkness seemed to draw raw emotions out of people in an irresistible way, and many would break down into tears or find peace. This process could take many hours to complete. The resultant feeling of release, relief and cleansing at the end was very satisfying for Roger. Some hardy types would come out of the intense heat and immerse themselves in the cold waters of the stream running nearby. Roger loved to do that too when he was in the mood.

One night he sat on his towel in the pitch black of the sweat lodge, breathing deeply and slowly. The heated steam from the stones rose irrepressibly around him, taking his breath away, lightening his head.

Drawing his consciousness out of his body and up through the top of the willow structure, on into the extremities of the earth's biosphere. There the quiet, still vast space was dark, vibrant and sparkling.

Roger floated.

Viewing it unafraid, unmoved by this immense miraculous transformation, just accepting, being himself.

Then a voice came to him:

'Plant the seeds.'

In his altered state of being his hands were filled with seeds of all sizes and descriptions and he bent down inserting them into thick, dark black humus. As he stood back up, he could vaguely see others doing the same around him.

In the next moment thick, dense foliage unfurled all around him.

It grew, thrived, danced with him. The people were creating a huge forest of beauty and desire. He stood and admired, overcome by the immensity of their actions. He was then drawn back down, through the soil, the biosphere, back down into the familiar landscape, through the top of the lodge, into his body once more.

Roger could hear the teacher, 'Thank your guides, thank your helpers, thank those who have assisted you.'

Just a day earlier he and the teacher had sat discussing the logistics of the sweat lodge. The teacher had told him there were to be two groups. The first would plough the soil, the second would plant the seeds. Roger was uncertain which group he should join, the teacher listened to his confusion, and then looked fiercely at him.

'Roger, how much longer are you going to spend preparing the fucking soil?'

Roger returned his glare with a little embarrassed shrug of the shoulders and a smile.

'I'll be in the second group then.'

They both laughed.

Roger didn't know how to thank his guides, but into his mouth came these words. 'Thank you all, I have found my new name, here amongst you, my pack.'

He didn't know what he was talking about.

The teacher calmly said 'I hear you brother, what is your new name?'

Roger hesitated, but then continued: 'My name was Lone Wolf, but as of now, I am Grey Wolf.'

Silence greeted this unexpected announcement from all in the lodge.

The teacher grunted his approval, and added: 'So, if you're now Grey Wolf, let's hear your name properly.'

Roger drew in a breath. In that moment he thought he would shout out 'Grey Wolf' really loudly.

He didn't.

He howled.

Face pointing upwards. Blood-chillingly. Authentically.

From deep within his diaphragm came his name, his call, his statement of being. His wildness, pride, love, passion for life. He announced to the world who he had become.

Roger the Grey Wolf slept deeply and well that night, and then rose early to return to work. The separation process soon kicked in, and within a couple of days he was back to his normal routines and didn't give this new name much thought.

He returned on the tube that Monday evening in a good mood after a stress-free day at work, and as he made his way up the underground tunnel, he suddenly remembered the beggar.

A while ago the beggar had called him Mr. Wolf. The Buddha beggar had known his name before he had known it himself.

His blood ran cold.

He pushed up through the crowd, to the corner where the beggar normally sat, there was no one. He had gone.

The next morning as he rushed to work he noted again the

man wasn't there. This was very unlike him, he was always there. That evening the same again, he had disappeared.

The next Saturday Saskia came to visit, she rushed in with a disappointed look on her face.

'Mr. Magic has gone' she announced.

'Oh, dear' replied Roger.

Mr. Magic, as far as Roger knew, was a fun character in Saskia's world, and had been around for some time. She mentioned him on an irregular basis as making balloon animals with her, showing her card tricks, magic singing and chanting even. Roger had presumed he was a feature of Giselle and Saskia's life together. Giselle had presumed that Mr. Magic was someone Roger and Saskia shared. Both parents had not really thought very deeply about Mr. Magic and presumed the other knew what was going on.

That day Roger replied. 'What a pity, you and your mother will miss him.'

'Why would my mother miss him? She doesn't know him' Saskia replied, surprised.

'I don't know, I presumed she knew him too.'

'No, Mr. Magic lives in the tunnel, he lives in the tunnel going up to your house, but he's gone now.'

Roger froze, a shiver ran down his spine.

'Did Mr. Magic have a big brown coat and string round his middle?' He asked tentatively.

'Yes, that's him, he was good fun, he was always there, but he's not there now.' 'Oh...my...God' was all Roger could say.

Roger had a lot on his plate at Unilever. The new responsibilities at work weighed heavily, and he struggled to keep up with the demands made of him. Each year on year he had to commit more time and effort to work. The job consumed a large amount of his life.

He was also very keen to spend his second weekends with his

daughter, and he kept them as clear as possible.

He was now no longer going to any New Age weekends, all he was attending were the sweat lodges, and he tried to do this as regularly as work allowed. When at the sweat lodges he had built a good relationship with James and Richard, he could discuss his problems with them in a mature way.

He didn't feel inclined to go to bars and clubs looking for women after his initial experience at Suzie's.

He wasn't playing on his Game Boy so much.

When he thought about all these changes, he realized he had a very different lifestyle to before: the selfish and indulgent, carefree conquests without consequence.

In many ways he was starting to mature, and this maturity was affecting his expectations. He felt it was connected to his expectations about being with a woman, being in a relationship.

He was no longer seeking one-night stands.

He knew deep inside himself, he wouldn't be content with continuing the pursuit of instant gratification.

If he wasn't seeking that, then what was he seeking? What was he capable of?

Maybe he was capable of having a longer, deeper, more meaningful relationship. Maybe that was the hole in the core of his being. Maybe his not being in a meaningful relationship with a woman was the pain he felt early in the morning.

Roger had always focused on his career. This seemed the right thing to do, and he'd been rewarded for his self-devotion. The pursuit of work and career had necessarily focused on his goals and needs, rather than the consideration of other people's. He'd lived a superficial and responsibility-free lifestyle. Giselle's intervention, and her forcing him to cope with Saskia had changed all that. He had to take others into consideration. Becoming a father had been a catalyst for many changes in his life, and he started contemplating what could be the next stage for his development. He felt he was ready to move on, to become something new and different, not so superficial. He was willing to consider having a relationship with a woman.

He had never really understood what it meant to be in a relationship. He'd not had such things role-modeled to him. His early recollections of his parents' relationship were missing. He couldn't remember what it had been like to have a father and a mother who interacted with each other. His mother kept her life very separate from Roger. He saw her as detached, in limbo, unable to start again. Walking head down on 'Lone Street'. He didn't know what his parent's relationship had been like and he hadn't bothered to find out.

Throughout his adult life he'd never tried for a deep or meaningful connection with a woman. Instead he'd had lots of pursuits, conquests without consequence. They hadn't taught him anything about the responsibilities of being in a relationship. They left him now feeling empty and shallow.

Saskia was the product of the longest relationship in his life, two weeks with Giselle. Not the best model of good practice.

His self-focus and lack of experience had left him emotionally immature and unable to relate to others. A consequence of this immaturity was his inability to understand how other people perceived him. He couldn't read the signs very well.

In his head he was the victim of Giselle. It fitted nicely into his worldview that she had forced him against his will. He still suspected she would start asking for money at any time. He didn't see that Giselle had completely softened towards him. She often thanked him for taking Saskia. She respecting and appreciated the stability he brought to her daughter's life. She even complimenting him on being a good father. Roger didn't hear these comments, he was too busy thinking 'poor me'.

'Roger, we need to discuss something.'

Saskia was perched on the arm of the sofa. She regally beckoned her father to sit on the sofa.

He did as he was told.

She smiled at him, slid across and onto his lap. She snuggled up to him.

'We need to discuss Christmas.' She looked at him earnestly.

'OK, it's a month away, but yes, OK.' He responded. 'I'm happy for you to spend the morning with your mother and then for you to come over here in the evening like we did last year.'

'Yes, I know you are happy with that arrangement.' She said abruptly. 'I'm not.' she paused to make sure she had his focus, which of course she did.

'I want it to be different this year.' She continued 'I want to spend the whole day at my mother's.'

'Oh.' Disappointment in his voice.

'Now, don't jump to conclusions, father.' She smiled. 'I want to spend the whole day at my mothers', but with you and your mother coming for dinner. Everyone together at the same time in the same house on the same day.' She concluded. 'That way we don't have to rush and drive, chop and change, everything all in the same place.'

'I see, no, that makes sense.' He concurred. 'Yes, that's a good idea, not so much driving would be better.' He was nodding, then added 'What about your mother?'

'I'll deal with her.'

From an early age Saskia had been adept at influencing and manipulating people. She was very strong willed, which almost invariably meant she got what she wanted. She didn't need to be mean or underhand, she was often very open and honest, and she allied this to her considerable charm and innate good sense of humour.

Roger found it very difficult to resist her, and she had found many ways to ensure he gave her what she wanted. The first few Christmases had been awkward and difficult affairs. Saskia moving from one parent to the other, trying to fit other relatives in, Roger seeing his mother, Giselle going to Paris to see her mother, it was very bitty and unsatisfactory. So, Saskia had decided how she wanted Christmas to be. She wanted the whole family together for one day. Roger had found that first Christmas under Saskia's new rules awkward. He wasn't comfortable being in Giselle's house. Giselle also found it difficult, but both of them realized their daughter had a point. After a couple of years it became a familiar routine, and the day went some way to reconciling Giselle and Roger. The two of them committed to being together once a year for their daughter.

The Lone Wolf

'The female wolves teach the young wolf survival skills through fun and play, he likes that. However, one day, he is thrown out of the family, he is no longer welcome. This can come as a huge shock to some boy wolves. Others are ready and willing to make the change. For all of them, the result is the same. He is left on his own, and has to fend for himself.

In this state he can either sink or swim, and many young wolves are unable to make the transition from dependence to independence. Those who make it through this rite of passage do so by toughening themselves. They become lean, they create a tough shell around themselves, and they become survivors.

As you know, there are inherent risks in this strategy. Often you can lose contact with your compassion, with your nurturing side by toughening yourself. This can lead to illness. In your culture you call it "depression".

Being alone is a good lesson, but you mustn't be alone for too long.'

Tsao Chinem Cllens

Chapter Twelve

Breakthrough time

The score so far:

Roger: 33 years.   The world: 2003.

Roger continued to go to the sweat lodge ceremonies every other month. They weren't always as eventful as the one in which he received his name, but they acted as clearing and cleansing times for him. He built a good relationship with Richard and James, and this sustained him. The three of them would chat on the Friday night, sitting next to each other on a long and very comfortable sofa, nursing cups of hot tea and eating chocolate biscuits, it became a familiar and welcome routine.

'Well, I'm sorry boys, but I've been given some pretty shit news,' blurted James as he settled on the sofa.

The other two exchanged a quick glance.

'I've been told I'm being made redundant at the end of September.' James continued. 'I've been given a good settlement, a nice package, but it's one heck of blow.'

'Dead right it is, that's crap news, mate,' concurred Richard.

'That's tough.' added Roger.

'I knew it was in the pipeline, but it is still such a blow when you get the news, know what I mean?' asked James.

'Yes.' Replied Roger. 'It must be bloody debilitating.'

Roger had no idea how James was feeling, but he knew he had to make sympathetic noises. Richard felt the same.

'Well, it's also an opportunity. You'll be able to start up your own business, you've been talking about that for a while.' Richard sought the silver lining.

Despite the other two sympathizing and made encouraging

noises about there being better jobs out there, James was very down.

He was 45, and he said his chances of finding another job were very limited. The other two could see the logic of this argument, but didn't voice it. They remained optimistic in the face of his obvious discomfort. James was badly affected by his redundancy and become fixated on his bad luck, which became a bit boring for Roger, he didn't have much sympathy. After a couple more sessions James left the group.

Roger thought, 'unlucky bastard', and congratulated himself on his job at Unilever.

The regular group of participants at the sweat lodges were about twenty in number, of these normally fourteen or so were woman. The three men called them "the sisterhood." At first they reminded Roger of the sinister women who had judged him, but as he got to know them, he saw them in a different light.

They were a close-knit community of women, mostly between the age of thirty and forty-five, one sixty-six-year-old. The group held a fascination for Roger, they were able to talk about deep and personal things together, share their tears and joys, laugh and shout at each other without harbouring judgments or feuds.

This amazed him. He couldn't understand how they could be so open, without being judged and without fear of being judged. For him such behaviour was unimaginable. Roger had never behaved that way. He had talked with Richard and James, but they didn't go that deep, they remained wary of each other, rivals. Amazingly, these women didn't appear to be rivals, they actually collaborated and mutually supported.

He would sometimes sit on their table at meal times and just listen in to their conversations. He felt in awe of their ability to be frank and forthright. He knew it was something he needed in his life, but he wasn't sure how to go about finding it. It again reminded him of the hole at the core of his being, something else that was missing. The sisterhood made him think about friendship.

Roger had work acquaintances with whom he'd sometimes go for a drink after work. They were mostly women. When he thought about it he realized he didn't have many male friends at all. Roger saw his relationships with men of his own age only ever as rivalries. He would invariably judge and make instant assessments of other men. If they looked like alpha males, they had jobs and status, he'd communicate as an equal. Otherwise he was not interested. He'd had no time for those poor seekers of enlightenment, the hippy New Agers, who struck him as being desperate and needy. He reassured himself that he would never be like that. He had some time for older men, men who had experience. He was often drawn to them. He liked his sweat lodge teacher, but he didn't really commit to any in-depth relationships with him, he didn't share anything too intimate.

James and Richard were acquaintances, the closest he had to friends. However, since James' redundancy Roger found it hard to communicate with him. James had talked about nothing else, and Roger found this difficult, embarrassing even. When James dropped out, despite the fact that Roger liked him, he didn't keep in contact. Roger felt he should be in contact with people who had jobs, in his terms, people who were 'well'. By losing his job, James had stepped beyond this, into another reality that Roger was not interested in visiting.

One week he decided he'd go to an evening talk in Piccadilly, at the Alternatives centre. He reassured himself beforehand that it wasn't a weekend workshop, it was just a talk, no being picked on by red headed women. Out of habit, Roger scanned the audience for nubiles and passion mothers. He rued to himself about the numbers of men coming to the event. He noted at least half the audience were men, and some of them looked very powerful and confident characters. How had this happened? 'They've all started copying me', he thought.

At that moment his consciousness honed in to the words of the speaker.

'What if Jesus were to be amongst us now? Would we recognize him as the Son of God. Would we follow his teachings and want to be with him? We'd all like to think so. We'd all like to think of ourselves as his disciples, wouldn't we? But how many of us would just think of him as a beggar, a hobo, a vagrant? How many of us would even give him the time of day?'

The speaker's words struck deep into Roger. He felt them resonate and disturb him in a way he had never felt before. In his mind he saw the Buddha beggar. He saw how he had dashed past the man, casting judgments every day, and now he was gone. Where had he gone? Probably he was dead, that was a real possibility.

Roger had been sickened by the beggar, but also drawn to him.

He shut his eyes and saw in his mind's eye the beggar sitting in the lotus position radiating love and compassion to the passers by. He remembered the beggar calling him by his name before Roger had known it. He saw his daughter call him Mr. Magic, and sit on the floor with the beggar.

Roger felt a surge of familiar pain in his body. It moved through his body until there was a huge pressure in his head. Emotions were surging and swirling up through his body, washing through him. Emotions he couldn't name or identify - they were despair, loneliness, dissatisfaction and unhappiness.

He struggled to control and suppress them but was overcome. He felt tired, exhausted, weary of the world. The world went black.

He opened his eyes and the male speaker was stood close in front of him. He was looking down at Roger with a crooked smile. 'That's it, brother, let it out, let those tears flow.'

Roger's face was wet with tears, they were spilling from his chin to his shirt. He'd been crying and sobbing deeply for some time. He felt ashamed, he struggled to regain control of himself. Failing, he stood up.

The man pulled Roger towards him and gave him a tight hug. 'That's it, let those tears flow.' The hug had exactly the opposite effect. It staunched all of Roger's tears and emotions. He felt squashed, oppressed by this stranger.

He sought to struggle free from the unwanted embrace.

Roger realized he was familiar with this sensation, he had felt this way before. His body desperately sought to give vent to emotions, and yet the hug was stopping the flow. Roger pushed the man away and struggled through the audience, out of the door into the cool evening air. There he realised he was in a deep emotional state, totally unfamiliar territory for him, and in that moment he had a vision.

He saw all the times he'd offered similar insincere hugs to women. He saw how he'd suppressed and oppressed their need for connection, or to express emotion. How he'd focused on squeezing and pressing himself up against them. He saw how many times he'd not listened to the trauma, but just sought to meet his own needs. He had felt it was fine to behave that way, but now such a response seemed empty and vacuous to him. He shuddered from deep within himself and instinctively looked up at the starry night sky.

'Oh my God, I'm having a fucking breakdown!' He screamed upwards, heaven bound.

Breakdowns were what happened to poor unlucky bastards like James, not him.

Roger spent a disturbed and unsettled night, worrying, being scared, and feeling out of control. He woke exhausted the next morning and called in sick. The first time he had ever done such a thing. He was not sick, he was just exhausted, but he also knew he would have been unable to do any work that day. He went back to sleep and slept all morning.

He dreamt of being in a long-term relationship. He dreamt of how comfortable it felt to be held by a woman. To be completely enveloped by her warmth and presence without a sexual agenda. He longed for that embrace. For the embrace to be about stability and depth, a deep open heart connection. In his dream he snuggled into the comfort and warmth for as long as he could, and gained strength and renewal there.

When he woke, he could feel the hole in the core of his being aching, longing for something more.

The score so far:
Roger: Mini-breakdown, temporary glitch

Note to self
What have I lost?
  Hairline
  Invincibility and king status at New Age workshops
  Marbles
  What have I gained?
  A daughter
  A lot of stress at work
  Sweat lodges
  What remains the same?
  Not a lot

Roger sat on the floor of his spare room. It had now been completely taken over by Saskia. The air was heavy with a cheap sprayed perfume, and laden with the pink dust from children's toys which had been played with and were now abandoned, scattered randomly over the floor. He had a brightly jewelled crown placed jauntily on his head, bright red lipstick sprawled across his lips and right cheek. A pink scarf wrapped round his neck and a series of plastic imitation pearl necklaces thrown around his upper torso. He was wearing a long blanket as a dress, and Saskia was trying to fit his gargantuan feet into her tiny plastic pink shoes.

Her forehead was wrinkled with serious intent, and she succeeded in squashing the first half of his foot into a shoe. 'There,' she said triumphantly as she rose from the floor. A big smile and laugh emerged as she surveyed her work.

'Come on darling, show me how you walk, show me how you dance,' she teased her father.

He tottered up onto the edges of his pink heels and wobbled around the room, as he did so he tripped over the leading edge of the blanket and fell in a heap.

Now they were both hysterical, laughing, panting and crying as she threw herself on top of him.

'No, no, no, darling, walk with style, walk with elegance, not like the ugly duckling.'

He sat on the sofa watching the television, laughing out loud on occasions, whilst watching his favourite show 'Two and a half men'.

Charlie was once again getting the girl whilst Alan was beating himself up. Suddenly Roger saw how his life was reflected in the show.

'I get it. I used to be the New Age Charlie Harper. The other men at the workshops were Alan Harpers. I was the successful businessman, serial pursuer of women, afraid of commitment, but…I always got the girl. The men punters were all unsuccessful chiropractors, how true to life is that! They were jealous of me. They weren't as successful in so many ways as me. I love it, makes the program even funnier!'

Roger chuckled to himself.

Chapter Thirteen

Jules the jewel

The score so far:
Roger: 34 years.   The world: 2004.

At the last two sweat lodges of that year, Jules, a new passion mother arrived. She was open-faced, wore a bright jewel in her nose, had long dark hair, and was seeking to change her life after going through a messy divorce. All music to Roger's ears.

He focused his attention on her, spent time listening, being supportive, and sure enough she started to melt towards him. However, she didn't succumb to his charms on the first or the second session as he had wanted, she had actually pulled back quite abruptly. He was disconcerted by her actions, he didn't know how to react. He hadn't been with anyone for some time, and there was touch of neediness and desperation in his pursuit of her. She had felt this, but had decided to go ahead anyway, not that Roger could tell.

Roger heard himself saying the words 'Yes, let's exchange numbers, I'll give you a call next week.' He had never uttered those words before, something was happening, something had changed in him. Jules lived in London, just half an hour away by underground.

He could phone her if he wanted.

He wanted.

He phoned her on the Tuesday, not the Monday, that would have been too needy. He'd spent the whole of Monday desperately waiting for it to be Tuesday.

They met up for a meal in a favourite expensive restaurant of his. He politely listened to her talking about her divorce, her teenage sons, and he talked about Saskia. They had got on.

Jules was happy for him to come round on the Saturday for a home-cooked meal at her place. Her kids were staying with her ex. The meal was accompanied by two expensive bottles of red wine he'd brought, and they'd ended up in bed together.

He thought he'd been in control and made all the running, she'd known otherwise.

He woke early the next morning with a start, disorientated, not knowing where he was, after collecting himself, he thought about how and when to get home.

She stirred and said sleepily, 'Good morning.'

They turned to face each other, and she kissed him on the lips, and then said, 'For being such a pretty boy, you're crap in bed.'

'What?'

He was shocked.

'You may have a reasonably big cock but you really don't know how to use it, do you?' She spoke in a calm and steady voice, a smile on her face, open and sincere, and yet the words struck him like a knife.

'I've…I've…not had any complaints yet.' he spluttered, under a deeply frowned forehead.

'That's because you probably never stayed long enough to hear them.' came her measured response.

'Shit, I don't have to take this.' he replied abruptly.

'So you're going to love and leave me, like all the others, are you?'

'What?'

'I was warned by the sisterhood about you, but I thought you might be worth the gamble.'

'God, you lot talk about everything don't you.'

'Pretty much,' she smiled.

'Come on, Roger, stay and play, stay and enjoy yourself, stay and have fun. The two of us can learn from each other, it doesn't have to be a wham, bam, thank you ma'am. I've got a few hours before my kids come back, let's do it properly this time.' She pulled him towards her and kissed him full on the lips.

He was baffled, startled, angry and aroused all at the same time.

He stayed. Not only did he stay, he returned.

Jules quickly became a feature in his life and this changed him in many ways.

Two months later as he ran and sweated on the exercise bike in his local gym, he assessed the impact Jules had on his lifestyle:

'Running on exercise bike: didn't used to do that.

Diet changed, eating healthy: blimey even eating vegetarian food.

In a relationship: actually enjoying it.

Used to think of them as 'man-traps'. Used to think that a man was tamed if he was in a long term relationship. Thought it would be boring.

It doesn't have the buzz of the chase and pursuit. But that was addictive and destructive in the long run.

Got security now.'

After a few more months with Jules he admitted to himself he rather enjoyed being tamed. Roger felt at ease with her, he was still on occasions shocked by her blunt manner, but he really enjoyed her company. He realized by being in a relationship he had undergone some pretty profound changes:

He had consciously allowed Jules into his life.

He was giving the relationship time, and by doing so he was growing to like her and the concept of being a couple.

He enjoyed it when they went shopping or went out for a meal together.

He enjoyed spending time with her two boys, and his daughter very much enjoyed them all being together.

They had a social life as a couple.

Jules had many friends, and they became an established couple in this circle, which he enjoyed.

And, of course, there was the sex.

Good sex between two grown-up people was an eye-opener for him. It actually felt different, easy, not fraught. It took time wasn't over in a flash. He also enjoyed the quiet restful times together, he enjoyed holding Jules in his arms and smelling her neck as they lay in bed. He enjoyed feeling the weight of her body resting on top of him, and the touch of her lips on his. He enjoyed stroking her gently curved hip with his fingers.

He liked the simple connections which were increasingly being made between them, in subtle and not so subtle ways.

This contrasted so starkly with how he used be when he was single. He used to have sex not make love. The crash and bang of a one-night stand, with it's desperate urgency, was being replaced by tenderness and empathy.

He liked it.

He liked it a lot.

The score so far:

Roger and Jules

Note to self:

OMG

I am in a relationship.

I'm a partner.

I'm a boyfriend.

I'm a lover.

I'm a half in a whole.

All with the one person.

What does this mean?

Does it mean the end of the League Table, will I forever remain:

Attendance: 86 Sex: 39 Success rate: 45%

Roger mused to himself:

'Will I never do that sort of thing again? I don't know, it is difficult to say. That's asking a lot. But, it has been a long time since I went and searched. Maybe I'm not that sort of person any more. I don't know. There is still part of me which longs for that stuff, for the thrill. But, there is also a part of me now which thinks it is childish, immature.

It is difficult to admit, but the truth is this. I may well have slept with about fourty women, but still I actually lack experience and expertise. Jules has quite clearly shown me that. That is weird, it's like all the previous women don't count somehow.'

Chapter Fourteen

Time to know the truth

The score so far:

Roger: 35 years.   The world: 2005.

Jules was different to Roger, she viewed the world differently. She brought a different way of thinking into his life. Her influence enabled Roger to question the values of his present lifestyle. By doing so, she brought some depth to him. She wanted more from life than just a job and fun on the weekends, she was seeking deeper meanings and motivations. This challenged Roger in a way he had never been challenged before.

Being in a relationship forced him to reflect on his life, he'd never really had the time nor inclination to do so before. He examined the internal book of his life, opened it up, and looked into the empty pages, and saw the wasted years. Where before he had seen success and kudos, he now saw loneliness and self-indulgence. Where before he had seen busyness, order and control, he now saw avoidance and lack of maturity.

He took the time and looked deeply inside himself, and once there, was struck by the hole that appeared at the core of his being. The ache and pain registering there was familiar, and yet this time it was subtly different. This time he saw a part of the overall pain was the lack of a father. He ached for a father. He couldn't remember what his father had looked like, how he had spoken, what kind of a man he had been. He realized he needed to reconcile himself with his father, in a sense, to go and find him. He didn't know how to do that, after all, his father was dead. He just intuitively knew he was aching to know who his father was. Paradoxically the older he got the more urgent this need became. He envisaged the hole in the core of his being to be shaped like his father. Roger realized he didn't even know the circumstances of his father's death, other than he died in a car crash. He couldn't remember their life before that event. This made him feel lost and sad, without a solid centre.

One Saturday he was lying on the sofa in his mothers' front room watching the football in between naps, when his eye settled upon an invitation to a wedding on the mantle-piece. He rose, picked it up, and read.

It was from his Uncle Jeffrey. He was getting married for the third time. Roger vaguely remembered his mother mentioning it.

He called to her. 'When's Uncle Jeff's wedding?'

'Oh, it's next weekend.' she replied from the kitchen.

'Oh, good, I'd like to go.'

His mother came into the front room from the kitchen, wiping her hands on a cloth. 'You'd like to come along?' She was astonished.

'Yes, it's been such a long time since I saw anyone. I'd like to come along and see everyone.' He too was surprised by his enthusiasm, but he knew it would be a chance to somehow connect back to his father.

'Well, well, I didn't expect that. You'll find it awfully boring, very dull…there won't be anything for you.' His mother was flushed, she looked as though she was hiding something.

'No, no, I'd like to come.'

'OK then.' she replied reluctantly.

Roger's mother, Janet, had an elder brother Jeffrey and a younger sister Maureen. Uncle Jeffrey had made his money trading stocks and shares. This was his third marriage and he had eight children and two grandchildren. He retired early from business life in his mid-sixties, and he continued to play the stock market. His new wife was, as he called her, 'a high risk investment.' A Tai girl called Susan, in her mid-thirties, about the same age as Roger.

Aunty Maureen, had, in Jeffrey's words, gone off the rails. She'd left home early and lived on benefits. She was addicted to sleeping pills, alcohol and cigarettes.

Janet was in the middle, trying to keep the peace between the two of them, but often failing.

Both her siblings felt sorry for Janet. When either of them mentioned her, she was 'Poor Janet.' 'Janet who lost her husband.' 'Janet who lost everything, and can't moved on.'

The wedding was in the church hall round the corner. The hall filled with flowers, bright bunting and streamers was a colourful and vibrant display of affection from Jeffrey's children.

This was much in contrast to the people who filled the hall. Mostly, their mood was tense and judgmental.

There were factions and splinter groups forming and fermenting, some on Jeffrey's side, others on Maureen's. Haughty looks, condescending chatter, and spiteful jibes were the order of the day. Parts were played and the large amounts of free booze drunk and spilled.

No grudges were forgotten or hatchets lay unburied.

'How lovely to see you, dear Janet, and if it isn't Roger the dodger, haven't seen you in years. Are you still in advertising?' Jeffrey, his arm around the young Susan, leered and smirked.

'I'm in marketing, not advertising.'

'Yes, poor you, whatever, guess these are hard times for us all.' Jeffrey looked at Roger's mother.

'Pity your Mathew can't make it to the do, Janet' she flushed and looked at the floor quickly. 'Ooops, have I put my foot in it? Hasn't Roger met him yet?' Sniggered Jeffrey, well aware of what he was saying.

'What?' Roger was confused.

His mother steered him away from Jeffrey.

'I was going to tell you, I've met someone. We are friends, just friends.' She was flustered and looked embarrassed.

'Well that's great, Mum.' Roger said in his confusion.

She brightened and looked up at him tenderly.

'I'm happy for you, that's good news.' he added quickly.

'I did mean to tell you, I was going to. He's a nice man.' she said slowly.

Roger was on automatic pilot, he nodded his head as his mother spoke but he couldn't really take her words in. He needed time to digest this surprising news.

After a short while he moved towards the bar, seeking a drink and time to think.

He surveyed the crowds and then froze as he saw Aunty Maureen making a beeline for him. He looked around, there was no escape. Maureen, already slightly worse for wear, pinned him to the bar expertly. She was used to people trying to make a quick getaway, her forefingers pinched into his arm.

'Roger, my dear. How lovely to see you. Where have you been?'

She had a captive victim whom she was not going to let go. She looked across the room to Jeffrey.

'Hasn't he got a cheek, an almighty cheek. She's about 12, have you seen her? Revolting, slitty-eyed, you can't trust anyone with slitty-eyes. Ugly, pig ugly. Well I suppose they've at least got that in common.'

Roger was silent as Maureen spat out a venomous stream of consciousness.

'He's losing all his money you know, losing the lot. He's going to be broke soon, you watch and then he'll be the one looking for handouts.'

She paused and surveyed the crowd.

'Is your poor mother with you? She's a saint you know. She

had to put up with so much, Jeffrey's much like your father in that way.'

This casual remark chilled Roger.

He realized this was his chance.

He held onto Maureen's elbow and accompanied her away from the bar.

'Let's sit down, Auntie, we can hear each other better over here.'

She was unused to anyone showing any interest, so she glided as best she could with him.

'Auntie, I can't really remember my dad and I'd like to know what he was like.'

She focused her slightly blurred vision on him.

'Your father was a bastard, just like Jeffrey. He made your mothers life a misery. He was off and out after skirt all the time. He never kept it in his trousers.'

She was enjoying herself now, in full flow, and Roger sat trying not to react, keeping an open expression on his face.

'He seemed nice enough at the beginning, friend of Jeffrey's he was. Well what do you expect, friend of Jeffrey's? All the same, just out for themselves. He's such a self-obsessed bastard, look at him now, dancing with her, what does he think he looks like.'

She was slipping away.

'Yes, Auntie, but what about my father?'

'Him, George. Well, there was always the accident, the car crash. You did that sort of thing in those days didn't you?'

Alarmed, Roger asked. 'What sort of thing?'

'Driving and drinking, drinking and driving. He'd had a few hadn't he, more than a few, we all knew that, we all did it in those days.'

'Yes, lots of people drink and drive,' agreed Roger.

'And then there was the woman,' added Maureen.

Roger could feel his heart beat increase.

'The woman?'

'Yes, you know, Mrs. Huddlestone. She got out of the car with scratches and bruises. Scratches and bruises. But she was in there with him. "Getting a lift home" she said she was. We all knew otherwise.'

His aunt's face started to glaze over.

'Poor Janet. Poor, poor Janet. But in many ways she was better off after. There was just the two of them then, her and Roger, a little boy. He was little at the time, they were both better off without that waste of space.'

Roger was reeling. He had been given a lot of new information in a very short period of time. He had been told his mother had a friend, and given a picture of his father, not a pleasant one, but at least he felt some kind of connection. He spent the rest of the evening waiting for his mother to want to go, and this didn't take long.

As he drove his mother home the two of them were quietly reflective, and then he spoke.

'Why didn't you tell me about Mathew?'

'I just didn't know when was the right time. I didn't want to upset you.'

'Why would that upset me?'

'Well you know, you were close to your dad, I don't want you to think I was forgetting your dad.' They were silent for a moment.

'Mum, he died over 20 years ago.' He paused and then continued. 'I talked with Auntie Maureen.'

'Yes, I saw.'

'She said my father was a bastard to you. She said he was no good and that we were better off without him.'

His mother was silent, she didn't react, she sat staring blankly through the windscreen of the car.

'She said he died drink driving. She said it was all his fault.'
The two of them stared forwards out onto the black night.
'She said there was a woman in the car with him.'
Roger felt dizzy and angry. They were silent for a moment, and then he added.
'What a bastard, what a fucking bastard.'
He could feel hot tears running down his face, he turned to look at his mother, and he saw streaks of mascara running down her face.
They both drove on silently whilst the tears flowed.

The following weekend Roger didn't visit his mother, he wanted to be on his own, he wanted time to reflect. On the Saturday afternoon he thought he'd visit his father's grave. He hadn't been to the cemetery for about ten years. His mother had taken him once a year on his father's birthday, but that had stopped.
The grey clouds scudded overhead driven by a fierce chill wind.
He turned up his collar as he walked down through the Victorian grandeur and decay of the graves and tombs. He headed towards the new area at the bottom of the hill. Here was filled with colour, flowers, decorative garlands, even a children's play area. It contrasted so vibrantly with the austerity of the formal graves above them. As he walked he could feel deep emotions stirring. He was choking back tears by the time he arrived at his father's grave, having not been able to remember where it was for some time. He stood before the grave, which felt like the greyest and most insignificant in the cemetery. He read the inscription.

'Here lies Harold Gordon Cologne
Born 13th June 1944
Died 25th May 1981'

He looked around, checked he was alone. He looked down at the gravestone and suddenly a thought came into his head.

Is this it? Is this all there is? My dad is just three lines, and I'm even less. Is this what it boils down to?

His sadness gave way to anger as he continued to think about his life.

All I've done is work in marketing. Spent all my life looking at graphs and pie-charts.

I've not managed any good relationships apart from Jules. Not had a family in the ordinary way. I've been forced to have a daughter. Not achieved anything. A life defined by the things I've not done, and this is how it all ends.

He looked around the bleak grey stones and figurines as he continued to contemplate, he said out loud.

'This is what I will become, this is the distinctive mark I'm leaving on the world.'

He took deep breaths to calm himself. Then he continued.

'Surely there is more to me than just this, surely, I can be more than this.'

He could feel the familiar pain in the core of his being, and he felt sick with frustration and anger. As he reflected, and went inwards, he saw an image in his mind's eye.

It was his father in the garage. He and his father were fixing something on the car, and the two of them were happily chatting away. His father had given him a big wrench, and his little hands could hardly hold and lift it as it was so heavy. The two of them laughed together. This image merged into another. The two of them eating cheese on toast, both watching the football results, cheering when Arsenal won. He remembered they'd both supported Arsenal. He burst into a smile.

He saw his dad. He could see him alive, not dead. His father had come back to life.

Roger staggered forward under the weight of this vision, he

almost tripped over his father's gravestone as the impact of the recollection hit him.

'I can see my father.'

He shouted in his frenzied excitement.

Now the tears flowed, Roger whimpered and cried copiously as he knelt in front of his father's grave. In his grief he put his hand on his heart, and he felt his heart beating. He felt the blood coursing through his veins, he felt alive. He laughed loudly through the tears, and bowed his head in respect before his father.

He stayed bent over by the grave for some time, and then he wearily stood back up. Before he left the graveside Roger resolved he was going to do something with his life, make his mark on the world.

'Dad, dad, dad.' He yelled out loud. 'Things are going to change.'

'No, I'm in charge, I'm the father here, I have an announcement.'

Roger sat at the table, in his hand a half filled glass of red wine.

He steadied himself, stood up, allowing time for his drunken focus to come back to the table. The four of them had left a half finished turkey, greasy plates and dishes, the strewn crackers and useless toys that came with them. It was a festive and bountiful scene. He smiled at his mother who sat opposite him.

He was in Giselle's house, he felt at ease, maybe because he had a full stomach and had drunk a lot of wine. He could hear Saskia and Giselle talking in the kitchen, and then the two of them came through to listen to him, giggling together.

'Fill your glasses please ladies, fill the glasses. I'd like to propose a toast to Father Christmas, thank you for coming by this year. You brought everything we needed.'

'Well almost.' added Saskia.

I'd like to thank my mother for being my mother, she's very

good at it.' They all cheered.

'I'd like to thank Saskia. Thank you for being my daughter, I love you lots' Saskia looked down at the table, she blushed, and demurely waved a hand at her father, whilst they all cheered.

'And, I'd also like to thank Giselle for cooking and preparing the lovely food, much appreciated as ever. I really appreciate it all. I really appreciate all of you.' She looked into his eyes and smiled, raised her glass to him in silence.

He raised his glass, then felt flushed, awkward.

'And I'd like to thank myself for being me...'

He raised his glass to himself, he had now forgotten what he was going to say.

'So, Happy Christmas everyone.' They all cheered.

'Oi, pisshead...yes you, pass the brandy butter.' chirped his daughter.

Roger sat down again, felt pleased with himself.

He reflected on how much his attitude towards Giselle had changed. The two of them had grown to mutually respect each other, enough to be at ease in each other's company.

He had softened towards Giselle, especially since he had started the relationship with Jules. He could now understand what a commitment it had been for Giselle to be a single parent, and how much she provided for their daughter. She had never asked for financial support. From the beginning she had sought her independence. She was far too proud to rely on Roger, and worked on at least two or three part time jobs to make sure she and Saskia had everything they needed. He was never sure if Giselle had lovers, certainly Saskia never mentioned anyone, and he presumed she was too busy trying to make ends meet.

Giselle in her turn, appreciated Roger and his relationship to their daughter. She saw how much he loved her, and how committed he had become. The three of them somehow functioned and made being a separated family work. In his drunken way he had wanted to honour that burgeoning new family, especially at Christmas time.

'Hi, this is Saskia.'

'Hello?' Said Janet.

'Just calling to see how you are.'

'Oh...thank you, yes, I'm fine.' Janet felt disconcerted, she'd never received a call from her granddaughter before.

'Good, because I'm on the 12.15 from Kings Cross, should be with you in about 45 minutes.'

Janet was stunned.

'Oh, OK, good. I'll meet you at the station.' She recovered herself a little. 'Is there something wrong?'

'No, granny, don't be silly.' Saskia chuckled to herself. 'I've not run away.'

Janet was relieved.

'I've decided that we should get to know each other.' Saskia continued. 'I think it's high time I got to know my grandmother.'

'Yes, that's a lovely thought.' Replied Janet, as a smile spread across her face.

Janet had taken her granddaughter to eat tea and cakes. The two of them chatted and gossiped all afternoon, they looked into many shop windows. She took her granddaughter to her hairdressers and introduced her to everyone. Janet hadn't smiled so much for years.

Saskia found the whole experience very amusing, but also very moving. The two of them connected on a deep level that afternoon, and their meetings became a once a month event.

Chapter Fifteen

Snakes and ladders

The score so far:

Roger: 36years.   The world: 2006.

On the morning of his birthday Roger's bald patch spread to over five centimeters wide. He'd meticulously measured it every morning for the past six years, and it finally edged over, for him, the defining mark. As he confirmed the measurement he felt his insecurity increase, he felt his fear and vulnerability multiply, he didn't know what to do. He resolved to give up measuring. The next afternoon he had a puncture on his way to a client, and was an hour late to their appointment, in doing so, he lost the contract. His boss was not amused. These negative events were hard to bear, but then they were compounded and magnified one hundred-fold.

The following week he was overlooked for promotion. This event pushed him to a place he had never been before, it felt very unfamiliar and frightening, a place where disappointment and failure lived.

The job of brand manager for Dove should have been Roger's just by default. He'd been doing the job for months already. He'd been certain it was his next step on the ladder, it was what he had been waiting for.

A twenty-seven-year-old was given the job instead. This was a thundering, crashing, disappointing event in Roger's life. He took it very badly.

He played out the scenario in his head a thousand times. How his boss had addressed him, the sharp and cutting way in which he had been cast aside. The guy who got the job had no loyalty to

Unilever, he had never worked for them. He was being bought in, transferred like some young, pricey and fancy foreign footballer into an English football team.

This was not how his life was supposed to pan out, this was not part of his plan. He had thus far only ever moved upwards. He had always been 'successful', and this was the first time he consciously experienced failure. He didn't know how to react to it, it was unfamiliar. He felt betrayed, and for the first time in his life, he felt he lacked a purpose, he felt de-motivated. Over the next months he started to come in later and later, he did his tasks without humour or enthusiasm. He returned home to drink too much whilst watching sport aimlessly on the television. He didn't want to go out, he didn't want to stay in, he didn't want to do much. He took a week off and lay sweating in bed.

Jules came round, and tried to be sympathetic, but failed. They were sat at his kitchen table, an empty bottle of red wine stood between their two full glasses. He'd been ranting about the person who got the job.

'He doesn't have a clue, he's completely a novice in marketing. He keeps coming round asking me to help him, I mean what sort of boss is that?'

Roger was walking a very well worn path.

'He is crap at the job, and everyone knows it, but they won't do anything about it. Oh, no, nothing to do with management.'

'I know, love, you've told me this.' She tried a faint smile.

'Sorry…yes, I'm ranting.'

He came up for air.

'What about if we go back to your place? I just want to be with you.' He pleaded.

'I've already got two moody teenage sons at home, thank you very much, I don't need a third.'

She fended him off.

Jules had little inclination to pander to Roger's self pity and wallowing, and she resolved to keep him away from her house. She had spent the last months since he'd not been promoted, battling against his indifference and moodiness. At first she tried to overcome the frostiness which Roger put around himself, by acting as if nothing had happened. But she quickly realized she couldn't reach him at the depths to which he had plummeted. She then tried to have a sense of humour and remind him of his blessings. But this didn't work, it wasn't well received. She eventually took to nagging and picking at him. This deepened his self-imposed exile, and made him start to resent her. He was unable to stop himself from spiraling downwards. She could feel herself slipping into her own despair and resentment whenever she was with him, she didn't need that.

She gave him a copy of a book called 'Eat, pray, love' about a woman on a journey of self-discovery. She said it might inspire him to do something positive with his life. He flicked through it and thought.

Women do the journey toward holiness, towards enlightenment, all very lovely. Very eat, pray and love, thank you very much. I'm a bloke, I don't do that, I move the other way. 'Drink, play, fuck' that's my journey.

This rather clever remark made him feel just a tiny bit better for a little while.

That night when Jules had gone he felt motivated to go out to 'Suzie's' which he did. He sat sullenly in the corner and watched the women chatting, having fun, laughing.

This breached deep primal feelings in him - repressed anger, desire and self pity, all stirred in an internal cauldron. He indulged himself in dark fantasies of failures and disappointments with the women as he sat in the corner.

After a while he remembered how it felt to hold Jules and to smell her neck, and he dragged himself home to lie sweaty and unfulfilled in his tousled bed.

In reality very little had changed, he was still in the same job as before, but Roger didn't see it that way. He felt his world was now falling, in descent, and there was very little he could do about it. He felt as though external forces were taking over, his fate was changing for the worst without him being able to intervene.

He believed he was being let down by everyone: the company which had not promoted him; in his relationship with Jules, who wasn't coming round so often; by his mother, who was now spending more and more time with Mathew. In this crisis his selfishness and immaturity came to the fore. He wallowed in self-pity and felt righteous anger at the world.

The only person who continued to love him was his daughter, but in his depressed state he forgot to pick her up one Saturday. He would never forget the look on her face the next time they met. She had very clearly been hurt and saddened by his forget-fulness.

The darkness of the winter afternoon had penetrated the fabric of the house. The depth of the winter was around them and between them. Roger felt the chill in his heart. Saskia sat on the floor of her room and he sat on the sofa.

The two of them had looked earnestly at each other.

'Right, Dad, I've got something to tell you, and I want you to listen,' she started. He felt ashamed, he held one of her Spice Girl dolls limply in his hand.

They sat in silence. He nodded. She sighed deeply as the rage began to surface.

'I DO NOT want you to forget to pick me up again!'

She shouted, red in the face, holding his eye with hers.

'You were VERY, VERY naughty,' she screwed up her face and glared at him.

'You will not do that again' she said sternly.

Both were now on the verge of tears.

'Say it to me, Dad, say it to me, repeat after me.' she urged.

'I will not forget to pick you up again,' he repeated through tears.

'Again.' She insisted.

'I will not forget to pick you up.'

Her face brightened and she smiled, the mood passing like a windswept cloud. She picked up a fluffy monkey, looked kindly down at it, deliberately and slowly patted it on the head.

'Well done, monkey, well done.'

She put him down, stood up and moved beside Roger on the sofa.

'Good. Now we've sorted that, I need you to know something else. When I move up schools I have decided to change my image. At the moment I am the girl who is always ill. I'm a wimp, I'm the wuss. I've decided I'm not going to be that in secondary school. I'm going to be the popular one, I'm going to be at the centre of the "in-crowd", street-wise and sassy.'

She clicked her wrist and offered her father a high five, he reciprocated, and she quickly withdrew her hand as he awkwardly swished thin air.

She laughed.

'So, I just need you to know that I won't be ill any more. I'm going to be someone else, better, and cleverer.'

She gave him a withering look. 'Unlike you.'

She did as she said. She reinvented herself. She did it with ease.

She was very determined just like her father and mother. Seamlessly she made the move up to the bigger school and there she transformed herself and settled as the girl to know, the person to be with.

In a dream Roger had, he was walked towards his father's grave. It was a bright sunny day, the air was warm, birds were singing, the flowers were all out. Everything was Day-Glo, almost fluorescent. He walked past happy families playing around gravestones.

He realized he was a small child. He laughed with the families as he passed them. They were happy, they made him happy. He walked on.

As he approached his father's grave the air grew chilled, the wind bit into him and clouds rolled in overhead. He looked along the path, there striding towards him was his father.

His father looked happy, content, but was limping. He had something attached to his right leg and it made him walk awkwardly.

The two met and Roger gave his father a hug. His father ruffled his hair. Roger looked down at his father's leg, and saw a red and black striped snake wrapped around the leg. It was alive and it had attached itself tightly to him. Roger asked his father about the snake as they walked away from the grave.

'Oh, that's my snake, he comes with the job,' replied his father. 'What job?'

'My job,' smiled his father enthusiastically. 'Didn't you know, I'm a snake charmer.' His father ruffled Roger's hair again, and put his arm reassuringly round Roger. 'When the time is right, you'd make a good one too' his father added.

They walked on a while and things changed. Roger looked down at his leg and realized the snake had slid from his father's onto his. He started to feel his right leg being constricted by the snake, rhythmically squeezed and compressed. At first it was a tickling sensation and didn't feel unpleasant. He looked around, expecting to see his father. But he was gone.

Roger was now in an unfamiliar part of the cemetery. The snake was growing, growing fast, squeezing not just his leg, but climbing up his body. He felt afraid and overcome by the snake. The snake rapidly put on weight and size and held him close in its' coils. It grew and grew until it was larger than him. Roger became rigid with fear. He could feel the snake pressing and squeezing his body, constricting the air in his lungs, he was being crushed and squeezed. He tried to shout, to call for help, but he couldn't make a sound.

In front of his face was the snake's face. The mouth opened wide and swallowed his head. He was covered in slime. He felt his face being sucked deeper down the snake's throat. The constrictions of the snake's hugely powerful muscles pulled his body deeper and ever deeper down the beast's throat and into its stomach. His body was being rhythmically dismembered.

His mind was still present, but his body was now crushed, shattered. Every bone broken. Every part of his being basted in a mix of acid and stomach fluids. He was transformed into a crushed and mashed cartridge. He had no arms or legs, he was just a pellet.

He lay still in the snake's stomach for some time. It was a densely dark place. After a while he tried to move and realized he could just about shift his frame. As he wriggled his limbless form he saw a dim and distant light. He shifted his head, or what remained of it, towards the light. He wriggled his body, moving like a maggot, undulating, towards the light. The light grew stronger, brighter, it drew him on, magnetically, drawing him on. He watched as through this hole came two strong arms. The hands grabbed hold of him firmly and pulled. This enabled him to be birthed through the hole. He was pulled out of the snake's body into a light and very bright room.

A tall man, very familiar to Roger, held his limbless form in his arms. He wrapped Roger in a white cloth, held him gently and smiled down at Roger benevolently. Roger kept thinking to himself, 'I know this man, I know him, who is he?'

As the man held him Roger felt his own arms and legs growing, reforming. He realized he was creating himself again as a human being.

He felt his limbs stretching and growing, he was starting to look like a man again.

At this point he regained consciousness.

He woke up with a start. Wrapped tightly, unable to move, in his duvet and bed sheet, Roger lay exhausted in his bed. As he slowly surveyed his bedroom and unwrapped himself, a nasty pungent smell hit him, it was piss. He looked down at the bedclothes.

He'd wet himself! In that moment, he remembered who the man in his dream was. He'd been delivered back to humanity by the Buddha Beggar.

Note to self:
What have I lost?
Status
Identity
Pride
What have I gained?
Fear
Weakness
Vulnerability
Despair
What remains the same?
Nothing
I'm still in the same job, but I have to get away from Unilever, the faster the better.

'Dad?' Saskia asked in her annoying, nagging, voice.

'Why don't we play with Ben and Stefan any more?'

She knew Roger and Jules had fallen out and weren't seeing each other very often.

Saskia was disappointed because she had enjoyed Jules' boys company. They were older and she enjoyed teasing them, flirting with them, confusing them, she enjoyed the power.

'Because me and their mother aren't getting on very well at the moment,' came Roger's sullen reply.

'Have you two like split up?' She looked intently across at his sad face.

'No, no, I don't think so, we're just taking a bit of time out.'

'Oh, good' her faced lightened. 'Does that mean you're like having "a depression"?'

He frowned.

'No…well, maybe…a bit,' he stuttered.

'Oh, great,' she perked up and came to sit next to him.

'Amelia's dad is like having a depression, and she said it's brilliant. He's buying her everything she asks for. He's like being really generous.'

She gave him a big hopeful smile.

Chapter Sixteen

All change

The score so far:
Roger: 37years.   The world: 2007.

Roger's wish to get away from Unilever was granted. He found a new job with Addis. He became brand manager for their outdoor range. He knew they were smaller and a less prestigious company, but he felt at least he was still in the game, still competing.

He tried to throw himself into the new job, suggesting TV campaigns and other exciting new ventures, but the recession was hitting home, and marketing budgets were being cut. He was no longer working at Proctor and Gamble or Unilever. The new company was unable to undertake the size of campaigns to which he was accustomed. That frustrated him, but he was also pragmatic. At least he still had a job. He soon realized his best policy was to keep his head down and not draw attention to himself. This was not the way he'd worked before, it was not in his nature even to think that way. It made him feel angry and bitter about what might have been.

'Douglas.' Roger shouted as he came into the office. Douglas was a marketing assistant.

'I'm disappointed in you.' he continued. Roger was intent on teaching Douglas a lesson. 'I've just come in through the car park and what have I seen?'

'I don't know boss.' Douglas was intimidated.

'I've looked in the window of your car and seen a complete and utter mess everywhere. Your car is your office. It's the first impression you make, it's what our clients judge you by.' Roger was thrilled by how angry he had become. 'Time to give it a clean, time to get it sorted, mate. You wouldn't leave this office in such a state now would you?'

'No boss.'

Douglas went out and opened his car door, found a map and a crisp packet lying on the floor and a plastic bag on his passenger seat.

He thought to himself: Fussy bastard.

For many months Roger blamed others for his misfortune. This stopped when he joined Addis. By joining them he became aware of how fragile his field of work had become. Whilst he had been at the big companies he'd been insulated from the full effects of the recession. Now he could see how deeply the cuts were affecting budgets, jobs and the economy. He appreciated for the first time what an effective job Stuart and the other managers had done in maintaining budgets and funding.

As a consequence of this realization he took the time to look at other aspects of his life. By doing so, he saw clearly how he had been treating Jules. Using her to dump all his pain and hurt. Continually going over the same ground with her. How boring and depressing that must have become for her.

He saw how he had cut his mother out of his life. Realizing he had done it because she was so happy with Mathew. He had been unable to be around happiness in his state of depression, he'd mocked it.

He shuddered as he recollected Saskia's reaction to him forgetting to pick her up.

He realized that in all the major relationships he had been stepping very close to the edge, to the end even, and he didn't want to do that.

He didn't want that at all.

What could he do to stop this behaviour?

When he reflected on this question, he saw something deeper stirring in him, and it started with the word 'maybe':

Maybe, just maybe, he was responsible for his failure at work. No one had done this to him.

Maybe, he was sharing his bad moods with all the important women in his life, when he should be supporting them. They had all tried to help him and he'd rejected them.

Maybe, he was to blame for the depressed state he was in.

Maybe, only he could do something about it all.

He remembered going to a workshop run by Byron Katie, at which she urged people to own their thoughts. Taking her advice he removed the 'maybe':

I am responsible for my failure at work. No one had done this to me.

I am sharing my bad moods with all the important women in my life, when I should be supporting them. They had all tried to help me and I've rejected them.

I am to blame for the depressed state I am in.

Only I can do something about it all.

These statements actually felt good, clear and true to him. For the first time in his life, in this state of heightened awareness, he admitted he had some deep-rooted problems and issues. He admitted he needed help in order to really come to terms with them, and to move on.

That night he woke in the early hours and lay awake, holding his chest, a pain throbbing inside him, a pain all too familiar and yet somehow softer, more gentle than before. As he lay there, he thought - I need help, and I'm the only one who can give it to me. He wrapped his arms around himself and gently rocked himself to sleep.

'Yes, Roger, I still care for you, of course I do. I just find it difficult being with you at the moment.' Jules was on familiar territory with him.

'I think I'm getting better, really,' Roger was begging. 'I've not drunk anything for a couple of days.'

'I know, love,' she softened. 'It's just I'm not the one you should be asking for help. You need serious help, proper help. You need someone who knows what they're doing. Please go and find someone.'

Deep down in the core of his being he knew she was right. She was too close, too enmeshed in the difficulties to give clear advice. He knew it, but he was terrified of actually asking for help from the wider world. Such an action felt like an admission of failure for him. If he actually sought help he was admitting his life was crap, he'd failed to hold it all together, he was not a success. To ask for help was going to be difficult, it felt nigh on impossible, but in the end, he knew he had to do it. He had heard there was a Spiritualist Church, and every Tuesday they offered free healing for people. He decided he'd go there. It felt safe. Safer than going to a psychiatrist. Safer than really admitting there was something seriously wrong. He imagined someone would hold his hand and offer him absolution from his sins. Or maybe they'd pray together and that would make it alright. He was looking for a short cut to redemption, and this felt like the easy option.

It was a small wooden building set back from the road, with a thick cover of evergreen trees hiding it from the busy traffic. As he made his way up the stony path he was formulating the reasons why he shouldn't go inside.

This is crap.

It's a shed, it's falling down.

It's not a church, turn back.

At that moment he thought of Jules and her demands. She had been urging him for many weeks to seek help, to sort himself out.

He thought - even if it is crap, at least I can tell her I've started to look for help.

He reluctantly entered the dimly lit building, and looking at the walls, realized it was a scout hut. He felt very disheartened. Heated by electric heaters, the draughty, musty, wooden building held a small group of people sat waiting. At the far end of the hall, there was a curtained area behind which the healers were working. At the other end two old ladies dispensed tea and biscuits. He made his way to them and asked for a tea.

'Hello, duck, not seen you here before.'

'No, I've never been before.'

'Oh, that's good. Just take a seat and someone will come and get you soon. Take your time, be at peace.'

Roger sat and sipped his tea. After about half an hour one of the women stood in front of him, smiling.

'This way,' she beckoned.

Behind the curtain there was a wooden chair. He sat, the woman stood behind him.

'Just relax, be at peace. Brian will be out soon. Please close your eyes and take some deep breaths.' He did as he was told. He felt her hand touch the back of his neck whilst he breathed deeply. He felt a calm warmth emanating from her touch, he closed his eyes, he waited. He heard the woman very quietly leave the space.

He sat with his eyes closed, his mind flicking from place to place, not settling, searching for a way out. He heard someone enter the space, and felt them gently lay hands on his shoulders from behind.

A man's voice said, 'Breathe deeply.'

He did so. He brought his consciousness to his shoulders and could feel the gentle touch of hands on him. As he sat still he started to feel heat being generated from those hands into his shoulders. The hands then started to move on his back and gently massage a large knot at the base of his neck. He could feel the heat increasing, he could feel the knot dissolving and diminishing.

'This bloke is good' he said to himself.

As he settled in his chair something strange happened, the heated hands came round to his face and settled on his forehead. But the man had not moved. He felt the heat from the hands become absorbed through his head and start to course down his body. It was like a waterfall pouring down from his head, into his stomach, into all his internal organs, warming and glowing it's way through his body.

The heat then seemed to settle and focus on the exact place where he hurt. The hole in the core of his being. Here it settled and then began to percolate deep into his tissue and fibre. He could feel himself being restored, he could feel himself being healed. As he realized this he became conscious of tears flowing down his face. They were literally pouring out of his eyes, he wouldn't have been able to see if he'd opened his eyes. The heat remained in his body for about quarter of an hour, but it felt much longer, and throughout this time, he gently and quietly cried. At first it made him feel awkward, but after a while he just let the tears happen, there was no way he could have staunched the flow.

He cried and he cried and he cried. Eventually, he felt the gentle pressure of the hands back on his shoulders, and he was able to stop. He felt at ease. Realizing for the first time in months he had not had any thoughts and distractions, he had been at peace for a few minutes.

'Welcome back, Brother Wolf, welcome back.' The voice pierced Roger's calm.

He spun round and looked up into a familiar face. He instantly recognized the beggar who was now clean-shaven, wore clean clothes, had a tight short hair cut. He had transformed himself.

'You were crying for England.' He gently smiled at Roger. 'You've done some wonderful work here tonight, take it easy.'

'But, it's you.' Roger was struggling for words.

'Yes, it is, and you are here too.'

The beggar offered Roger his hand and helped him up from the chair. 'You're going to be a bit wobbly for a while, let's have a cup of tea together.'

Roger was feeling weak and weary but also slightly euphoric, it was a strange combination, and a cup of tea sounded just right.

'What is your name?' asked Roger as he nurtured a warm cup between his hands.

'I'm Brian,' came the reply.

Roger took some time to contemplate the man before him. He saw how much the man had changed, how light and clear his face was, how much younger he appeared. As he looked at him Roger recollected their first encounter and suddenly he felt ashamed.

'Oh my God. I was a right bastard to you the first time we met.' Roger blushed deeply.

'You were a little impolite,' responded Brian gently.

'You tripped me up!' Roger exclaimed. 'Oh my God you stank to high heaven,' he added rather sharply.

'Yes, I probably did, I'd just been beaten up by a gang of kids, and they pissed on me,' Brian added calmly, almost gently. 'That sort of thing used to happen on an all-too-frequent basis.'

'I am so sorry. God, I am so sorry.' Roger was genuinely distressed. 'I didn't know.'

'I know,' came the simple reply. 'You saved my life that night, Brother Wolf, little did you know it.'

'What? I saved your life?'

'Yes, in a way. What you said to me that night was one of the main reasons I changed. You were really angry with me, and you were incredibly honest with me. You said you were being chased by the police, by the social, by the tax man, by everyone. You told me how miserable that made you feel. I'd seen you pass a few times before and I'd always thought that you had it easy and good. It made me think maybe being a beggar wasn't so bad after all. Beaten by kids is a hazard, begging is only a temporary step. But you were so miserable despite your lifestyle. You had everything and yet you were more miserable than me. You said you were always being chased, always running away, always looking over your shoulder. That made me sad. I didn't want that kind of life. So, I started to accept where I was, who I was, who I still am. And it was the start of my recovery.'

'Blimey, I remember it differently,' muttered Roger.

Chapter Seventeen

Learning what is important

When Roger arrived home that night he slept peacefully and for many hours. He awoke clearheaded and full of energy the next day. He phoned Jules and told her about the healing with Brian and how much better he felt. She was cautious, not sure about Roger's conviction he was now back on track, but knowing it was good to hear him being optimistic again. He wanted to come over. She put him off.

'Why don't you want me to come over?' He insisted. 'I'd like to see the boys again. How are they doing?'

'They're both good, well done for remembering to ask,' Jules was impressed. Over the last months he'd never mentioned them.

'I need to know you are really better Roger before I re-introduce you to them,' she added.

'What do you mean by that?'

'I mean you are a role model for my boys, they were used to looking up to you, and over the last months you've been role-modelling some pretty crap behaviour to them.' An emotional charge tinged her voice.

Roger was silent, absorbing the message.

'Yes, I see,' he replied. 'I understand. Thank you for that, it is a compliment in it's own way.' He'd never thought of himself as a role model to her sons, he was shocked.

'Yes it is.' Jules was left feeling something had changed in him, that a move had been made. She hoped it would be sustained.

Roger didn't visit his mother as often as he had in the past. He'd avoided her for some time because he was so down and he didn't like being around her and Mathew, as they were so happy together. She'd moved on. In his own way he had too. He wasn't the faithful son lying on the sofa any more. He didn't enjoy coming to the old house, it brought him down even further. It didn't come as a surprise when one day, his mother phoned and told him she was selling the house and moving in with Mathew. Roger was genuinely pleased, and offered to come over and move some things for her. He didn't need to, was the reply, but it would be good if he and Saskia came over anyway.

He and Saskia arrived. They all sat in the front room drinking tea in stilted silence, and then Roger blurted.

'I'd like to go up into the loft.'

'Really, dear, what on earth for?' His mother couldn't understand his request.

'There's that box of Dad's stuff up there, I want to see it.'

'What box?' His mother was still confused.

'Don't you remember, we put a wooden chest of his things up there when he died.'

'Did we?' His mother looked bemused. 'Well, if you say so.'

'Woah, yeah, dad. Let's get it. Is this like a chest full of bones and treasure maps?' Saskia piped up.

Janet nodded her head, giggled, and smiled.

'No, it's probably full of dust' Roger looked down at the two of them as he got up from the sofa.

He leant a ladder to the attic and after shining a torch around for a while, he recognized and brought down the box. The three of them searched through drawers and eventually found the key that unlocked the padlock. He pushed open the top.

Inside were some sweaters, a few greying shirts, a pair of trousers. He pulled them all out. Beneath these was a layer of papers, forms and official documents, as well as a newspaper cutting telling the story of his death.

This fascinated Saskia and she sat reading it.

His mother pointed.

'Oh, yes, look dear, there is your snake.' She smiled as she pulled out a battered old paper snake attached to a stick.

Roger shuddered and stepped backwards in alarm 'Oh my God,' he exclaimed. Saskia couldn't help but stifle a laugh at Roger's antics.

His mother said 'Your father used to love to torment you with this. He'd chase you round and round with it. You used to shriek with excitement, and that made him do it even more. It was a little game the two of you had together.'

'After all these years still afraid of paper snakes are you, Dad? Traumatized for life by a snake on a stick, what a wimp.' Sniggered Saskia.

'As it happens, yes.'

Roger went to receive healing from Brian every week. He also joined Brian's Saturday classes. The two of them were becoming close, but Brian always remained a little distant, detached. Roger realized this distance was important, he needed it.

He needed a teacher, not a mate. If he was to really change his ways and to rebuild his life, he needed help, and who better to help him than someone who had been a beggar and was now a healer and teacher. Roger was hungry to be taught and he came to Brian with a proposal. He wanted Brian to become his personal trainer.

'I need you to be my teacher, to be my trainer. I want to learn the things you know. I think you can teach me how to sort myself out.'

'Yes, that's true,' replied Brian calmly.

'Good, then how do we go about this?' Roger was in a very positive and assertive mood. 'I want to be trained in how to get better. I need you to show me the way.'

'That would be lovely and simple,' smiled Brian. 'I'll sort you out, you can rely on me, I'll show you the way.'

Roger fell silent.

'All I can do my lovely wolf friend is to share with you what happened in my life. How you get yourself sorted is up to you. I can't help you with that. Is that good for you?'

'Yes.'

'OK, I'm happy to do that.' Brian looked him in the eyes. 'First question, do you need sorting? Aren't you just fine as you are? Aren't you already healed?'

'No, my head is shit, I feel like crap, I'm useless, I can't hold a relationship for more than five minutes, I'm in a crap job, and I'm on the scrapheap.'

'Fine, I can't work with you. Go away and come back when you've come to terms with the fact that you are perfect as you are right now.' Brian smiled and settled in his chair. 'I can't help you until you start loving yourself.'

'Fuck, this is going to be hard,' replied Roger.

'Only if you believe it is,' came Brian's sharp response.

'How can I love myself? I feel like crap, I feel like a failure, I'm not happy with any aspect of my life,' Roger whined. Brian grasped Roger's arm, stopping him from talking, and looked intently into his face.

'Let's remember some things from our past. How did you feel about me when you first saw me? Be honest, what did you really think?'

'OK, I was disgusted by you. I hated you. The way you looked, the way you were dressed. I hated the fact that you didn't have a job, how you were scrounging.' Roger looked down, feeling ashamed of those thoughts.

'Good. You hated me. Now let's take that in two different directions.'

Brian moved forward on his chair and folded his arms.

'Firstly, your story. You hated me so deeply, so intensely

because I was your shadow. You projected onto me all the things you feared about yourself. Right now you are feeling very depressed and unhappy, you don't like your job, you're more than likely going to be made redundant soon, and then you'll be even more like I was. You will become me, and that is scaring you. You are on the edge of being on the dole, becoming a scrounger yourself.' Brain paused.

Roger sat silent, his fingers entwined, slowly twisting them as if in pain. 'Now, let's look at it from my perspective. Not only was I begging, but I also hated myself very deeply. I was so far gone into addiction, into self-loathing and self-hatred, I was a beggar on the streets, I didn't and couldn't work. People would beat me up, piss on me, and in many ways I brought that on myself. I accepted that as right and fair. That was how little pride I had, how little self worth I had. How far gone I was. You are nowhere near that place, and yet you tell me you can't love yourself? You can't pick yourself up. I was so deep and yet I found the ability to love myself. You can do this work, you can find the love, you are the same as me. Believe me you can do this.' Brian smiled as he urged Roger on. Brian then took a deep calming breath.

Roger knew to keep quiet at this point, as something important was about to be said.

'Roger, you've done the most important part of the work already. You have asked for help. Most men find it difficult to ask for help, they are normally too proud or too stupid. The consequences of asking for help are very far reaching. When you ask for help, you are admitting that you don't know all the answers. This leads to the understanding that you need to learn. Such thoughts radically change who you are.'

He grinned widely at Roger before continuing.

'You used to think you knew it all, now you are seeking to learn, that is a much more positive place to be. Instead of being fixed or solid, you are becoming flexible, you are becoming porous.' To illustrate his point Brian expanded his chest, and took another deep breath.

'In a sense, you are opening your pores and starting to absorb lessons, wisdom, knowledge and skills. As men grow up they tend to become hardened to life, they develop a tough outer skin. This is very useful for getting ahead, reaching pinnacles, accumulating money and status, but it is blinking uncomfortable! By asking for help you have re-opened your pores and softened your skin. This means you are able to breath properly again. You are absorbing the lessons you need, and exhaling the poisons and damage from within. By starting this process you are on the way to becoming a more mature, whole, human being, becoming more rounded, not so sharp. If you keep on doing this, one day you might even start to love yourself.' Brian laughed and settled back into the chair.

'If you really want to love yourself maybe you need to start seeing whether you are loved by other people.' Brian continued.

'Let's look at your relationship with your lady, what's her name?'

'Jules.'

'Does she love you?' Brian asked. 'Or should I say, has she changed recently?'

'Uum, I do know she came very close to splitting with me, but something has kept her in the relationship, and I do remember her saying that was because she was now seeing the start of real changes in me.'

'In other words you've recently moved towards being lovable.'

'OK, if you say so.' Roger said shyly.

'What about your daughter?' Brian pushed. "Does she love you?'

'Oh, yes, I love her. She's wonderful.'

'That's not an answer to my question. Does she love you?'
Roger paused. 'I Guess so. Saskia doesn't talk that way, she
just bulldozes me, she flattens me. But, yes, I think she appre-
ciates me, loves me, and wants me in her life.'
'Good, she loves you' continued Brian. 'What about the
mother of your daughter?'
'Giselle?' asked Roger. 'Oh, she doesn't love me.'
'OK, but does she appreciate you, has she changed towards
you recently?'
Roger paused to think. 'Yes, you know, that is actually true.
She's been very kind recently, and she said that she really appre-
ciated me the other day.'
Roger looked up and smiled.
'You know, you're right, she does like me.'
'Good.' Brian encouraged him by nodding several times.
'You see, there are people in your life who love and like you.
That probably wasn't true a few months ago. The first step
towards loving yourself is to make yourself loveable. One way of
measuring that is to see yourself the way other people perceive
you. Often we are too busy berating ourselves to notice people
liking and loving us.'

Note to self
Spent some time with Brian and we talked about how he had
been my shadow, I really like that concept. He was my shadow. I
didn't like things about myself, and I transferred them onto him.
As we were talking I thought about all the men I've classified
and categorized. When I first went to New Age workshops I
classified the men as "lost souls" or "dragged men". And yet
here I am, I'm a "lost soul". I spend the whole of my time
thinking about the past. Thinking that it was all so much better
back in the day when I was with Proctor and Gamble, when I was
the king of the scene. I'm also a "dragged man", it was only after
Jules insisted loads of times that I got help. She didn't go with

me, but I was definitely a "dragged man" unwilling and stubborn. I get it now. All those judgments I made were not about the men, they were about myself. I have to admit who I really am, the wholeness of me, not the narrow restricted view I had in the past. Blimey that seems very profound right now.

Chapter Eighteen

The canary sings the blues

Roger sat poised in his manager's office, his sweaty palmed hands gripping the cold black leather of the creaky chair. He cast furtive looks around the room he had entered so often, with which he was so familiar. He took it all in, as if for the first time. The impressive oak desk, the glass side table and comfortable sofa, the framed photos on the table, the framed certificates on the wall. The view of the City of London, the high-rise blocks that almost blocked the view. He knew all of this.

It was familiar territory, and he had never felt intimidated or scared like this before. He sat in the chair, trembling, on the edge of his seat, head down, trying to stop the quaking.

He knew what was coming.

He knew why he had been called.

There had been rumours for weeks.

Now it was about to happen.

'Sorry to keep you waiting, Roger.' His manager walked in briskly, shut the door, and patted him on the shoulder as he moved past Roger to his seat. The manager sat with hands touching in a triangle in front of his chest, leaning forward. He looked intently across the table towards Roger. 'I think it's time we talked about changes.' Roger didn't, couldn't, wouldn't hear what was said after that.

His consciousness became very small. It shrank and curled itself into a small ball in the middle of his chest. It turned into the throbbing pain in the core of his being.

He could hear words being spoken, words from his manager, even his own responses, but they might as well have been in a foreign language for all he was able to take in.

'I'll do whatever you suggest,' he heard himself say.

'It is a very reasonable redundancy package,' said the manager.

'We really appreciate all the effort you have put in.' There was a pause.

'What plans have you got?'

'I'm fine,' he replied. 'I've got some ideas.'

He hadn't.

As far as he was concerned this was the end.

The end of Roger Cologne - the marketing guru.

Beyond this moment he could not see. He had never considered anything beyond this moment, he had never considered this moment as ever happening. He felt deeply sorry for himself, and was desperately searching for someone to blame for this disaster. He went home, it was all he could to make it to his front door. He was drained, exhausted, completely broken. On his return journey, he had convinced himself he had lost everything, he had no identity, he now felt bereft. This was far worse than before. At least he'd just missed promotion and was still in a job, but now, as far as he was concerned, his career was finished. The pain in the centre of his being throbbed and pounded, he could barely open his eyes. He curled up in bed with a bottle of Jack Daniels, and he slept on and off for two days.

'Are you always going to be this sad?'

'No, Saskia' he smiled.

Somehow she always knew how to make it light again.

'I'm just having a hard time, I've been made redundant, so there isn't lots of money.'

'Yes, but no...hold on, when you're made to be a redundant you're paid lots of money.'

'Well, yes, not lots,' he was struggling to remain serious. 'But, the money I've been given I'm saving. I've put it away for a rainy day.'

Her face darkened, she sat thinking.

She then looked out of the window and walked slowly over to it. Saskia pressed her hand against the window pane and looked up.

'Those clouds over there are very dark, it looks like it's going to start raining any minute now.'

She turned and looked imploringly at him.

The two of them laughed.

Roger stood in the bathroom, he was naked. He'd just toweled himself after a shower. He instinctively checked his bald patch, fingering the smooth skin where there used to be hair. His hand then slid down his face and touched under his chin, pinching at the layer of flabby skin. It then slipped down his chest, through the graying hairs and rested on his belly. He felt the slack distortion of his stomach where before there had a been a six pack of sorts.

He had spent the last two months struggling with the pain in the core of his being. Alternating from feeling sorry for himself, to feeling lost, or in anguish about the future. He wallowed in ways he had never experienced before. The man who was always in control, let go, and in letting go, he descended into a dark place. There he felt abandoned and isolated, unable to impose his will on any of the circumstances of his life. In this place he raged, felt angry, was frustrated, and was on the verge of tears almost all the time. And then he let them lose. He cried bitter tears as a marketing manager who no longer had a job, and he cried as a small boy who had lost his father a long time ago. He was unable to stop the tears, and they represented the flow of feelings, raw emotions and desperate scenarios playing out in his head. He was in this place for a long time, it felt like years, but it was just months. Whilst there he lost control of himself, and that scared him deeply, but he had no alternative. It was irresistible. He went insane with despair. He let go. He was lost.

He kept returning to the same question:

'What do I do now?'

The only answer he could find:

'I don't know.'

Throughout these difficult times the one thing Roger regularly attended was Brian's Saturday workshop. He had let go of the sweat lodges a while ago. There were no prestigious New Age workshops for Roger any more. A draughty, creaking wooden scout hut was all he had now.

Brian taught a small number of people basic healing techniques. He demonstrated the laying on of hands, working with crystals, reading auras. On average 7 or 8 people would attend. Some came just for one session and didn't return. However, there was a small core who kept returning. They really saw what Brian was doing and Roger was one of them. This group had earnest discussions about Brian. They felt privileged to know about him, it was as if they were part of a special secret club, because so few people knew about Brian. He was a brilliant and very effective healer and yet he lacked any ego, he was content as he was, unknown. The privileged few would discuss in depth the weird and wonderful things Brian had manifested in their lives, they talked about him as if he were a mystical guru. Roger couldn't believe how few people knew about him, how few people attended his classes, and how unconcerned Brian was by the lack of attendance.

'I've been to see Ken Wilbur, I saw Satish Kumar, a thousand people turned up to see Deepak Chopra. None of them were as good as you, none of them have a better way of teaching,' Roger raved. 'I don't get it, you should be teaching hundreds. You should be out there, you should be on the telly.'

'Should, should, should,' mocked Brian with a smile. 'Maybe I'm happy with things as they are my friend. Maybe I am grateful for what I've got.'

'I know all that humility stuff, but you have a responsibility to get this stuff out there. How do you make ends meet? You could make a go of this, you could really make an impact on the world.'

'Maybe I already have,' Brain looked up at Roger's anxious face. 'Roger, you need to come home with me and see what I have. Then you might understand.' Roger was shocked. When he and the little group had discussed Brian they all remarked on how no one had ever been invited to Brian's house, no one had ever met Mrs. Brian as Brian called her. This was something special.

'Yes, thank you,' Roger responded. 'I'd love to.'

At the end of the session they packed up Brian's equipment and tools, closed the hall and walked to his house, which was nearby. Brian lived in a small terraced house on a quiet road, nothing extraordinary, tucked away behind a hospital and it's grounds.

They entered the cluttered hallway.

Brian shouted out: 'Hallo, I'm back' to no one in particular, as he ushered Roger into the front room. A small smiling friendly woman came in. Mrs. Brian, Roger presumed, she said hallo, was not introduced, and offered to make them a cup of tea.

Brian sat in a battered armchair that had seen better days. Above his left shoulder was a birdcage hanging from the ceiling, and a beautiful yellow canary was flitting and perching in it. Brian got up and picked up a pipe and some tobacco from the mantle shelf.

'My one addiction I can't give up.' He said as he sat back down, pulling the tobacco into his hand and rolling it before filling the pipe.

'At least it's not crack, eh.' He smiled to himself.

Roger sat on an equally old sofa, and said nothing.

He felt warm and cosy, the house enveloped him, he could feel it's peace and calm. He didn't want to get up, afraid it would break the spell.

'Very nice bird you've got,' he ventured.

'Yes, it's a canary, he'll sing for us now.'

The canary bounced around as they both sat watching. He settled on his perch and then began to sing, chuckling and burbling to himself at first, and then singing a distinctive melodic song.

Roger was transfixed. 'He's beautiful.'

As the bird began to repeat his original song, the door opened and two young girls appeared, maybe 8 and 10 years old. They both greeted their father and Roger, and sat under the birdcage listening to the canary.

All four of them were silently reverential.

After a few minutes the canary flitted from his perch and drank some water, then picked at seeds. The performance was over, the two girls left the room and the men were alone again. Mrs. Brian brought in two cups of tea and some biscuits. Roger sat perched on the front edge of his sofa, silently taking it all in between sips of tea.

Brain put his pipe down, looked across with a smile and said to Roger, 'You see, this is simple. This is heaven on earth for me. I don't need anything more than this. I've been in a very dark and desperate place, and in that place the idea of me being together with a woman, having lovely children, even living in a house was a complete impossibility. For me this is the pinnacle of what I want and what I want to achieve. I certainly don't want to be famous, I would hate all that stuff.'

Roger nodded, 'I get that, I see that now.'

They continued to drink their tea and eat biscuits, then Brian rose from his chair and went to his small CD player.

'Do you like Neil Diamond?'

'Errr, do you want an honest answer?'

'Of course.'

'No.'

'Good, then listen to this.'

Brian put on a CD of Neil Diamond songs and his face lit up as each song began. He sung along, accentuating the meaning of the words, bringing out the nuances of the songs, and by the third song, it was irresistible, both of them were crying, sobbing along to the sentiments being expressed. When they then started singing 'I am...I said' the canary joined in, the three of them singing out of tune along with Neil Diamond.

Roger had never sung like that before, he had never appreciated the words of Neil Diamond's songs, he was amazed.

As he stood up to leave, tears of laughter and release rolling down his face, he felt transformed as he so often did in the company of Brian.

He was renewed and humbled.

The next day he awoke refreshed and determined. He went through his diary, making calls, pulling in favours, and at the end of the day he had two possible consultancies. No one from work had phoned or contacted him since he had been made redundant. He'd been dropped like a hot potato. He thought about James at the sweat lodges, Roger had dropped any contact with him once James had been made redundant. At the time it seemed like James had contracted an infectious disease and Roger had stayed clear hoping not to catch it, but Roger had well and truly caught it now. He saw his work acquaintances were treating him the same way and he couldn't blame them. He resolved to phone James and see how he was.

Jules and her best friend Steffi, a writer and yoga teacher, sat facing each other over the kitchen table. Large wine glasses, crusty plates, an empty chocolate box and a vase of wilting flowers were between them. Jules was, as usual, complaining about Roger.

'Well, he's just not very attentive, he doesn't really notice anything.'

'Typical man.' Steffi looked down at the table, and twisted an empty chocolate wrapper. 'if he's that bad, why are you two together still?'

'Oh, well, he's not really that bad.' Interjected Jules. 'He has been getting a bit better recently.'

Steffi leant across the table and clasped Jules hand. 'Look either work with what you've got or move on. At least you've got someone.' She was looking intensely across the table as someone who has drunk too much does. 'At least you've got some bloke interested in you.' She added with feeling.

'I know, I know, it feels good sometimes, and then other times I feel like I'm hanging in there because I don't want to be left on the shelf.' Jules took a sip from her glass. 'I don't want to be stuck on the ledge, or whatever you call it.'

'What, on the book shelf, like me?' Steffi laughed.

'Yes, ooh, good one.' Jules laughed.

'The chances of you, the Goddess of Loveliness, being left on the shelf with me are very slim, very slim indeed.' Steffi reassured her.

'Thank you, darling, that's very kind, and Roger does have his moments.'

'I should bloody well hope so.'

'He's very caring with his daughter.'

'Kind to small animals and children.' added Steffi.

Jules ignored her: 'And, you know even though he's out of a job, I know he's going to sort himself out, I can just feel it.'

'That's good.'

'Yes, he's much better that way than their father. He just gave up, lost his job, and now he's a complete waste of space. Roger isn't like that, He's a go-getter.' Jules said proudly.

She thought for a moment. 'Ever since he started hanging out with Brian he seems to be better, which is a good thing.'

'But, I thought you didn't like Brian?' Remarked Steffi.

'Well, I don't know, he kind of gives me the creeps sometimes. He's in the room and then disappears, and then reappear again. It's all very odd, very strange. He can say some profound things and then other times he doesn't say anything.'

Jules wrinkled her brow as she thought about Brian. 'He's a blinking mystery, but if he's good for Roger, then he's good for me.' She concluded.

'Yes, at least you've got a man.' Steffi concurred.

'Yes, at least I've got my man.'

She was thoughtful again. 'He's getting much better in bed as well.' Jules added with a wry smile. 'He's getting much better at licking pussy.'

'Well, that's always a good thing in a man.'

They both laughed and then took a pensive sip of wine.

'To be recommended.'

Grey Wolf

'If the wolf can survive being alone, he will do so by learning sufficient skills and strategies for survival and he will become self-reliant. When the wolf gets there, paradoxically, he becomes a worthy member of a pack. He then knows it is time to go look for his clan. He pursues and courts existing clans, and eventually, he is accepted into one of them.

When he is accepted into a clan, he must learn how to run with them. He must share his skills and learn new ones. He needs to know what place he has in the pack, where he stands in the pecking order. He is no longer alone, he has found his pack, he becomes part of a family, he fits in, and now he is the grey wolf. The grey wolf learns how to combine his first lesson from the female wolves – being nurtured - with his second lesson – being alone - to create the third – being of service to others.'

Tsao Chinem Cllens

Chapter Nineteen

Men at work

The score so far:
Roger: 38years.   The world: 2008.

'I'm scared by it all,' Roger said quietly.

'What are you scared of?' Brian asked.

'I'm scared that it will all end badly, very soon. The world will become an apocalyptic mess, we'll all end up fighting, killing. I'm scared that we'll just run out of resources and that will be it.'

'Have you been reading newspapers again? Roger, please don't believe everything on the news,' Brian smiled. 'I know, it is difficult right now to stay positive, especially when you don't have a job and feel shit about yourself.'

Brian's voice was reassuring. 'Let's just keep it simple. The point is what applies within can be applied without. Let's try to keep a positive mindset. Besides, there are millions of people out there doing incredible, brilliant, life-transforming things, they just aren't in the press right now.'

Brian sipped his tea, and continued:

'There are people who are incredibly positive about life and there are those who are very fearful and worried. The last lot seem to be in the majority at the moment, but that may well not be the case. How do you know what the billions of people who don't have access to the media are doing or thinking, or, most importantly, what they are capable of?' He waved his hand at Roger.

'You've traveled the world, you've seen people from other cultures who don't rely on money and banks. They operate in a very different mindset, they have completely different world views.'

Brian paused and then continued as he held Roger's arm. 'Those people who are fearful and have a negative mindset believe that within two days of the banks falling there will be anarchy on the streets. Chaos will ensue, dog will eat dog. It will literally only take two days to become anarchy. Agreed?'

'Yes, agreed.'

'At the other end of humanity, operating from a different mindset, full of compassion and love. There is the experience of being in nature, fully committing yourself to nature and beauty. When you spend time in nature within two days you fall in love with nature and yourself. It takes just two days to change your experience of the world. These two events will both take two days. Do you see?'

'I think so.' Roger was confused.

'Roger, believe in the innate good of humanity. Believe that we are all able to collaborate, share and mutually support, don't fall into the trap of fear and lack. You and I, we have plenty right here and right now. I know my job is to role-model being happy, and to live it, embody it, whatever happens. If I experience the world in a positive and loving mindset, then the world I encounter is positive and loving. Simples!'

Roger laughed, but his furrowed brow showed he still didn't fully understand.

'OK, let's go at it from another angle.' Brian continued patiently: 'When you worked at Proctor and Grumble you felt secure, didn't you?'

'Yes.'

'What was that security based on?'

'I don't know, job security, money, pension, stuff like that.'

'Yes, all those temporary and irrelevant things. And now, all those things have been taken away, but they have also been shown to be no longer safe and secure.'

Brian smiled to himself. 'Money in the bank is not as secure as it used to be, having a job is not as secure as it used to be. We can either worry about that or we can move on to the next currency. The next, and actually more important, currency.'

Brian looked up and he could see Roger was attentive now.

'So what's the new currency, what is it?'

'It's relationships, it's community. Your security is no longer gained from money and material goods. You can gain just as much, in fact much more, from having good friends and relatives, from living in community.'

Brian laughed 'That's much better than money, it always has been. We all just forgot that for a while.'

Note to self:

What have I lost?

Stress

Pressure

Superficiality

Cold-heartedness

What have I gained?

Contact with my fear

Vulnerability

Empathy

What remains the same?

Self-belief

Drive

I am still the man I used to be, just a bit wobblier and more prone to crying.

Roger contacted James and they arranged to meet in London for lunch. James was still unemployed. Roger expected him to look terrible, thought he'd be suffering like he was. James had been through hard times, he had his house up for sale, he had been separated from his wife for a year. He was re-training as a counsellor. James looked good. He was fit, had a sparkle in his eyes, and an aura of vitality. Roger was impressed. James said he had fought against his fate for a while, but eventually had resigned himself to whatever was going to happen, and now felt much better about everything. He'd realized losing his job wasn't such a bad thing after all. Roger laughed and said he hoped it would be true for him as well.

They arranged to meet regularly, sharing a take away or watching some football on the television. Roger enjoyed James' company, and the two began to share more intimate and deeper experiences with each other as the trust grew.

James attended a men's group every first Wednesday of the month and suggested Roger should come along. Roger was reluctant. He thought only wimps went to men's groups. It all smacked of therapy and another admission of failure as a man.

After persuasion from James, and especially from Jules, he went along. What had he got to lose?

Eight men attended on a regular basis, and the group was facilitated by a poet in whose rambling, clutter-filled house it took place. They met in the upstairs front room, filled with shelves of intellectual and obscure books, musty chairs and busts of famous poets and composers. Roger liked sitting in the room and breathing in the intellect, he felt clever just by association.

Roger was pleasantly surprised to find some professionals and businessmen amongst the attendees, and was quite taken aback by their honesty and frankness. At first it disconcerted him, but after attending three meetings, it started to inspire him.

Maybe this was the way that men should talk? Maybe this was actually how men were supposed to be?

'OK.' The poet pulled the men's attention to silence.

'Let's talk about pornography.' Some of their heads went down nervously.

'I'm guessing we all use it?' He continued nonchalantly.

'So, how damaging can it be?'

There was a pause.

'Well, it's not damaging at all,' asserted an earnest short man who had the haunted look of a geek, the hunched shoulders, the dark shadowed eyes. 'I think it is a public service. Think of all those perverts out there who would be exploiting women but who now use porn to satisfy their needs instead.'

'So, porn isn't an exploitative industry?' The poet rather briskly replied.

'Yes, some of it is, but not all of it, I'm not doing any damage,' came the slightly cowed response.

'Are we doing damage by looking at porn on the Internet?' The poet pressed on. 'What do you think, Roger?'

Roger, flustered, looked down, but gathered strength.

'I know it's bad, but I still enjoy it. I'm a man and I like to look at naked women.'

'Yes,' agreed James. 'I saw something on the net the other day that said men who look at women's breasts live longer.'

'And a lot of those breasts you are looking at belong to women who are very happy for you to see them. They're being paid good money and they enjoy doing it,' the man with a beard added.

'Yes. I don't think there's anything wrong with it. Anyway, there's so much of it out there. Aren't 90% of hits on the Internet on porn?' asked the tall thin athletic man.

'I think that's a bit of folk legend' replied Roger. 'Some people say that porn sites are actually in rapid decline.'

'We're off the subject,' interjected the poet.

The conversation meandered and wandered for a while and then the poet, increasingly frustrated by the men's lack of responsibility, interjected.

'OK. Let's get back to the point. The porn industry exploits women. You are supporting the porn industry by looking at images of women on porn sites. It is irrelevant whether you are choosing not to go to "snuff sites" or fetish or bondage sites. By clicking on any image from a porn site you are supporting and perpetuating the exploitation of women. Many of those women may feel in control of their image and their level of participation, but it's a well-documented slippery slope from control to exploitation.' He looked around the circle of men and many were now looking at the floor, not raising their heads.

'As men we need to take responsibility for our actions, we need to be aware of the consequences of our deeds. It's not good enough to say you're not doing anything harmful. You are. You are encouraging the continuation of the porn industry by clicking on images of any kind. It's like saying you're a vegetarian because you only eat pre-packaged meat, you don't participate in the killing of the animals. You do, the meat comes from somewhere.'

The other men sat silent.

'Hey, sorry, guys, but it was time for a reality check.' He looked around with a smile.

'No. Good point, much appreciated,' James responded. 'I'd not thought of it that way.'

'Hey, yes, I get it,' added Roger. 'But at the beginning you said we all use porn, does that mean you do too?'

'Yes, I used to,' the poet added. 'Nowadays, I don't use porn, but it was hard to stop.'

'How did you do it?'

'I weaned myself off it by only going to public domain sites where there were images I knew weren't exploitative.'

'What do you mean?' asked the athletic man.

'Well, instead of googling porn, I'd google bikinis or lingerie. Those images weren't supporting the porn industry, they were supporting Marks and Spencer.'

They laughed.

'Once, I'd made that move, I realized what I was really looking for when I masturbated was the relief of an orgasm for me and not for anyone else. I was seeking to please myself, and I realized I could actually do that without images, my imagination didn't need photos. I built up a new relationship with myself, one that excluded others, women even. It was about how I feel about myself and how I want to be.'

Roger was impressed.

'Roger, why did you first come to see me?' Brian asked in his quiet way.

'I was feeling shit, I was very depressed, I needed help,' Roger replied.

'Yes, and how did you used to describe that state of being to me?'

'I don't know, I felt very alone.'

'Yes, but you used to use a very specific phrase,' Brian persisted.

'I think I said I had a pain in the core of my being,' Roger remembered.

'Yes, that's it. You kept talking about the hole in the core of your being. Think a little about the symbology of that statement.'

Roger closed his eyes for a moment.

'What were you really saying about yourself?' asked Brian.

Roger's face lit up. 'I know, I was talking about my heart.'

'Exactly, you were talking about the pain in your heart. You had a hole in your heart. Like so many men, you were so unfamiliar with your heart you didn't even recognize it when it was talking to you. Few men actually recognize or honour their heart by listening to it. So many have hardened their hearts, and don't know when it is trying to communicate.' Brian smiled. 'Do you get what I mean?'

'Absolutely,' Roger felt elated by this revelation.

'In the past you identified yourself as the hole in your heart, by doing so, you identified yourself with pain and suffering. Now we need you to identify yourself with your heart, the healed heart, not the hole and the pain.'

Note to self:

I need men

I never realized it before. I have always thought I was good, I was cool, I'm capable of looking after myself.

I thought men who went to men's groups were wimps, fools, who needed therapy, who had something wrong with them.

I realize I need the company of men.

I enjoy spending time in an all-male environment, and I get a huge amount from it. I'm able to talk with such sincerity, authenticity, and without censor, it is really liberating. I'm becoming a liberated man.

I need men.

'Your mother sent me a letter from the school again. A begging letter for contributions to the new wing they're building. Bloody cheek, I pay my taxes, I pay all the fees.' Roger was chatting to his daughter.

'Dad, I can't believe you said that. The new wing will be brilliant, it's going to house a proper drama department.' She looked angrily at her father.

'Oh, I didn't know that.' He could feel her hurt, he added, 'Giselle didn't tell me that.'

'No. Dad, she didn't tell you that. Why should she have to tell you everything? Why didn't you know?'

She darted another dark look at him.

'Do you know anything about what I do? Me and mum may not always get on, but at least she knows what I'm up to, she actually knows who I am, and how a new drama department would like be good for me.'

He bowed his head.

Chapter Twenty

Angela's eightieth

'I come from Barry, I was born and bred here. I didn't have a good childhood. As a child I was sexually abused and severely beaten by my step-father.'

Five people were taking a brisk walk across the windswept beach at Barry Island in South Wales. The little group had travelled from London to celebrate Angela's eightieth birthday. She was a well-known healer and friend of Brian who lived in South Wales.They all enjoyed tea and cakes at her house, before stepping out into the brisk sunlight.

In the summer the beach was packed with holiday makers, full of sun tan lotion, ice cream and fish and chips. Now, deep in winter, the beach was deserted and the sand was whipping up into their faces by a chill wind as they strode out to see the sea. As they walked, heads bent. Brian was talking.

'It became such a problem for me that I used to sleep at night with a knife under my pillow. The atmosphere in the house meant that I became very violent.' This came as a shock to most of them, never having experienced Brian as anything but the mildest of men, never having heard about this side of him.

He continued, 'I ran away from home when I was 14, I didn't really learn to read or write, and I was homeless. I would sleep rough on the streets and in the fields. I became addicted to alcohol and to violence. I fought my way around Britain. I was angry and addicted.'

They were all stunned into silence as they continued walking.

'I begged on the streets, I sat and had a cap and would ask for money. I was alone, I was on my own, and I blamed everyone else for my predicament. This went on for many years, but eventually I had to stop blaming others. When I stopped blaming others I realized I had nowhere to go other than inwards, I could only look into myself. By looking inwards I started to see the patterns in my life. The ways in which I was avoiding pain, the ways in which I was bringing pain to me.'

He looked out across the bleak sands to the grey sea in the distance and continued to walk and talk.

'I spent about ten years turning inwards, listening to myself, hearing my patterns as I sat begging on the street. I watched as people passed me by, ignoring me, deliberately abusing me, choosing to mock me. They reinforced my separateness.' He snuck a shy smile at Roger, who, head down, was wrapped up against the cold wind.

'Then I had a spiritual awakening. It wasn't all love and light, these things aren't like that.' He chuckled to himself.

'It was definitely more hate and darkness, but it was a huge awakening. In it I went mad. I went insane, I lost everything, I broke down.'

He pushed his hands deep into his coat pockets.

'I was institutionalized for a year and given all sorts of drugs and poisons. I ran away and got into a fight and almost lost my life. Somehow I survived. Not only survived, but I started to thrive.' He laughed to himself.

'I thrived by adopting a personal spiritual discipline, nothing too complex. I didn't go to meditate for twenty years in a cave in Nepal. I didn't even know what meditation was then.' He looked out to the sea again.

'I developed my spiritual practice here in Britain, and I did it because I could do nothing else. I was sort of forced to because I had gone insane. The practice just came to me. One day I heard a voice and it said, do this every day. It's not difficult. I started to do things every day.'

He walked on and they followed.

'By doing things I mean breathing, just breathing, and listening to my body. Very basic. Everything started with that. And by doing it every day I changed from the darkness to the light, I was filled with light. I burst through the old self and became someone else. I became one with myself and most importantly with everyone else.' He stretched his hands out to illustrate the expansion.

'I found that I could love myself and everyone else. I continued to sit and beg on the street, but I was now sending healing out to the people as they passed. I would unreservedly send healing to people, and as I did this they changed in their attitude to me. Suddenly, people would come up, they noticed me, and some would ask for healing even. I had changed and they noticed.' A brief smile flickered across his face.

'I realized I was a healer, and I was meant to do that kind of work. Everything about me changed, I was transformed and the world transformed itself. I married, had children, I set myself up as a healer.' He gave a big smile up to the sky.

'I pray every month we have enough money to pay all the bills, and we do. I have a box by the side of the phone which is for money to pay the bills, and each month there is just enough in it to pay them all, sometimes a little extra. That is how I live, and I am very happy.'

They were all speechless, few of them had any idea this was his past. None had heard the full story before. Some, who had thought about it, had presumed he had an idyllic childhood and upbringing, because he was so kind and gentle. He had struck them all as a very placid person, and yet this colourful and violent past had formed the man with them on the beach.

'In those times of enlightenment, I was given some information, which I've written down, as best I could. They're very rough notes. I can't write very well, so I want to give these writings to

Roger. I hope he will do something with them.'

Roger flushed, he felt very proud as they continued to walk to the sea.

'What happens to the writing is irrelevant to me, I pass them on, see what you can do with them.' He continued to walk head down into the sand and wind.

'I have always chosen to live and be on the edge of society. I don't live in the mainstream. Most healers live on the outskirts of their culture, but every now and again we can be of service to the greater good.' He said, smiling enigmatically at Roger.

Shortly they arrived at the edge of the sea, the waves lapping at their feet. 'Please keep looking out to sea' he requested and they did as asked, looking for signs or boats.

'While you're looking out to sea, tell me how many of us are there here?'

'Five,' came the puzzled response.

'Good. Now turn round slowly and tell me how many foot tracks are there leading up to us across the sand.'

They turned and counted, there were four distinct tracks in the sand. They all looked at Brian in amazement. Angela poked her foot onto his to check he was really there.

'Ah, now you've noticed, brought consciousness to it, I can't do it any more' he chuckled to himself.

'How do you do that?' marveled Roger.

'By relaxing' came the simple reply.

As Saskia made her way through her teenage years she became, as she said she would, the centre of the "in-crowd" for her school. She was tall, skinny, wore all the latest fashionable clothes, vivacious, cutting and charming. She was also studious and conscientious at school, but had a tendency to drink too much at parties, however, she always got by on her charm and looks. People wanted to be with her. She was very popular, she wasn't used to people ignoring or avoiding her.

Roger had been struggling with his redundancy. Despite the work he was doing with Brian, he was still sabotaging himself. When he thought of Saskia, he felt embarrassed, he felt unworthy of her. He thought of himself as a failure as a father, he felt he had let her down by losing his job. Consequently didn't want to see her, didn't want her to see how low he was. He avoided contact, made excuses, tried to avoid her. He wanted his daughter to see her father as a success, and he felt nowhere near that. He was not available, in a meeting, unable to meet with her when she rang.

This had been going on for two months, she was not happy about it. Only after Saskia had persisted and insisted they had arranged to meet at a local café, he'd run out of excuses.

They sat outside in the sunshine. Sharing a coffee and awkward silence.

A young man in his early twenties was walking past and he and Saskia made eye contact. He started engaging Saskia in conversation.

'Wow, did you see them last night, they were brilliant.'

'No, I've never seen them live.'

The young man was very interested.

Roger sat and waited for the young man to move on, but he persisted, and Saskia was enjoying the attention.

'I love the colour of your hair.'

The man stroked her hair away from her face, smiling and flirting.

Roger couldn't contain himself any longer.

'Er, yes, thank you. Her father also present,' he announced.

The two of them looked askance at him.

'Yes, alright old man,' the young man sneered.

Saskia blushed and pushed the man away.

He retreated with a last lingering glance. She turned to her father.

'I think you're jealous of the attention,' She laughed.

Roger looked down at his coffee.

'Yes, sorry, just a bit awkward,' he mumbled.

'I know Dad, it's all a bit awkward isn't it. Your daughter growing up, becoming attractive. Getting on with her life. Having a life you know nothing about,' she smiled. 'Does it make you feel old?'

Roger couldn't suppress a smile. 'Yes, really old, ancient!'

'Time waits for no-one, especially an absent father.'

She looked hard at him.

'A father who doesn't turn up.'

There was an emotion-filled silent pause between them.

He spent those moments in reflection, feeling into a deep hurt, and then he started. 'Saskia, you don't know how important you have been for me over the last years, I owe you so much. You have been a brilliant daughter and I've been a crap dad, I realize that, and I want to thank you for all your patience.'

A silence followed, the two of them continued filling it with emotion. She turned to him.

'I know, dad. You have been a crap father these last months, it feels like you've been away, as though you've abandoned me, you just haven't been present.'

She was on the verge of tears.

'I've been hanging in there hoping you'd get through the bad times. I know it has been tough for you, and you've been through a lot, but you didn't half lose sight of what was important. I'm not just your daughter. Your dutiful daughter. I'm also someone who cares, who loves you. You could have shared it with me, you know, I'm not a child any more.' She smiled through the tears as they moistened her eyes.

Roger choked as he watched her struggle.

He breathed shallowly and with effort. He realized he had shut himself off again from the people who were trying to love him.

His voice came to him, as he looked her in the eyes.

'I'm just very sorry, I'm so sorry,' he muttered. 'I know you would have helped, thank you.'

'I don't want you to be sorry,'

Saskia glared at him.

'I want you to be proud of yourself and of me. I want you to be you, not a pisshead. That way I get a dad and you get a life. It's too late for sorry, it's time for you to start taking your responsibilities seriously.'

Her eyes burnt brightly.

'Come on, Dad, pull yourself together, get your arse into gear. Stop feeling sorry for yourself.'

'How come you're so blinking clever,' he spluttered, 'and I'm so thick?'

'Because you're a miserable git and I'm a genius!'

They sipped their coffees in reflection.

'Why did you used to go to all those New Age Workshops?' Brian was probing again.

Roger didn't pause. 'Because I could pick up women easily.'

'Yes,' Brian smiled. 'But, was that all?'

'Yes. I didn't attend for the message or the experiences. I never thought those messages were for me. I was alright, I had a great job. The workshops were for all the poor people who hadn't got a life.'

'So you missed the messages and the teachings?'

'In a sense I was never present at a workshop I was just an observer, I didn't hear or see anything. I was watching for my next conquest to reveal herself.'

'The thing is, Roger, despite what you say, you were absorbing the messages and the experiences. You were unconsciously seeking enlightenment whether you knew it or not. You attended meetings and workshops by some of the world's leading thinkers, and on many levels you absorbed the lessons anyway. You have a huge amount of experience and knowledge in you. We need to get that out. To share it with the world, as you say.'

Roger laughed at Brian's impersonation of himself.

'OK, so how do I do that?' Roger asked.

'Well, do you remember what I said when we were on Barry beach?' Brian brought out a plastic folder with scribbled notepaper inside as he spoke.

'Yes, you talked about the things which came to you, and how you wrote them down.' Roger looked at the pile. 'Are these them?' he added reverentially.

'Yes, these are they' laughed Brian. 'They are just some things which came to me and I'd like you to have a look at them and put them in order, and then share them with other people.'

'But, they're yours, they're not mine!' exclaimed Roger.

'They're just the thoughts of a beggar who was going insane. They may well be rubbish and of no use, I haven't looked at them in years.' Brian smiled at Roger. 'I know that you can put them to much better use than I can. Maybe they're only good for burning, who knows.'

'Wow, the crown jewels,' said Roger with genuine affection and respect.

'Yes.' Giggled Brian. He looked up at Roger and put he put his finger to his lips to indicate they should be silent for a moment. The two of them eased their bodies into their chairs and deepened their breath.

They sat in quiet contemplation, and then Brian started to speak again.

'Right. Before I go any further I need to explain what this is all about.'

Roger nodded and waited.

'I've said before that I went through an enlightenment process, which superficially looked like insanity. That concept is a very important part of what I am sharing with you.' He paused to allow his words to enter Roger's consciousness.

'During that time I was given the realisation that people who live on the outside of society, who are outcasts, can be of great value to society. I understood that me being a beggar, me being a violent bastard, was actually of value to society.'

He paused and smiled to himself as he recollected how he had been. 'I was so far outside society that I could actually look into society from a long distance away. I gained perspective.'

He closed his eyes and drew in a deep breath.

'The perspective I gained goes something like this.' He relaxed his shoulders and settled into his chair.

'At the present time we are busy, busy, bustling everywhere, doing things. The things we consume and fill our lives with are actually completely irrelevant. They mean nothing. All of it. All of this means nothing.' He swept his hands round in front of him.

'If you can detach yourself from this stuff, as I did you, then see what is actually important, what actually has value.' He relaxed his shoulders again and drew another deep breath.

'The things which are of value are community, love, collaboration, sharing, friendship, nothing else matters. You'd think people would like to hear that message. The trouble is bringing back such a message actually makes you unpopular. People don't want to be reminded that they are spending all their lives being busy with things that are irrelevant. That doesn't go down well.' Brian paused and smiled at Roger.

'They don't want to hear that they've spent the whole of their life pursuing irrelevance, and you're the same.'

'Absolutely.' He nodded. 'But I would have thought people would like that message if they understood it.'

'You'd think so wouldn't you? The message is not new. It's

been around for a long time. Jesus was preaching it, and look what they did to him.'

'Yes, I suppose so.' Roger was in thought about that remark.

'Good.' Brian relaxed his shoulders and drew a deep breath again.

'So, I realised if I'm going to be of any value to other people I needed to create a message which could be understood without being too confrontational.'

He shut his eyes, drew in another deep breath, and then continued slowly.

'So, I created the Core Values. Basically, what you need in your life in terms of beliefs and concepts. These are:

"Acceptance of self totally

Take full responsibility for your thoughts and actions

Every act has a consequence

Non judgementalism to everyone and everything

You can only ever change yourself

Every day is a clean fresh new day

No matter what happens give thanks

Accept your human limitations

The law of correspondence

Until you are committed there is no movement at all".'

Brian settled in his chair and took a deep breath, then asked.

'It would be good if you were to write those down, and then spend some time absorbing each of those statements, and seeing how they can be linked together to help people.' Roger scrabbled for a piece of paper and wrote the ten statements down as Brian repeated them again to him.

'Once you have absorbed those messages, you and I can then move onto The Practice, the doing of them.' Brian smiled.

Chapter Twenty-one

Achieving success through empathy

Roger walked past the executive car sales rooms. He pressed his face to the glass on a regular basis. This day he saw a young man in his early twenties being fawned over by the sales staff. He was trying out the latest models, moving from a Ferrari to a Porsche. Roger watched him slipping in and out of the comfortable leather chairs, pressing the gear handles, reflecting on his image in the rear view mirrors.

'Lucky bastard'.

Later that day Roger was at Jules' house, the sun was shining and the warm air wafted with the smell of newly cut grass. He had been helping Jules out in the garden, and he'd just put the lawn mower away. Doing such small jobs around the house for her felt good, made him feel of value. As he started to prune an over-grown bush by the kitchen he reflected on the changes in his life over the last years.

He knew he was no longer the master of his life. He had definitely lost control. Previously, he had spent inordinate amounts of energy and time controlling and compartmentalizing his life. He didn't have the strength nor the inclination to do that any more.

He was now behaving in a more intuitive manner. He was allowing his emotions to have an input, not just his head. All his life he had thought his way in and out of situations using logic. Compartmentalizing as he went along, keeping everything separate. Now he was listening to his heart, sometimes acting on his intuitions, seeing the bigger picture. It felt good to behave in this new way.

He certainly wouldn't and hadn't chosen such a path, he still felt like it had been forced on him. As he thought that, a sharp branch jabbed him in the arm while he tried to reach up with the pruning shears. He took a deep breath and stretched again.

He continued. There were advantages to this new way of being. He felt more alive than he had in years and years. He felt happier despite no longer owning the most up-to-date material goods, he didn't miss them. He felt more content and at ease with himself than when he had been financially secure. His relationship with Jules had been rocky for a time, but as he improved so had their relationship, they were now in a good place. He was a lucky man.

As a child, Roger had thought if two people fell in love then all their problems were over. By being in love everything became well in their world. In his adult life, before Jules, he had only ever indulged in very brief affairs, conquests without consequence, so he never really tested his earlier belief. Now he was in a deep and meaningful relationship with Jules. His hypothesis was being tested, severely. 'If two people are in love, they have to work very hard at it', he thought to himself, as he gathered up the cut branches and put them in the wheelbarrow. He saw that a relationship wasn't all fluffy and lovely. The two of them had struggled to maintain the ties during Roger's troubled times, but he was now through them, and the bond between the two of them was growing. As Jules had said, what doesn't kill you makes you stronger, and the two of them were coming together in a more honest and loving way. This led him to question his exact feelings for Jules.

What did he feel for her?

Did he love her?

He had never told anyone, apart from Saskia, that he loved them. He leant the wheelbarrow upright against the wall of the garden shed. As he walked back to the house, he asked himself,

'What is love?' The intuitive response came back instantly. 'It might as well be this'.

He stopped on the path to listen to a blackbird who had started singing in the tall tree at the back of the house. The melodic song was beautiful. He allowed himself to absorb the candescent subtleties of the song, encouraging them to resonate deep into his body. He felt into the moment, and another message popped into his head.

'Now is the time to tell Jules you loved her'.

He had been pondering these question for months. Did he love her? How could he tell her? What could he say or do?

He'd been waiting, hoping, for leadership from Jules, but none had been forthcoming.

He resolved he now had to take the plunge. He stepped back into the warm glow of the kitchen.

The two lovers lay in each others arms, draped across the bed. Tousled bedding intertwined with limbs and tousled hair.

The sunshine streaming in from an open window.

It was Sunday morning.

Jules' boys were away with their dad, they had the house to themselves. Both were sleepy but awake. Roger looked lovingly into her eyes.

'Wait here a moment will you?' he asked as he slipped out of the bed.

'I'm not going anywhere,' came her muffled confused response.

He padded across to the sitting room where he had secretly placed some flowers.

He entered the bedroom with the blooms covering his groin and stood smiling in front of her.

She looked bemused, and then surprised.

She thought, Roger doesn't do this - gifts, presents, surprises!

'What's this?' She asked. She was awake now.

'This is a symbol, a token, of my love for you,' he said, despite his attempts to keep it light, he could feel tears welling in his eyes.

'This is a little gift for you, to say thank you so much for loving me, thank you so much for your patience. I love you.'

He handed her the bouquet and continued:

'I know I've been a crap boyfriend recently, I know I haven't been paying much attention. I know I've been feeling very sorry for myself.' He smiled at her. 'I am going to change, I am going to be different, I am already different.' He said firmly.

Both had tears welling. Jules was struggling for words as she admired the flowers.

'Oh, Roger, I don't know what to say. Thank you. You didn't have to…'

'Oh, OK, I won't…' He laughed and made an attempt to take the flowers back.

'No. no, no.' She smiled, and held the flowers firmly, before putting them down. 'Do, do, do, do, be the change.'

She stretched out her arms for him, and he gently lent down to be held and kissed by her.

'That is wonderful. This means so much to me,' she spluttered.

'Me too.'

The men's group was gathered as usual. The poet looked around the expectant faces.

'What is success?' He asked. 'How do we know we are successful?'

They all gave it a few minutes to consider their responses.

The athletic man replied first, 'It's temporary, it's fleeting, it comes and it goes, it doesn't last forever. You can be successful for a moment, but then it changes, and you have to strive again.'

'That's beautiful, I agree,' responded the man with the beard. 'However, I think success is more permanent, I think of my success in terms of my children. I see them as my success, I have brought them up and enabled them to fly the nest and I gain a huge amount of pleasure from seeing them out in the world.'

'Yes,' agreed James. 'I think I measure my success in terms of my children, and how proud I am of them. But, also I measure it in terms of my ability to help others. I see success as the changes that occur in my clients' lives. I'm not saying it's because of me, but it gives me great pleasure to see them grow.'

'Yes,' piped up the geek. 'To be of service to others, that's success. To have transcended the personal and to now be of service to the greater good is the goal.'

The other men were a little stunned by the man's eloquence, he hadn't spoken like this before.

He continued. 'It reminds me of Osho and when he told me the story of Zorba the Buddha, you know that one don't you?'

The men all looked blankly back at him.

'Oh, OK, I'll tell you the story as best I can remember it.'

'Good, please do,' encouraged the poet.

'Well, you see, there is Zorba. Zorba the Greek, it's a book by…by a Greek author'

'Nikos Kazantzakis' the poet tossed in.

'You knew Osho?' asked the athletic man.

'Yes, I stayed with him in the States for two years.' The geek stared blankly, as though everyone had done such things.

'Wow, cool.' replied the athletic man. 'Tell us the story.'

'OK. I think it goes something like this.' The other men settled down on their chairs. 'Zorba the Greek is a womanizer, singer, poet, general bon viveur, if you see what I mean. He lives a life of plenty and lives it in the physical. He experiences life as a very grounded, very earthy character. He gets into fights, he chases women, he enjoys life completely. A bit like all of us.' The geek joked.

The other men smiled, still amazed at the man's sudden eloquence.

'This carries on for many years. But, at a certain point he realizes there is something missing in his life. I think Osho put it this way, he realizes there is a heaven as well as an earth.' As he said this the geek rocked his head from side to side, imitating Osho's typically Indian gestures.

He continued 'Zorba is living the life of the earth, but he is not experiencing the life of the air. He is connected to the planet but not to heaven. He has only ever considered his own needs, he hasn't thought of others. He understands he could consider others, and by doing so, he could connect himself to heaven. So, resolving to do the work, he undertakes a spiritual or personal development practice, he studies and betters himself. He starts to pray and think about more than just the physical. He connects the two aspects of himself. He doesn't throw away his past, he uses it as a stepping stone to enlightenment. He transforms himself from Zorba the Greek to Zorba the Buddha.'

The geek calmly looked at his rapt audience, and then continued.

'Osho used to say that the best monks were those who had followed such a path, and that the Lord Buddha himself took that path. He was of the earth and then looked up and sought the heavens. By doing it he became of service to his people, and I guess, in that sense he became a success.' The geek finished, and looked around at the spell bound audience, and then added.

'It's a parable.'

'Wonderful, thank you so much,' the poet complimented the man. 'Let us take some time to reflect and consider these wise and wonderful words.'

Note to self:

Walking down Camden Road today, saw a couple of very lovely nubiles chatting, on their phones, holding arms. I was roused, the old beast within me stirred, and I lusted after them. Most definitely lusted after them, especially as I was behind them. Both in short skirts with dark tights on. Oh, how I love the fashion for short skirts and tights this winter. Walked behind them for a while, musing to myself, and then they both stopped and went into a café. They were about 14! They were younger than my daughter by a long way. OMG. Felt very strange, disturbed by it. I have changed, something has moved in me. I am not ever going to be interested in a girl younger than my daughter, it made me feel ill.

Saskia took her GCSE's. She didn't get the high grades she could have, but she passed them and was now studying Sociology, Art & Design and Geography at A level. She wasn't sure where these subjects would lead her. She chose the subjects she was most keen on and felt she could pass the easiest. She had no aspirations to go to University after school. She was more interested in taking a few years off. Giselle came round to Roger's to discuss their daughter's future. This felt like a big step for Roger, she was asking him for his opinion. It made him feel very 'grown up'.

Giselle spoke first. 'She needs to go to University to get a proper education, she needs to study more, she knows so little, she is so young.'

Giselle was sat on the sofa, balancing a cup of tea on her lap, whilst looking up at Roger, who was stood at the kitchen door.

She continued passionately: 'What kind of life will she have if she doesn't? She'll just drift from job to job, she'll not master anything. She needs to settle down to work, and she can have adventures later in life.'

Roger thought about it and then replied.

'Oh, you know, I think our daughter knows what she wants and is very capable of going and getting it.'

He stood tall in the frame of the door, the light from the kitchen window shining behind him.

'She's a bit like her father and mother, she's very driven.' he added with a smile. 'Really, I think, Giselle, our daughter can go to University at any time in her life. She doesn't want to right now, and I fully support that. She should take a year or two out, find out about life and the world, spread her wings.'

Giselle looked down at the carpet mournfully, tightly holding on to the cup on her lap. 'Roger, I know you want the best for our daughter, please, University is the best. It is the best for her.'

She pecked at the cup as she brought it to her mouth.

'No.' Roger smiled whimsically down at her, but remained firm.

He realized he was standing up to Giselle for probably the first time, and he felt in control and calm.

'I know you have done a wonderful, wonderful, job of bringing up our daughter. Giselle, you have done all you can, but you now need to have a bit of faith and trust in her ability go out there and make something of the world.'

He moved to stand in front of her and attempted a weak grin.

'I know I have only played a bit part in all this, but the day that you told me I was a father was actually, in hindsight, the best day of my life. It transformed me, it made me into a man. I can now really appreciate and thank you for doing what you did. It has been a very rocky road, but I have learnt so much from you and my daughter, and one of those things I've learnt, is that you just don't know what will happen next. You need to have faith in the bigger picture, and that everything will actually work out fine. So, I trust Saskia to do what is right for her.'

Giselle shook her head. ''Yes. I know, but what is right for her is to go to University.'

'What you think is right for her is for her to go to University. Please have faith in Saskia, she is very capable of doing great things. She is very intelligent, she has charm, wit and lots of ability, let her go out and find herself. I want to help her become fully Saskia, not conform to someone else's expectations.'

Giselle didn't agree but she was impressed by Roger's calm authority. She'd not seen that in him before.

Roger contemplated the piece of paper with the ten statements from Brian.

He thought to himself, 'It's all a bit biblical, the ten commandments. I guess I need to look at myself and apply them to me, which should give me an understanding of them. Well, here goes':

Acceptance of self totally

'I see now I have been good and bad, I've had my ups and downs. I've been a naughty boy and I've been a good boy. I've tried my hardest, I did my best, given the knowledge and understanding I had at the time. I'm doing alright.'

Take full responsibility for your thoughts and actions

'That's a tough one. Can't I blame my parents for my terrible upbringing? Can't I blame my work colleagues for my unhappiness at not being promoted? I guess I'm the one who created my world, no one else was actually involved. I can also change my reality by thinking positively rather than negatively about it.'

Every act has a consequence

'Blimey, that strikes a cord. Every time I had a conquest without consequence there were actually consequences I chose to ignore. Sleeping with Giselle had a consequence, although I didn't think about it at the time. Every little thing I do affects other people.'

Non-judgementalism to everyone and everything

'This so applies to my relationship with Brian. How much did I judge him? If I'd stayed in that frame of mind I would never have been on this journey, I could quite easily have rejected him. I can also try to not judge before something happens, that's hard. You never know what anything will be like until you've tried it. Custard - yuck!'

You can only ever change yourself

'Ouch! I always wanted other people to change, for them to change me on my behalf, to do all the work. I guess I'm the boss of myself and I can change me for the better. I need to stop trying to change other people, or assuming my life will be better if they change.'

Every day is a clean fresh day

'Very Buddhist. If only it were true! I don't have to bring all my past into this lovely new day, what a concept. I can make this happen by being a bit more spiritual, a bit more focused, maybe meditating every day.'

No matter what happens give thanks

'On the day of my redundancy, on the day that I was overlooked for promotion, I should have given thanks! Wow. That would have saved me a lot of heartache, pain and depression.'

Accept your human limitations

'I guess this means there are things beyond my control, beyond my understanding. There are forces at work that I can't master. I am in a physical body that is changing all the time. My body is choosing to lose hair, there is nothing I can do about it, I should stop worrying about it.'

Law of correspondence

'Everything on the inside is the same as the outside. I create my world and everything is perfect right here right now. That is so true.'

Until you are committed there is no movement at all

'I need to start walking my talk.'

Brian sat facing Roger. The two of them drew in deep breaths and relaxed into their chairs.

'How are you getting on with the core values?' Asked Brian.

'Good.' Roger smiled. 'I'm really getting my head round them, but they're also quite tough.' He laughed.

'Fine.' Brian smiled. 'So, it's time to move on.' He settled his shoulders down as he relaxed.

'It's very simple to talk about these things. It's beneficial to have an intellectual understanding of these concepts. But, what is most important, is the embodiment of them.' He drew a deep breath.

'You now need to start doing and being all of those things every day. You need to find some personal discipline and to stick at it.'

'Oh, that sounds tough.'

'Only if you want it to be, it should be a very joyous practice.'

Chapter Twenty-two

The teacher leaves and leads

The score so far:
Roger: 39 years.   The world: 2009.

It was once more the date of his father's birthday. Roger decided he'd visit his father's grave. As he walked down the concrete path between the brightly coloured flowers and memorials he remembered his snake dream. He allowed himself a smile, and placed his hand on his heart. He continued walking down the path to his father's grave, smiling and feeling his chest. And then it struck him.

There was no pain. He hadn't felt the pain in his core for a long time now. The pain was gone, he was free, he had freed himself. He broke into a bigger smile as he continue down the path, he swung both his arms as he walked, he felt like a little boy. He started to whistle to himself, and then louder. He thought of his father, he saw the two of them in the garage. He knew he would always have a gap where his father should be, he'd never fully connect, but he was much more accepting in his own way. He knew his father had given him life.

Roger felt he needed to show his gratitude for this, acknowledge his debt to his father, so he had brought a bunch of flowers wrapped in cellophane. When he arrived at the grave there was a small bunch of daffodils laid on the gravel. He thought they must have been blown by the wind from another grave and he picked them up.

There was a card, it read:

'In memory of George.
With love from Janet and Saskia.
Loving wife and granddaughter.'

This little token, touched his heart. It made him feel very emotional, both sad and happy. 'Typical, typical, women,' he said out loud. 'They know what to do, they get on and just do it.'

'I'm leaving London to go and live in Barry.' said Brian matter-of-factly. He continued, with a quiet smile on his face.

I've put my house up for sale and we'll be off soon.'

'Oh, my God.' Spluttered Roger. He felt as though an electric charge had been put through his body.

'But you can't. What about London? There's nothing in Barry, you can't do it.'

'It's where I belong. It's where I come from. I know and love the people there. I'm not from London. I have never felt completely safe or at home here.'

'You can't leave, I need you,' gasped a desperate Roger.

'Exactly. The right time to leave my friend.' interjected Brian quickly.

'Look, Roger, we've been over this before. I am no guru, I'm no New Age sage, I'm just an ordinary bloke. I can best teach people like myself. They are the ones who get the most from me. That's why I'm going back to South Wales. Here in London there's loads of people who need help but I'm not like them. They go to Mind Body Spirit shows, they love the light but don't want to face the dark, I can't understand them. They're all seeking the short cut to enlightenment, not prepared to do the work. I can't work with people like that.' Brian held Roger's arm and sat looking at him.

'All those business types, the corporate people who want to be taught in a certain style and use a certain language. I don't have that either. I can't talk the way they do. Remember, I'm just a beggar at heart.' Brian paused and then smiled.

'But you can do the work here. You can teach corporate stuff, Roger, you'd be brilliant at it. Think of the numbers of businesses you already know and how you could introduce them to techniques and disciplines. I know some of the messages I have here are relevant to that kind of work. Please use them, use them to help other people.'

Brian was definitely leaving. Nothing Roger could do would change his mind. He felt a great sorrow and anguish about the imminent parting. He shared this with Jules, who in her down-to-earth way, reminded him he needed to now stand on his own two feet. Roger felt the loss of Brian as if he were his father, it hurt. After a few days, he reflected, at least Brian was still just three hours' drive down the motorway, and at the end of the phone.

Roger began urgently working on Brian's writings. He started to write them up and transfer them into his computer. It was quite a task to decipher Brian's scattered and disparate notes. Some sheets were clear, full of diagrams and figures. Others were cramped, covered by spidery handwritten miss-spelt text, making it a very painstaking process. He had his piece of paper with the ten commandments on it as a starting point. He transcribed the commandments into the computer. Brian looked over Roger's shoulder at the screen and silently read the statements checking they were all there.

'OK. These are the Core Values. They are the beliefs I was given when I went insane, and I think they apply to everyone's life. They are principles on how to live a good life. I guess they give guidance about what you need to think about in your life and how you should behave. Now I'm going to introduce you to the next stage on from that.' Brian pulled out a small bundle of A4 sheets with headings and simple statements scrawled across them.

'These are what I call The Practice. This is what you need to do and think about all day long, every day. They are what I call states of doingness. Each of them relate back to how I was during my enlightenment. They came to me over a period of months. They came in a specific order. I have developed them into, what you would call, a daily spiritual practice for myself.' He handed the papers to Roger.

'I've stuck to this personal discipline for years, it works for me. I know they can be used as the foundation for personal development work for everyone. I'm not saying everyone needs to follow what I do, but the practice can be used as a guide. You will be great at teaching stuff like this.' As with all things associated with Brian, they were very simple and also personal.

Roger spent the night deciphering the headings and statements, and the next morning was scanning through the notes he had made on his I-pad. He felt he now had a grip on what Brian had written.

The Practice comprised eight 'actions', numbered from one to eight.

They were defined and expanded by a statement by Brian, these related how he had been at the time he received the 'action'.

Brian followed each of these statements with questions that sought how to get a deeper understanding of the 'action'.

Roger had spent many hours deciphering Brian's hand written notes, wanting to replicate them correctly. He took his time to read the text Brian had written again:

'The Practice

Each of these are states of doingness. They came to me in this order:

I Breathing

I was lying on the ground in a park in London.

I'd been in a fight and I'd probably broken a rib or two, all I can remember is my breath was very short because of the pain.

It was night-time.

I was looking up at the stars.

The pain was very bad and my whole body was aching, I'd been badly beaten. I was thinking that maybe I was going to die, die alone in a wet and soggy field.

I had those thoughts a lot, and I used to want to die, but this time, I didn't want to die, I wanted to live, which was unfamiliar.

I was breathing really shallowly because of the pain and I decided if I wasn't going to die then I needed to lengthen each breath I took, because I didn't know how many more I had.

I made myself as comfortable as I could.

I just started to lengthen and deepen my breath.

It was very painful at first as the raising and lowering of my diaphragm hurt my ribs. I didn't sleep that night.

I was just lying there breathing deeply for hours.

Sometime in the morning I became aware that my ribs didn't hurt any more.

I could even stretch my arms out without pain.

By breathing deeply I'd repaired my body.

My breathing had healed me.

I realised I'd experienced something miraculous.

I knew it was the start of something. I wanted to find out more.

So I asked myself:

How do you breathe properly?

How do you breathe naturally?

How do you control the breath?'

Roger thought of all the yoga classes he'd attended and how this simple lesson was always one of the key elements. He marvelled at how Brian who had never been to a workshop or class in his life had plugged into this rich vein of knowledge. Roger took some time after reading this first short section to calm himself and to lengthen his breath. After about five minutes of doing this he felt refreshed and invigorated. He was ready to read on.

2 Relaxing

When I used to beg, I would sit very awkwardly against the wall of the underground tunnel.

You can't really beg when you're standing up.

Sitting down for long periods used to make my legs and back ache. I used to have severe pain in my lower back and calves.

After the breathing experience I continued to beg, but something in me had changed.

I sat in a different position, with my knees pointing outwards and my feet tucked under my knees.

Only later I was told this was the Lotus Position, I didn't know about that stuff, it just felt natural.

I realised after a few days that by relaxing into this position, by really releasing all the tensions in my body and sitting, I was again healing myself.

My relaxed pose became easy to hold for hours without getting any aches or pains.

I was changing, and I wanted to continue learning:

How do you rest and sit?

How do you control your movements?

How do you calm the body?'

Roger moved away from his computer. He went upstairs to his bedroom cupboard. Rummaging around in the dark space for a while, he eventually returned back with his old yoga mat. He'd bought it years ago at a yoga retreat, but had only used it a couple of times. He lay it out on the floor of his room and sat, attempting to stretch his legs. The stiffness of his thighs shocked him, in order to reach the lotus position he was going to have to practice long and hard. He stood up awkwardly and returned to the notes.

3 Balancing and grounding

I became aware of the connection between myself and the earth.

When I sat and begged in the lotus position I connected from the top of my head to my bottom.

At some point I realised the connection wasn't just to my bottom, it was through my bottom into the earth.

If I thought about that connection it made me feel very grounded, solid and happy.

It made me feel balanced, and I realised I needed to connect to the earth through my mind and my body.

I wanted to get better at it. I really enjoyed connecting to the earth and wanted to do it more often:

How do you ground yourself?

How do you re-align your body?

How do you put yourself into neutral?'

Roger stood up, moved to the window and looked out. The street below was awash with water, it had been raining very hard all morning. Now the sun was now coming out. The reflection of the sun on the water everywhere was very attractive. The whole scene seemed to be illuminated by thousands of tiny candles flickering. Roger put on his walking boots and raincoat and went outside to enjoy the brief sunshine whilst it was there. As he walked he brought his consciousness into his feet, and spontaneously a smile came to his face. After a while he returned to his reading.

4 Mind body connections

When I started to make the connection through my body to the earth I became conscious for the first time that I had a mind.

I'd never thought about it before.

I connected to the earth by using my mind to shift and focus my consciousness.

Whilst doing this I became aware of the separate nature of my mind from my body.

I realised I had been listening to voices in my mind all my life, they were so familiar I'd never disassociated myself from them before.

I started to listen to my mind's voices and realised they were pretty terrible, very intimidating and destructive.

I decided I didn't want to have them rule me any more.

But, I didn't know how to change that, so I wanted to learn:

How do you identify your internal messages?

How do you replace 'negative' messages?

How do you control the sound?'

When Roger returned from his walk, he re-opened his I-pad and saw there were some e-mails. He replied to a couple as he did so he started to think about what work was coming his way. He then began to worry about his redundancy money, how long would it last? What would he do then? He caught himself, stopped the internal messages. He re-opened Brian's pages and settled back down to read the notes.

5 Growing

I realised even though I was an adult, I was growing, and I thought about growth.

When I did my breathing, relaxing and listening every day.

I starting to heal not only my body but also my mind.

For the first time I made a connection between the healing of my body and the healing of my mind, the two were linked.

In order to grow I had to listen to my body and my mind, not just my mind.

I realised I was starting to grow as a human being, as a

person, really for the first time in my life.

I then started to think about how I could grow further:

How do you listen to your body?

How do you take your time?

How do you live in the 'now'?

How do you allow others to grow?'

Roger stopped reading and straightened his back. He felt a tension in the base of his back, so he stretched upwards in the chair. He then stood up and bent over to touch his toes, releasing the tension from his back. He shook his shoulders and walked around the room a couple of times. He then returned to his chair and screen, and The Practice.

6 Self-discipline

I developed an about two-hour routine for me each day.

That included breathing, consciousness changing, meditation, lots of stuff.

I knew if I stopped doing this daily practice I would return to the violent world I'd previously inhabited.

It took a lot of resolve, but I quit the underground tunnel.

I quit begging.

I changed everything.

I didn't know anything but how to survive on the streets, but I also knew I had to get away, break the ties.

I was certain that I would be able to make those changes stick, but only if I continued to breath, relax and listen to my body every day.

Only later did I realise that other people call some of my practice meditation, I didn't know what meditation was.

I was just following my instincts, and by doing so, I found self-discipline:

What is self-discipline?

How do you enjoy self-discipline?'

Roger resolved to practice some meditation, yoga and deep breathing every day. He wanted to really absorb Brian's messages and knew the only way was to do it himself.

He knew he needed to develop his own programme, and make sure it was achievable and enjoyable. He sipped his coffee, and then continued reading.

7 Identifying the truth

As the days turned to months and years, I thought it would get simpler and easier to continue on this new path, but it wasn't.

I continued to be wracked with painful thoughts, memories and past ways of behaving still arose.

Each time I thought I'd dealt with something it would be replaced with something equally painful or damaging.

In those moments I doubted what I was doing.

I thought I was deluding myself about being healed, and those thoughts would drag me down.

I realised I had to have faith in my bodies ability to show me the way.

I had to listen to my body and not my mind.

In the more lucid and happier times I was able to share some of my thoughts with people I met, and I wasn't rejected as a madman, that encouraged me.

So, I thought about how I could interact with other people, and it boiled down to telling the truth:

How do you tell the truth?

How do you listen to others?

How do you encourage others to tell the truth?'

Roger took a while to consider this section. It didn't resonate in the immediate way the others had, and then he thought about the word 'truth' and what other words could Brian have used. He remembered having gone to a workshop about 'authenticity', and that gave him a clearer understanding. He remembered the teacher said if you are authentic you can be vulnerable or scared. The teacher had said it was brave to be vulnerable. Roger sensed his recent life has confirmed that. He carried on reading.

8 Making it real

I lived as a beggar on the streets.

I was addicted to violence, drugs and alcohol.

During that lifetime I was just following the voices in my head, I ignored everything else.

At some point in time I broke down.

I went mad and by doing so, I found sanity.

I found it in my body, by starting to breath deeply I accepted that I wanted to live rather than die.

It took a lot of self-discipline and a few years, but my life became worthwhile.

I was able to disassociate myself from the voices.

I use the personal daily discipline to keep reminding myself of the positive and good aspects of myself.

Lurking in me is the person I used to be.

As all alcoholics know you are never rid of the addiction, it only takes one drink to be right back there.

I want to be able to continue to apply the lessons I have learnt for myself, and to share them with others.

In order for them to work, the people need to know the answers to the following questions:

What if you are struggling?

How do you document progress?

How do you make ceremonies, rituals and rites of passage?

How do you integrate all this information?'

Roger put down his coffee, and smiled to himself. He loved the messages and the simple truth of Brian's work. He felt very honoured to have the opportunity to work with him in this way.

Roger also realized he had a lot of additional work to do. He needed to fill in the gaps around each statement, and especially around the questions. He saw he had to expand and make accessible the information, and give some examples and hints of best practice. To do this he would have to research other practices, and also draw on the extensive knowledge he had picked up from the workshops he'd attended. He now recognized how much information and knowledge he had retained from those workshops he'd attended all those years ago, and how it complimented Brian's work.

Roger knew these simple instructions could be used in the business and corporate setting, and he started to fantasize about running workshops and weekend retreats.

For the first time in a long time Roger felt excited about his life and the future. These fantasies filled him with hope, and most importantly with confidence. He felt he could forge a new career. One which actually suited him better than his previous incarnation as the assistant brand manager to nowhere.

Chapter Twenty-three

The Maturation

The score so far:

Roger: 40years.   The world: 2010.

As he worked late one night with Brian, Roger shared how happy he felt, and added with a smile. 'Things have changed so much.'

'Yes,' added Brian, as he leaned back in the chair. 'What things have changed where?'

'How do you mean?' Roger was confused.

'What things have changed where?' Brian repeated as he sat looking at Roger.

'Oh, everything, my relationship with Jules, Saskia, my mother, my career, everything.' Roger waved his arms enthusiastically.

'Yes, they're external to you, but the only thing which has really changed is you. Your mindset has shifted. The change has occurred in your head. By shifting thought patterns you have altered the world around you. You think differently about yourself now. That's the only change you needed to make.'

Brian bent forward and looked intently at Roger.

'That's the only change any of us need to make.'

He pointed at Roger's head.

'The only changes which really happened are all in here. Remember the fifth of the core values.'

Roger couldn't, and looked blank.

'You can only ever change yourself.' Brian smiled at his pupil. 'So, what is the most important change you've made recently?'

Roger was a bit frazzled from all the work he'd been doing and he looked dazed.

'I don't know, you tell me.'

'OK, for once, I'm going to tell you something that I've observed about you, and how important I think it is.'

'Cool.' Roger settled back in his chair.

Brian looked around the flat and he pointed out the big flat screen television, the I-phone, the large designer sofa. 'What do all of these things mean?' He asked.

'I don't know, I've got too much money, I'm greedy?'

'No, they mean success.' Brian smiled. 'For you, they are the outward signs of success. You have always wanted and needed success. You wanted to be seen as successful.' Brian leant back in the chair. 'For you, success was very important, it was how you measured your life.'

'Yes, I think so.'

'Well, for me, what makes and defines a man is not how he reacts to success, but how he deals with failure.'

Brian paused, and placed his hand gently on Roger's arm. 'You have become a far deeper, more mature man, by dealing with and accepting failure, than when you were successful. Your successes were only ever going to keep you shallow.'

The next morning Roger woke at 7.30, he showered, and then squeezed some fresh orange juice. He sat down on his yoga mat, crossed his legs as best he could, and calmed his breath. He shut his eyes and instantly recognized that the sun had just broken through the clouds and was now shining into the room. He didn't open his eyes to check he contented himself with the knowledge that it had happened. He brought his consciousness to his breath and started to deepen his in-breath, thinking about drawing in clean, fresh restorative air, and then lengthening his out-breath and thinking about expelling old and stale air.

He sat and breathed. As he did so a slow reflective smile crossed his face as he recalled the day he had first seen "The Buddha Beggar", he remembered what kind of judgments he had made about Brian then. He remembered how dismissive he had been of the beggar. And, now he was the pupil to Brian the teacher. He continued to lengthen his breath. Core value number four, he thought to himself.

'How do we become mature men?' The poet addressed the men's group.

'What is the difference between an immature man and a mature man?' He paused.

'How do we know when we reach maturity?' He turned to the right.

'Is it possible to reach real maturity, or what indigenous people would call - eldership?' He turned to his left.

'What are the signs, the markings of a mature man, and would any of us recognize an elder if we saw one?' He opened his hands out inviting answers.

The circle sat for a while, thinking and feeling into the questions.

'Blimey, that is a tough one. It's not something I've given much thought to be honest,' started the athletic man. 'I once knew an old policeman who worked as a volunteer in schools. He was in his seventies and a typical white working-class lad. He and I worked in a school with a lot of Somali kids. I didn't really give the old boy much attention at first. It was difficult enough to keep the kids under control. Turned out he was really good at drawing and painting, and he helped a lot of the kids. Very quiet man but he had depth. After a week or so he suddenly started talking in Somali to these boys, we were all shocked. None of us thought he'd know other languages, we presumed he'd only know English. We all just saw him as white working class bloke. We'd all judged who he was, and what kind of life he'd led. Being fluent in Somali, and, it turned out, several other languages, being able to draw, didn't fit with who we thought he was. He never bragged about it. He was just very interesting and really quite an amazing bloke. I was really impressed by him, I had to re-appraise who I thought he was, and he struck me as having been a really wise man. A mature man. He's dead now.'

'Yes,' said Roger. 'I have a friend who was a beggar. The first time I met him he was begging in the underground. He's turned his life round completely. He works as a healer now, he's sorted his life, he has kids, he has changed completely. He is the most modest, humble and ego-less man I've ever met. I think he's also the most mature man I know. He doesn't have wealth or status, but he has dignity, he knows who he is, and that inspires me.'

'Absolutely,' the poet nodded his head. 'Mature men inspire us by their deeds and actions. Not by how much money they've accrued, or how many women they've shagged, or how powerful they are. Mature men are not celebrities, nor do they seek that kind of fame. Their actions may well be tiny, insignificant and unseen by others, but they are able to influence us in subtle ways. A mature man doesn't need to be ruled by his ego, any other thoughts?'

Brian and Roger worked hard to make sense of the writings, they covered many wide subjects and matters. The two of them spent many evenings poring over the notes and papers. Brian said not all of them were his and he had also been given some teachings by people he had met along the way.

'Some are from my good friend, Tsao Chinem Cllens. He's a wonderful Mongolian Shaman. He's very on the ball. He sent me some of his teachings and is very happy for them to be used, if you want to, they are powerful. Read one out for me, I love hearing his stuff.' Roger shuffled the papers and piles of sheets, looking for a quote.

As he did this, Brian added 'He always draws parallels with animals in his work. You'll like them.' Roger picked up a handwritten note, titled 'The Short Cut', and he read it out loud.

'Right now, human beings are like caterpillars crawling around in the bushes. Caterpillars are eating machines. They live for nothing but to eat. They don't spend time to notice the beauty of their surroundings. They don't take time to reflect on the wonder of the world. They just eat. They eat what is in front of them and what is behind them, until there is nothing left. They will consume the whole plant on which they live and then die of starvation. They don't think long term. They are destructive all-consuming beasts, and we want them out of our gardens.' Roger paused, thought of the damage they'd done to Jules' cabbages, and nodded his head. 'Too right.'

'The butterfly however is beautiful, it's very graceful. They are delicate sippers of nectar, a blessing, a welcome visitor to our gardens. We like having butterflies, they pollinate our flowers, add beauty and colour.' Roger paused, took a deep breath, and then continued.

'Good.' Interjected Brian.

'Right now, in evolutionary terms, human beings are cater-pillars. We're certainly behaving like them. Most of us caterpillars would like to become butterflies. We want to transform ourselves, we've heard there is a connection. We want to change instantly without any loss or discomfort. Many of us are desper-ately seeking the short cut to becoming a butterfly. Unfortunately, there isn't one. There is only one way, and it is the natural way, through the cocoon. We are afraid of the cocoon, because we know what happens in there, and we just want to get on with being a butterfly. It doesn't work like that. Metamorphosis doesn't happen that way. The caterpillar will die if it stays being a caterpillar, so we all have to submit ourselves to the cocoon.'

Roger paused and took another deep breath.

'Within the cocoon we become milk, our bodies loose shape, we literally melt. That is the part we are afraid of, the melt down. But what can we do? We know we will re-appear as beautiful butterflies, we have to be fearless.' Roger let the words in and felt their truth resonating in his body.

'To be fearful seems natural to us, but we really are not observing nature well if we are fearful. The DNA of the caterpillar is the same as the butterfly. Once you commit yourself to the process, there is no other end result other than a butterfly. You can only ever end up as a butterfly. So, please, do the work, create the cocoon. Do the work that is necessary, and have faith in yourself. You are worthy of becoming a beautiful butterfly.' Roger took his time over these last words, he sat and thought deeply, and then said: 'I am worthy of becoming a beautiful butterfly.'

Note to self
I've spent a lot of time as a caterpillar, starting on the cocoon, not a lot of faith in the butterfly.
  What have I lost?
  Hairline
  Money
  Job and identity
  Pressure to succeed
  What have I gained?
  Calling and identity
  Different status
  Pride
  A heart
  A daughter
  Love for a woman
  Love for myself?
  What remains the same?
  Ambition
  I want to be the best (there's still no short cut past the ego!)

Roger visited Jules a few days after the men's group. They sat in her kitchen discussing what it took to become a mature man. He shared with her the differing opinions of the men. She listened with interest. He described how they had come to the conclusion that a mature man should be responsible and of service to others, and he opined that such a man would be attractive to women. She disagreed.

After taking a deep draught of fresh water, she smiled brightly at him.

'He sounds like a real boring old fart, full of responsibility and duty, no good for me. You men, you really don't have a clue what women want or what women find attractive.'

'You're absolutely right,' he smiled. 'You remain a huge mystery to me.'

'Well, I can tell you what I think a mature man is and why he's attractive,' she enthused. He nodded in encouragement.

'A mature man is still a boy, he has a sense of fun and adventure. But, not all the time, only when it is appropriate. He also still needs to be ready for an adventure, up for a challenge, willing to take a risk. But, at the same time, he needs to be able to take responsibility for his words, thoughts and actions. Whilst not taking himself too seriously, he needs to be reliable and authentic.'

She giggled, reached out and held his arm.

'He needs to be able to care and empathize, be good with children...look after pets and animals...be rich and good looking...'

The two of them laughed, she moved her hand along his arm and interlinked their fingers.

'Yes, in fact, a lot like you.'

He smiled inwardly at the compliment. 'Too many men become boring old farts, too many become bitter about life, and stay like it. You've had your bitter time, but you've come through it. That's why I love you, that's why we're together, because you've been through bad times, not because you avoided them.'

She looked him over with warmth and affection, she squeezed his hand.

'You've still got ambition, you still want to get on with life despite being hurt and damaged. You've been through the mill and come out the other side, that gives you perspective.'

'Wow,' he gasped. 'That makes me quite a dude!'

'Yes. You are.'

Saskia sat on the sofa, laptop on her knee. She was pretending to be doing her homework, but she was on Facebook.

She was bored.

'God, dad, were you good at doing revision and all that?' She asked to the empty door of the kitchen.

Roger walked through with a towel in his hand.

'What did you say?'

'Were you good at all this revision stuff?' She repeated waving the laptop around. 'You know when you were at school.'

'Oh, well, we didn't have computers in those days.' he answered.

'I know and you all rode to school on horses.' Saskia couldn't resist.

Roger smiled. 'Well actually, yes, I was rather brainy at school.' He replied happily knowing his daughter would pounce upon such a statement.

'Brainy, or do you mean lonely geek?' She snapped.

He attempted to look wearily at her, came and sat next to her on the sofa.

'No dad, go on, tell me how you were when you were younger, I'd like to know.' A sincerely interested look flitted across her face as she put down the laptop and turned to him.

'I guess I was just very competitive when I was at school, and yes, that made me also lonely. I didn't have many mates, instead I got very good grade at O and A level. They took me on at LSE because I was so focused. You know, I was quite relentless and I always wanted to be best, very competitive. Driven I guess you could say.'

'God, you sound very dull as well.'

'I know, it's hard to think about it now, but I was very thrusting.'

They both laughed. 'I was scouted by Proctor and Gamble after LSE, they put me through the fast-track scheme. I got my diploma in quick time, I was marketing assistant before I knew it. Wow, it all happened so fast.' He reflected.

'Yes,' Saskia held a pretend microphone to her father's face. 'But were you happy?'

'I though I was happy, but I wasn't really.' He looked stunned as he thought back to those days. 'Blimey, I was a miserable git, and I made other people's lives a misery. I was a very bad boss.'

He sat for a moment with this statement.

'I wasn't good at managing people, I didn't have that kind of skill at all. I only ever knew what I wanted, I didn't really allow anyone else an opinion or time to share their thoughts or ideas. I was crap at delegating.'

'So, Mr. Grumpy Boss, what changed all that? When did you see the light?' Saskia asked into her pretend microphone.

'When I was made redundant I guess, and when I met Brian. That was a huge turning point.' He got up and moved back to the kitchen to continue the washing up. 'Blimey, I was a miserable bugger.'

'Yes, you are, put the kettle on.'

As he stood at the sink pondering his work life, he made a link between his career and his love life. He saw how the actions of his youth, the pursuit of conquests without consequence, had mirrored his upwards trajectory at work.

He had relentlessly pursued women. He had never been satisfied, always moving on.

He had been incredibly competitive, comparing himself to the other men. He hadn't always succeeded in seducing every woman, but he had taken pride in being able to have a lot more success than others. He hadn't loved any of the women. He had deliberately kept them at arms length. He had been a heartless and selfish lover, just like when he was the boss. He'd not been able to delegate or listen well.

Then things had changed, he'd been confronted by failure. The argument with the red haired woman, his decision to stick to the sweat lodges, his loss of status at work, had all contributed.

And then he had met Jules.

She had taught him a different type of lovemaking and consequentially a different type of relationship. In this new configuration he learnt about being open. He learnt to love someone. He gave her time and consideration. All the things he hadn't done in relationships before. Both Saskia and Jules had taught him to have empathy, to listen to people. He was now having to adapt himself to new circumstances and learning to be flexible.

He was in loving relationships in which vulnerability and humility were important. He had never considered such things as strengths in his previous life. These realisations about his personal development gave him strength, and made him feel proud of his own journey, his own transformation. He realised he had now found 'meaning'. His relationships with his partner and daughter were meaningful, they carried weight.

And finally, all the different aspects of his life were moving in the same direction.

The skills he was learning in relationship were the skills he needed to hone in his new work. He was learning all the time. He was moving away from work with no meaning and moving towards work that had a positive impact and meaning. Work in which he was going to have to listen to others.

Chapter Twenty-four

Light a candle for me

Roger was in the kitchen, he opened the door to the fridge and as he did so a sheet of paper fell onto the floor, it had been held up by a magnet which had moved. He picked it up and inspected it, he instantly smiled. He recognized it as his affirmation, completed fourteen years previously. He sat at the kitchen table and read it:

'I'm good. I'm great.

I've done what I set out to do.

I'm here.

This is where I wanted to be.

I went out and I got it.

I'm not going to let any of this slip.

I'm going to continue upwards, outwards.

I want more. Much more. Much more of the same.

I'm not going to lose any of this. This is all mine.'

He laughed out loud at his naïve arrogance, the assured presumption, his blinkered certainty. 'Wow, I need to update this', he thought. He went into his living room and decided he'd sit and meditate for half an hour, to focus on the creation of a new affirmation. When he came round after the half hour, he sought out paper and some coloured crayons and he drew a decorative border onto his paper. Then he wrote:

'I'm who I am.

I've achieved a lot.

I'm here for now.

I don't mind where I am.

I went mad, and I lost it.

I'm happy to give it all away.
I'm going upwards and downwards.
I'm happy with what I have.
I'm happy and willing to share.'

He put this new piece of paper on the fridge, next to the old one. He stepped back and looked at the two of them, and thought something was missing. He created another. On this one he drew a colourful, abstract, wild decorative border and located it between the two affirmations, in the middle. On it, in big bold letters, he wrote:

'I am happy.'

'I want us to focus on this first candle which I am about to light. I want us to bring the energy of Jesus Christ into our minds and to bless this candle with his energy.'

The group focused and Brian lit the candle. He had invited a few people round to his house for a final meeting. Roger and Jules came for a cup of tea and a sandwich. The small group were treated to a lovely long song from the canary as they sat around the central table in the front room. On the table Brian had placed a circle of tall white candles. He had asked people to put down their tea and food and to concentrate on the candles.

'Right, now, I want us to focus on the second candle which I am about to light. Bring the energy of Adolf Hitler into this candle. I want us to focus on his energy as I light the candle.'

The group did as asked, a little perplexed, but all knowing Brian had his ways.

'Good. Now let's bring the light of the Buddha to the third candle. We'll bring the light of Ivan the Terrible to the fourth.'

And so it went on, a positive candle followed by a negative candle, until they had all been lit. They sat and watched them burn for a moment before Brian invited the group to go out into the back garden to watch the sun begin to set.

They stood looking to the west over the grounds of the hospital. The clouds and sky turned into a beautiful mix of light blues, oranges and reds over the roofs of the nearby houses. They all stood in silence as the sun dipped down over the horizon. After about half an hour they were invited back into the front room. As they entered, the flickering flames of the candles wavered and swayed, filling the room with a beautiful silver and gold light. They stood and looked at the candles. Each had burnt differently. The positive candles had burnt further than the negative ones. Each positive candle was distinctly burning brighter and quicker than the negative ones. They were burning down in an undulating circle.

Brian smiled at their incredulous faces.

'You see. This is just a physical manifestation of the power of the mind. Please remember this. The mind is much more powerful than you presently know. You can change physical reality by applying your mind and consciousness. We have all come together because in many ways we have been hurt, damaged or treated badly.'

Brian invited them to be seated again.

'Over the last years we have brought consciousness to those states of being, and we have transformed them. We have, all of us, made a brilliant and beautiful journey and we have all shown that is possible for our minds to change, for our mindsets to be altered. Each one of us can and does burn as a positive candle rather than a negative one. If we had the time, we could all sit here now and give positive energy to those negatively imbued candles, and in time they'd catch up with the others.' He smiled his shy smile. 'From this point on, don't ever underestimate yourself.'

Later, as they all left Brian's house, Roger grabbed his teacher by the shoulders and hugged him enthusiastically, he held him for a long time.

'I'll miss you so much,' Roger managed to speak through the tears. 'You are the most important person in my life, you mean so much to me.'

'Thank you, Roger. But I know you are in very good hands now,' Brian said as he extricated himself from Roger's embrace. 'You have Jules,' he said as he looked at her, before turning back to him. 'And you still have the one person who has loved you the most and given you the most support.'

'What...my mother?' asked Roger a bit confused.

'No, your daughter.' He replied. 'Saskia has been the one person who has loved you unconditionally. She will look after you, she will always be there for you, just as you will need to be there for her.'

Brian squeezed Roger's hand and looked deeply into his eyes, as he spoke he shook Roger's hand to emphasize his words. 'Don't ever forget how much you owe your daughter, she has been there through thick and thin, you will need to be there for her.'

Roger took out his yoga mat and sat, bending his legs and relaxing into the shape and form he required. The sun shone into the room, and he relaxed his face muscles, he heard Brian's voice in his head. 'Relax the jaw.'

He sat and brought his consciousness to his breath, drawing in a deep draft of clean air, and then slowly letting it go. His mind flickered forward in time to the coming workshop, he tried to let the thought go. The practice didn't get any easier, but at least he was persisting. After an hour of sitting, deep breathing, followed by some yoga stretches he sat at the computer. He was preparing for the workshop he had organized. Twelve people were coming for the weekend. It was an introduction to the Core Values and The Practice, and incorporated a wide mix of exercises and relaxation techniques. He had chosen a big hotel, set in nice grounds with trees and lots of space. He thought the venue would enable him to introduce the participants to the concept of spending time in nature whilst being on their own. They were all from the corporate and commercial world, business people, and he knew they would need time to adjust to the slowing pace of the workshop.

The participants arrived on the Friday night and spent that evening settling in with a few introductory exercises. They were given a splendid vegetarian breakfast, and then assembled in the workshop room.

As Roger looked around the expectant faces, five men and seven women, he silently watched the actions of a young man. The man was in his late twenties, smartly dressed, clean-shaven, attractive. He was casting his eye around the room, alighting on the faces of the women who were present, and very subtly noting the shape and figure of each woman. When he'd checked the room out, he looked over at Roger and smiled, a very self-satisfied smile.

'Oh my God,' thought Roger, 'it's me!'

That afternoon he sat with the group. He'd given them time alone out in nature in the morning, and it had been very challenging for some of them. They had found it difficult to turn off the urgent voices in their heads, to ignore their future appointments, and had become bored. He thought about how many times in his own life, he'd felt that way. So, he had now arranged them in a circle, each sitting comfortably, each breathing deeply and consciously. They had all closed their eyes and were listening to their own breathing.

He heard himself say gently as they sat, 'Being in a job, being in the corporate world, is like having an itch. At the beginning the itch is mild and when you scratch it, it makes you feel good.

Itching can be very pleasurable. That's fine and you think you are in control, you only do it when you need to. However, the more often you itch the more often you need to scratch, and also the more painful the itch becomes. Often you develop a dependency on the itch, and you need to scratch it all the time.'

Roger paused and theatrically adjusted his posture and then had a little scratch of his neck before continuing.

'It becomes an addiction, then it becomes stressful. In the world you inhabit you will either be at the stage where you are in denial – "I'm in my ideal job, I can control the levels of stress I experience, I'm feeling good about the work I do". Or, you will be slipping into dependency, addiction – "I need more money, I need a better job, I've got to keep moving, this job no longer satisfies me, I want more, I want bigger, better". Or, you will be itching all the time and hurting yourself – "I'm stressed out, but I can't change, it's impossible to change, I'm stuck here for the rest of my life". Brian smiled at the group, they remained breathing deeply with eyes closed.

'Such addictive behavior is seen as normal in our culture, but it isn't. It's not normal to be stressed and unhappy. These behavioural patterns emerge within us because we didn't get what we wanted when we were younger. For many people what was missing was recognition from their parents. They didn't love us enough, they didn't comfort us enough. We spend the rest of our lives trying to compensate for this perceived lack. We fill our lives with completely pointless tasks, goals, and achievements in an attempt to feed an addictive pattern which only damages us in the end. We are told it is the pinnacle of our life to become the CEO, to seal that million-pound deal, to have all the latest toys and gadgets. It's not.'

He paused to check he had their attention, looked round the group, and saw a few eyes were open.

'Please keep your eyes closed, keep focusing on your breath.'

He took a moment and then he continued.

'The pinnacle of life is not itching any more. It is being content with who you are, with the cards you were dealt, not trying to trade them in for better ones. The pinnacle is to be able to see yourself as good enough, happy enough, right here, right now. Not some time in the future or in the past.' He paused again. 'The pinnacle of life is to be loved and to love, nothing else is of any value.'

On the Sunday night Roger returned to London, triumphantly. The feedback forms were very positive, several people had signed up to participate on the next course. He was proud of himself, he had achieved something very different to anything he had done before. He went to Jules', and they shared a very loving, warm, celebratory meal, both felt moved. They sat with wine glasses in hand and pushed the chairs back from the table.

'Well, it all sounds very good and very promising for the future.' Jules cooed. 'I'm very proud of you.'

'Thank you, you know I'm very proud of myself too,' Roger added 'I've done something which has had an impact on people's lives, and it feels blinking good. It feels like this is the work I'm supposed to be doing now. This is the stuff which will not only make me happy, but it will also help others. God, I wish I'd done this earlier in my life.'

He thought for a moment. 'No, actually, I wasn't capable of doing this stuff earlier was I?' He asked.

Jules nodded her head. 'I am only now capable of doing this stuff, and I should just be happy about that.' He smiled and held her hand, he kissed the back of her hand gently. 'Thank you for all your support.'

That night they had a bath together. Jules brought candles into the bathroom and placed them on the windowsill before lighting them.

Roger watched the curves of her body as she moved about. He loved watching Jules.

She drew out an incense stick from it's blue packet, she placed it between her fingers and held the lighter under the end until it started to smoke. She glanced towards him, and smiled, knowing he was watching her. She fixed the stick in the soil of a plant pot on the sill. Roger saw the smoke curve upwards in a delicate dance as she turned towards him, and turned off the electric light.

The sparkling candles brought a shifting, dancing iridescence to the room. Their light reflected in the tiles and mirrors. The room filled with steam, aromatic scent and giggles as they took it in turns to test the heat of the water gushing from the shiny taps.

Roger gently pressed himself up against her responsive body as they stood together in the slightly cramped room. His hands searched around her back, slowly rubbing her shoulders, squeezing her to him. She kissed him gently on the face and around the mouth, before they both kissed. Their lips caressed each other as they held each other closely and gently. She sucked gently on his top lip, letting out a small sigh. They pressed against each other, exploring, teasing with tongues and hands, gradually kissing with more depth, their sighs becoming longer as they slowly roused each other.

They started to pull each other's clothes off. He pulled her top upwards and off, and then gave lingering kisses to her arms and neck, lingering with his mouth just under her breasts. She pulled down his trousers and gently caressed his thighs. Teasing him she stroked right up close to his crotch. As each piece of clothing came off they slowly and lovingly licked and stroked each other, taking little nibbles, brushing their hands lightly against each other's bodies.

Roger slid down her knickers. She kicked them off as they fell to her ankles. They stood fully naked, not quite touching. They both smiled, looking into each other's eyes. The longing between them was palpable.

Roger took the time to enjoy the coursing energy moving through his body, he felt aroused, very happy and content in that moment.

'In you go, my lover.' Jules entreated. He stepped into the warm bath, and lay down.

He smiled up at her. She leant forward over him, reaching for the soap behind his head on the side of the bath. Her breasts were tantalizingly just inches from his face.

She could feel his breath on her nipples as they hardened even more. He gently lifted her left nipple to his mouth, sucked on it, while teasing and licking it with his tongue.

She smiled, her mouth open as she delicately pulled herself upright.

She moved back with a subtle groan of pleasure and then stepped into the bath. She gently sat on him, lowering herself onto his wet body. Slowly she rubbed herself on his hardness. Gently, slowly, she reached down. She started to draw him into her.

The lubrication of their lust and the water mean he slipped inside her quickly, despite the cramped and tight confines of the bath.

They slowly rocked together, both staring into each other's eyes. They kissed long and deeply, their tongues darted and danced with each other. Their bodies rose and fell together in one rhythm. The water gently sluiced around them. She moaned with the pleasure of having him inside her, feeling him residing inside her, feeling their two bodies melting into one.

Afterwards they lay together in the bath for a long time until the water became lukewarm. He thought about how comfortable, how secure he felt, in the embrace of Jules' arms. How satisfied he was with his life. A huge grin crossed his face.

They got out and toweled each other dry. Gently. Lovingly.

They paid attention to each other's bodies, before padding into the bedroom, and lying in the warm bed, wrapped in each other's arms. As they fell asleep Jules nuzzled in to his chest and Roger held her in his arms. He allowed a feeling of completeness to wash over him and grinned as images of the weekend workshop briefly passed through his mind before he fell asleep.

Roger slept long into the morning, he woke refreshed and joyful. He lay in the tousled sheets and contemplated his life:

He was in a good place with Saskia.

He was in love with Jules.

He could see a way of earning a living.

He had made some huge changes in his life and they had all come off. He felt very content with himself and the world.

He travelled on the tube back to his house, and as he walked back up the familiar underground passageway he turned on his phone to see if he had any messages. There were three, all from an unknown number, and one answer phone message. He listened.

'Hello, is that Mister Roger Cologne? This is Sergeant Brown from Kentish Town Police Station. I'm calling about your daughter Saskia Cologne. We have her here in custody at the station. You need to phone us immediately, or come down the station.'

He turned and started to run down the passageway to the trains. As he hurried to Kentish Town his mind desperately sought answers to unknown questions.

'What had she done?'

'What could she have been up to?'

'How terrible could it be?'

He was in a fever, and in the middle of that fever he remembered Brian's last words to him.

'Don't ever forget how much you owe your daughter, she has been there through thick and thin, you will need to be there for her.'

He settled down on the tube seat. He deepened his breath. He closed his eyes.

In his mind's eye he saw Saskia and wrapped her in a bright pink blanket. He repeated a mantra under his breath, 'I love you, it is fine, everything is alright.'

By the time he had reached Kentish Town his heartbeat was back to normal and he strolled into the Police Station smiling to be greeted by Sergeant Brown.

'So, Sergeant, what's happened?' He asked in a friendly tone.

'Oh, her. Your daughter was part of a "flash mob action" outside a games shop and we've had to take them in because they were causing an obstruction.'

The Sergeant was reading from a sheet of paper, but then looked up at Roger who was smiling.

'To be honest, Sir, I completely agree with what they were doing, and I'm in no mood to press charges or take any action. Me and the missus won't let our eleven-year-old play them, because I think they're awful. He's got lots of mates who are addicted to the games.'

Roger was completely mystified, he didn't understand what was going on, couldn't understand what Sergeant Brown was talking about, but he continued to smile, breathe calmly, and nodded encouragingly at the Sergeant, who continued.

'See, they stood outside the place for too long, and in the end we had to move them on, and the two of them didn't. I think a bit of time in custody might encourage them to take heed next time, that's all that's needed. We've got enough on our plates without having to deal with these minor incidents as well.'

'Excellent, I completely agree, thank you so much for your understanding, Sergeant Brown, I much appreciate it.' Roger kept eye contact, remaining positive. He still didn't have a clue what his daughter had been up to, but he continued. 'I'm sure she's learnt a lesson, and I'm just anxious to take her back with me now.'

'Yes, of course, Mr. Cologne.' Sergeant Brown looked up and shouted; 'Billy, get Saskia Cologne from cell one to come up the front desk. Her dad's here, lets get a move on.'

Roger greeted his daughter with a huge smile and hug, he whispered, 'You're my hero,' as he bundled her out of the Police Station and into the bright sunlight of the pavement outside. Saskia broke down into tears as they walked hand in hand away from the Police station. She explained what had happened as they travelled on the tube.

'Welcome to my world Dad. Me and Mike were just doing an action outside the games shop in Kentish Town. We protest, but in a humorous and entertaining way, we've been doing it for a few months now at loads of different places. It's like ironic what we do. You know these games that boys play, dad, they're disgusting, and parents are doing nothing about it. They're like porn, they are just despicable. You've got boys and some girls nowadays playing games all day long, and all they're doing is killing people. They spend hours on end killing people in virtual reality, and no one thinks this is wrong?' She was energetically making her point, waving her hands around as she sat in the tube.

'The boys in my school are completely addicted to it, they've been doing it since they were really young, and their parents don't care. What kind of parents are they? They're just happy their boys aren't "getting into trouble," instead they're sitting in their rooms killing people. What's getting into trouble? I think it's sick, that is just corrupt.'

'I agree,' said Roger. 'But what did you and Mike do?' Throughout this tirade from Saskia he had been thinking, 'Who's

Mike?'

'We just stood outside the shop and started shouting through a megaphone,' she continued. 'We shout all sorts of stuff. Like…come on parents, buy your young children more of these games, our children need to practice killing people in the privacy of their rooms. Roll up, roll up, turn all our children into killing machines. Keep spending money on virtual death games rather than anything of educational or ecological value. Stuff like that.'

She smiled wearily.

'You can see that some people really get it, and they encourage us, but as ever in the end the shop tries to get us to move away, we're bad for business, surprisingly.'

The two of them laughed.

Roger sat and thought about what his daughter was doing.

'I'm very proud of you,' he smiled at her. 'I don't think I'd have the balls to do that.'

'Thank you, Dad, that means such a huge amount to me. You weren't all angry and cross, you've been really supportive, I really appreciate that. Mum won't be like that, she'll go ballistic.'

Saskia returned to Roger's flat and phoned her mother. Roger was in the kitchen away from her, but could hear the ferocity of emotions and opinions being expressed, and finally Saskia lay sobbing on the sofa. He came in and held her. Giselle drove round to the house. Giselle was very flustered and red in the face. He diverted her into the kitchen before she confronted her daughter.

'She's fine, she's tired, but she has been very brave and good.' Roger started.

'Brave? Good? She has been ridiculous.' Giselle let fly at him. 'What has happened? She has been arrested, she has been in prison. Why? She has been doing these actions behind my back, I knew nothing. She has done some criminal actions, she has been illegal, and you think it is good?'

From somewhere Roger found his strength, his calm, he took deep breaths, and responded to Giselle from that inner place.

'Look, Giselle, that's not fair.' He said with feeling. 'You are obviously frightened and upset by this, and I understand why, but there is much more to this than just a superficial act of a child.'

'Oh, yes, much more. You don't mind your child is a criminal, you don't mind if she has a police record, maybe you encourage her to do these things!' Giselle was livid and worked up. 'Just like with University, you take her side and the easy option.'

'She won't have a police record, nothing like that has happened.' He replied, remaining calm and centred.

'She did this without telling me, did this without letting me know.' Giselle moaned.

Roger remained calm in the eye of the storm. 'I know, I didn't know about these things either.'

He looked at her and smiled, his voice was steady, this disarmed her. 'That is our fault not hers. We should know what she's doing.' He felt slightly giddy with this new-found inner strength, and could see the effect it was having on Giselle, she was visibly calming, the colour leaving her face. 'Giselle, you have been a wonderful mother to Saskia, you have done everything you could for her, and you have brought her up really well.'

Giselle quietened.

'So, whatever your daughter does is a product of her upbringing, she does what she has been taught to do.'

This didn't please her.

He drew breath deeply and continued quickly. 'She saw an injustice, saw something which was not right, and she has taken action against it. Her behaviour has been very commendable, and actually very right. She remains your and my daughter, she remains our child, and she will always be that whatever she does. I know you will always love her, nothing can change that. In time you will see this, you are just worried and angry right now.' He could see the tears welling in Giselle's eyes as she absorbed Roger's message.

'I want to see my daughter now' she hissed.

Roger was amazed by his resilience and sensible reaction to such a stressful and confrontational situation. He had not panicked at the Police Station, and it had paid dividends, he had stood up to Giselle, and she had appreciated his views and thoughts. He acknowledged his newfound inner calm and strength and realized it came from his daily practice of the Core Values. By having a self-discipline he was starting to find himself, and by doing so he was changing his relationships with other people.

As a reward for himself he decided to use the last of his redundancy funds to travel to Hawaii to spend some time with a famous teacher there. He told Saskia of his plans and she seemed crest-fallen, which puzzled him.

'Don't you like the idea of me going off to Hawaii and learning more about stuff?' He asked.

'Of course, I don't mind that.' She replied. She then looked appealingly at him.

He was puzzled, but then it dawned on him.

'Oh, I get it.' He smiled. 'You want to come with me, don't you?' Her face lit up.

'Let's do that then.'

'Hurray.'

Chapter Twenty-five

Stop trying to save the planet

The sweet nectar-filled Hawaiian night air was humid and warm. The buzz of cicadas chirped a consistent rhythm in the background. The fire warmed their feet, and the sand of the beach supported their bodies. Roger and Saskia, were staying with a renowned Kanaka Maoli, two days before Saskia's eighteenth birthday. That night the three of them lay looking up at the stars. They were contemplating in silence the immensity of it all, absorbing the interconnected matrix of possibilities.

After a long while Saskia slowly sat up.

Her eyes focused back into the dancing complexity of the flames licking the wood. She remembered how the British and Europeans had brought these wonderful people nothing but illness and disease. In that contemplation she realized these people had been faced with the destruction of their culture for hundreds of years, and yet had survived. They'd managed to preserve their way of life despite our best efforts to destroy it. Surely, such experiences could now be applied to the whole planet.

'Mumma, how can we save the planet?' she asked.

Mumma was a tiny, wrinkled Polynesian woman of an indefinite age, somewhere between 60 and 200 as she kept saying. She had been lying contemplating the stars, her belly draped by a rainbow coloured hand-woven scarf and shawl she had been given by her granddaughter.

She giggled.

Then she laughed out loud, genuinely, in childish mirth, at this serious remark. She rolled and then raised herself, looked intently across at the father and daughter. They both shrank back, feeling something important was about to happen.

'You lot. You always want to save something, don't you. Always seeking to save something outside of yourselves.'

Her focus came deeply into their being.

'You lot need to save yourselves before you can save the planet. Really, Saskia, the short answer is this:' Her sparkling eyes bored into Saskia's. 'Stop trying to save the planet.'

Her intensity made the father and daughter both feel uncomfortable, they squirmed.

As they sat looking at the grains of sand that covered their feet, they knew a story was coming.

'Four hundred years ago you came here for the first time, actually, that's not true you visited many times before that, but let's say it is. When you came that time you said to me, "I want to save your soul". You tried to convert me to your religion, but really you wanted my land. You didn't want to save my soul, you just wanted my land and minerals. You exploited my land, took my minerals, stripped my resources, and by the 1960's you'd depleted me pretty good.'

She grinned at them both despite the emotional charge and intensity of her words.

'Then you came to me and you said, "I want to save your culture". But, you didn't want to save my culture, you had no interest in the complexity of my culture. All you wanted was to make sure there were plenty of bare-chested native women in grass skirts to given you a Lei of flowers around your neck when you stepped off your great big airplanes.'

She pretended her hand was an airplane and she flew it around her head a few times before crash landing it in the sand.

'We stopped doing that, so you came to me and said, "I want to save your whales". We have a sacred agreement with the whales and we honoured and respected them in ways you have no idea about. Part of that agreement is the willing sacrifice of their lives to allow us to continue living. This is a symbiotic relationship far beyond the confines of your intellectual comprehension. You didn't understand or respect our relationship, you just told us to stop being ourselves. If that wasn't enough, you then came back and told me you wanted to save my rainforests.'

She kicked a stick that was poking out from the fire, it sprang back into the heart of the flames, and began to be consumed in the flickering orange light.

'You have no interest in saving my rainforests, at the same time you were telling me to plant non-indigenous crops – coffee, beet, all these other cash crops. Cash crops to pay back your banks for the loans of money you gave me to buy the equipment to clear the rainforests.'

She paused and placed another log onto the fire, and then looked across the flames seeking out their souls.

'With you there has always been a hidden agenda. For once be honest with me...that is all I ask. When you say you want to save the planet, what you are really meaning is, you want to save your culture.' She smiled inwardly to herself.

'You want to preserve the way you live - selfish capitalism - the one way of being which has done more damage to this planet than anything else, that is what you want to save.' She rubbed her hands as she warmed to the subject.

'You were comfortable, you have become uncomfortable, and now you want to return to your former comfort. That's bullshit.'

She squinted into the licking flames of the fire, and continued.

'Well, news flash, I don't want to help you. If your culture sinks below the waves of the ocean, I'll be happy. I ain't going to weep tears.'

The two nodded their heads in agreement, the three of them sat looking into the fire.

'Hey, you lot even made a great shamanic film which told the story of your culture.' They looked bewildered. 'What film was that?' Asked Roger.

'It was that big boat film, you know the one...Titanium,' she added mischievously.

'Titanic,' Saskia corrected with a smile.

'Yeah.' She continued whimsically, 'that's the one. The one with the naughty boy, and the English woman with the great boobs.'

'Kate Winslet?'

'Yeah, them's the ones...Kate and Winslet' she giggled, and wobbled her chest theatrically.

'But, I don't get the connection,' Roger blurted.

'Oh. What did you all shout when the boat hit the iceberg?'

'I don't know, "help"?'

'No, this is a symbolic film, you shouted, "women and children first". She leaned forward and held Roger's thigh to press home her meaning. 'Women and children first.' There was a pause.

'I don't get it.'

'Well, who are the women and children on the planet right now?' She winked at Saskia conspiratorially.

'I suppose the vulnerable people,' Roger spluttered.

'No, the indigenous people. They are the equivalent of the women and children. They are the precious ones who hold the future of this planet in their hearts and bellies. They are the ones who will save the planet.'

'Yes.' Roger nodded, still baffled, he sat upright by the flames of the fire, confused.

A wicked smile crossed her face, as she remembered the final scenes of the film. 'We, the indigenous people, know where the lifeboats are. We built them a long time ago. You lot don't know where the lifeboats are. You were so cocky when you built your culture, you didn't even bother to build lifeboats. You were so convinced your culture was unsinkable you built it big out of metal.'

She dragged a thin stick along the sand and then pushed it hard into the earth, it snapped.

'Now, you've hit the iceberg and are starting to sink, but most of you are still in denial. Most of you are still playing the same tune. The band plays on. You're ignoring what is right in front of your eyes. I can hear the band playing all around me right now.' She paused as if to listen.

She looked deeply and warmly into their faces.

'When your culture is long gone, on the bottom of the ocean, gathering weeds and fish. I'll still be here, living on this island, watching the sunset...' she turned to them both. A warm glow surrounded her.

She smiled deeply as they absorbed her message.

Then from nowhere they all set about laughing, joyously from within their bellies.

'...I'll still be here when you lot are growing corals at the bottom of the ocean.'

Roger's mind reeled as he tried to digest her message. It fitted so perfectly, we've hit an iceberg, we're sinking. Even the iceberg, as she later explained to them, was an ironic shamanic symbol - it represented global warming! So, where are the lifeboats? Would he even recognize a lifeboat if he came across one?

They slept out around the fire, under the stars. That night Roger had vivid colourful dreams of joy, beauty and growth, impossible abstract images, blurred, out of focus, lines, circles and spirals which bounced and sprang, somehow familiar and welcoming. When he woke in the fresh dawn light he lay looking into the ashes of the fire for a while.

The three of them got up and scoured the sandy coastline for driftwood. They built the fire back up, onto which they would prepare their frugal breakfast. They were all quiet and thoughtful. Roger was pondering what a lifeboat would look like. Mumma looked at him, and instinctively said, 'Yes, it is up to you to now start making a lifeboat.' He was too familiar by now with her ability to read his mind to be surprised.

'I am talking metaphor, mystery, magic when I say lifeboat,' she rattled.

'The kind of lifeboat I'm talking about doesn't look like a boat, don't get literal on me!'

'I know, Mumma, I know.'

'Well, stop looking so down, stop looking so glum, what a joyful thing to do, start building your boat.'

'But, I don't know where to start,' Roger squealed unappealingly, like a little child.

'I don't know where you need to start either,' she raised her voice, mockingly. 'You can't copy mine, you have to make your own.'

She added. 'Like I said, stop trying to save the planet and try to save yourself, by doing this, you'll save the planet.'

'Yes, but do I start by doing the internal work, by dredging up the past. I've done that so many times. Or, do I ignore the past and just get on with it, in the here and now. Or do I take into consideration the future generations needs, accommodate them. I don't want to hurt anyone, I don't want to ignore anyone's needs.' Roger said looking at his daughter.

'All three,' Mumma said with glee.

'I knew you were going to say that,' Roger said moodily as he reluctantly added another log to the fire.

She looked sternly at him. 'Stop looking outside of yourself for the answer, it is within. Bring it up and out, share it with the world.'

'Yes, but how?' he moaned.

She glared at him, and started to stir the contents of a very blackened pot.

The three sat looking into the fire for a while.

'I'll help you,' said Saskia quietly.

The Alpha Wolf

'The Grey Wolf runs with his pack for many years, he makes himself useful to others, he is of service to the clan, and he is happy with his place in the pack. For some male wolves there comes a day when he has to step up again. In those moments he has to take full responsibility, he needs to become the Alpha Wolf. Our understanding of this is maybe different to yours. You believe the Alpha Wolf acts from ego, he is selfish. We believe the wolf has to take charge of his "internal" pack, as well the external one, before he can become the Alpha.

The Alpha Wolf is content and at peace with himself. He has dealt with his shadow and his ego, and the paradox is, at that moment, he becomes an elder. The man who knows himself and doesn't take himself too seriously, is then ready to take on serious responsibility. These are the lessons from our brothers the wolves, they teach us how to become a man. Remember how it goes.

A man needs to have been nurtured, to have been alone, to have been of service, to eventually become in charge. We wouldn't allow a man, or a woman, who hasn't learnt these lessons, to be in charge. We learnt these lessons by observing the wolves in the wild, maybe you need to observe and learn from the wild more often.'

Tsao Chinem Cllens

The Practice

As with most works of fiction there is a great deal of truth in the story being told and in the characters portrayed. The Core Values and The Practice described in the book are based loosely on the work of a healer who was a beggar for many years. Nick Clements, the author, was given his writings many years ago, and has delivered workshops for over 20 years using these teachings and other practices from a wide range of people.

What follows is a more detailed explanation of The Practice, and some exercises which are linked to it. This is offered as a guideline and discussion document for those interested in such work. You may take what you need from it. Listen to your body and only do those exercises you feel comfortable with. You are responsible for what you chose to practice, just as you are the one who will feel the benefits if you do so. As with any programme you may wish to consult with a healthcare professional before undertaking the exercises or following any of the advice given here.

Brian:
'In order to be of value to the world and to increase your wellbeing, you need to do certain things. They come in a natural order.

The first thing to do is to lengthen and become conscious of your breath, that is simple, everyone can do it.

Once you have got that as a routine, you can practice relaxing, trying to be relaxed at all times.

Then you can become conscious of how balanced you are at any time, and how connected to the ground you need to be.

All of these actions establish strong and viable connections between the mind and the body, they encourage these two parts of you to work in harmony.

Once this becomes second nature you will start to grow, because you will have established a self-discipline.

By practicing every day you will be able to search for the truth about yourself and others.

When you do all of this you...you are making your life real.'

The Practice

I Breathing

How do you breathe properly?
How do you breathe naturally?
How do you control the breath?

2 Relaxing

How do you rest and sit?
How do you control your movements?
How do you calm the body?

3 Balancing and grounding

How do you ground yourself?
How do you re-align your body?
How do you put yourself into neutral?

4 Mind body connections

How do you identify your internal messages?
How do you replace 'negative' messages?
How do you control the sound?

5 Growing

How do you listen to your body?
How do you take your time?
How do you live in the 'now'?
How do you allow others to grow?

6 Self-discipline

What is self-discipline?
How do you enjoy self-discipline?

7 Identifying the truth

How do you tell the truth?
How do you listen to others?
How do you encourage others to tell the truth?

8 Making it real

What if you are struggling?
How do you document progress?
How do you make ceremonies, rituals and rites of passage?
How do you integrate all this information?

In order to retain the essence of these original statements and questions, I will first explore the eight actions in terms of their importance and effect on us. Then there are suggestions for a wide range of simple exercises relating to them. These are included in an exploration of the questions posed with regard to each action.

I Breathing

Breathing is good for you.

On average a person living to the age of 80 will have over 600 million breaths.

As the Buddhists say once you take your allotted number of breaths you die, so use them wisely.

Breathing comes naturally to you, you're good at it, you could be an Olympic champion, you've had that much of practice.

You do it all the time without thinking about it.

It is the first thing you did when you were born.

How do you breathe properly?

You are probably not breathing correctly or deeply enough most of the day.

Exercise:

Check it now, how shallow is your breath?

There is a huge difference between the shallow breaths you take on a regular day to day basis and the deep draughts you take when in exercise. The lung capacity of an adult is about 6 litres of air, but during normal breathing you consume far less than this.

A shallow breath expends little or no energy, no muscular movement is needed, so nothing changes.

If you deepen your breath you will exercise your diaphragm and rib cage, they have to expend energy, in other words, breathing deeply can keep you fit!

By breathing deeply you are, in a sense, forcing yourself to notice your body. When you breathe deeply you are remembering the totality of who you are. You are connecting your mind to your body.

Practicing conscious breathing can be done anywhere and at any time.

You have only to perform two tasks:

The in-breath should start at the belly, move up to the stomach and lungs and then finish at the mouth. If you place your hand gently on the belly it will help you to feel the breath starting. The in-breath can come through the nose or the mouth, it is best through the nose.

The out-breath starts at your mouth, moves down to the stomach and finishes with the belly. You can do this through an open mouth best.

Exercise:
Take four or five deep and calm breathes, each one getting longer.

Notice at the end how it can calm the mind and put you into a relaxed mood.

Notice your body.

How do you breath naturally?

The above exercise, breathing in and out consciously, will enable you to extend the length of your breaths, thereby extending your life, always a good thing. The exercise should be easy, not competitive or a cause of discomfort.

You need to practice doing this on a regular basis throughout the day, it is not a great effort. However, if you do it, you will greatly enhance your lifestyle and behavioural patterns.

When you bring consciousness to your breath you can also become aware of the effects of the air on your mind.

Exercise:

This exercise will alter your consciousness.

Takes some more deep breaths.

By bringing consciousness to the breath you will become aware of your body.

Feel the gentle rise and fall of your belly, the lungs filling and expelling air, feel the air in your throat and mouth.

You may feel relieved, lighter, better, calmer, all of which are good states of mind.

Relax.

As each breath comes and goes you can then add gratitude.

In your mind offer gratitude to your lungs, diaphragm, rib cage, muscles for supporting the breath of your life. The body will respond to such attention.

You can then think of the expelled air as the removal of old patterns and habits, and the inhalation drawing new ideas and ways of being into your body.

Every breath you take offers the chance to change, take it.

How do you control the breath?

As we all know, it's all about length.

By increasing the length of the in- and out-breaths you can enable yourself to feel at ease and be calm. By not straining, just lengthening the breath, and bringing a consciousness to that lengthening, you are improving your health.

If you exhale as much air as possible from all corners of your lungs it is very beneficial. By consciously emptying your lungs you are ridding yourself of old toxins and staleness that have lurked inside you for a long time.

You need to experiment with what feels natural for you - how long these breaths should be, how deep you want to go.

By lengthening the breath you will be affecting the functions of your brain. By increasing the oxygenation of your blood and nervous system you are stimulating your brain and replenishing yourself.

You are lengthening your life, becoming healthier, and brainier.

Brian:

'I think of the in-breath as self worth, and the out-breath as doubt. I breath out doubt and replace it with worth.'

2 Relaxing

You carry all your stress and strain with you all the time. Your body may well be continually contorted into strange positions due to stress and worry. In time these abnormal states can feel normal.

It is possible to live your life another way: to be relaxed at every given moment, to be flexible and comfortable.

How do you rest and sit?

The way you carry yourself directly reflects your developmental history. Those of you who have rounded shoulders can blame them on the chairs in which you sat, or on the way you were brought up. They are probably the result of both.

The spine is the first bone structure in your development as an embryo, and often any pains and problems you suffer in your back can be traced to trauma whilst in the womb.

There is a lot of work you can do to change this and it all comes down to posture.

Good posture is vital for your longevity and wellbeing.

If you ignore this. You will pay the consequences with back, neck or leg pains and discomfort. These inconveniences, when mild to middling, are often adopted and compensated for by your daily posture and bearing. You accept the inconvenience and perpetuate the resultant bad posture.

When the pain and discomfort becomes middling to severe you use painkillers. Painkillers do not change your posture, they only enable multi-billion dollar corporations to get richer. Indeed the prolonged use of painkillers may well aggravate the problem further.

The treatment of back pain has become a major industry. In February 2008 researchers from the University of Washington, Seattle, estimated the total medical cost for back and neck pain had risen by 65% between 1997 and 2005. They claimed it was now a $86 billion a year industry in the USA. The researchers concluded this increase had not been met in any way by a similar percentage improvement in patients' health after these pharmaceutical interventions. The pains remained, because the pills were not dealing with the causes.

Those of you without major trauma in your back can still improve and maintain good posture by doing simple exercises. By doing so you can prevent further or new damage, you can also improve your wellbeing and flexibility.

Those of you with re-occurring and chronic problems; please look around, slowly, gently!

There are any number of people who can help with your posture from physiotherapists, osteopaths, to chiropractors and beyond. You can have any number of treatments - kinesiology, acupuncture, Alexander or Bowen techniques and so much more. Or you can take exercise - dancing, yoga, pilates, Tai Chi, aerobics, all of which may or may not help. Try to find what suits you the best, maybe a combination of two or three of these.

Exercise:

One exercise which is good for the posture is the semi-supine posture from the Alexander technique. The pose is best practiced on a carpet or yoga mat, a supported but not too hard or soft surface.

It entails lying on your back with knees bent.

Resting your head on a book or towel to support it, without it being too high or too low, in what is called the Head Neck Back relationship. You'll know what that is when it is not a strain.

Arms by the side and hands placed on the torso.

Legs hip width apart, and feet on the ground.

Once there, use your conscious mind to let go of the muscle strains and stresses gently without force...relax. Listen to your body, let go of any places where tension can be felt.

Relax and use consciousness. Bring awareness to your body and let the places of tension release simply and naturally.

In this position small changes can bring huge relief. If you do this posture once a day for 15 to 20 minutes it will help your back and posture. If you want to advance that practice, you can undertake the exercise frequently throughout the day for shorter periods of time.

How do you control your movements?

To improve posture you need to be able to relax. Most people associate being relaxed with lying in bed and falling asleep. That is fine, but the key to making a real change in you life is to be relaxed anywhere and in any position, whilst being awake. If you observe cats. They are able to relax in the most difficult, awkward and inconvenient places. Their bodies melt, drop, shape themselves to the contours of their position and then they are content and happy. You must have seen cats fall asleep in the most superficially awkward and uncomfortable places.

In order to relax like that you need to bring consciousness to bear on your body. You can do this sitting, standing or lying down, even walking or running. The key is to use your mind to check out your body from head to toe for pains, aches and tensions, and to release each one of them as they are encountered.

When you let each tension go your body will make minute adjustments. Each of these adjustments will then release tension in other parts of your body. You will often feel a cascade of tensions and pains being released, as one move affects another.

Exercise:

Stand up and relax into a soft posture.

Bring your consciousness to your head and neck and check out to see if there are any tensions. If there are, bring your mind to bear on that spot and let it go. For more physical interventions, bring your hand to the area and give yourself a little rub and release.

Then check your shoulders, see what they are registering.
Then your lower back.

Almost invariably we only need a minute adjustment to change the ache into a release. Enjoy the release.

Sit down again.

How do you calm the body?
Relaxation is about remaining calm, being serene.

You can reach such a state very simply and quickly. The easiest way is using consciousness to check for stress or tensions throughout the body.

Exercise:
Once again, stand up and relax.

Check your body now, as you did just a minute ago.

Now perform a cascade of consciousness from the brain down through the eyes to the mouth, to the jaw, to the neck into the shoulders, onto the arms and hands, into the chest, stomach, belly, hips, legs, feet. You will be amazed at how many places have already lapsed back into tension. Such a check takes less than a minute.

If you were to combine this exercise with conscious breath lengthening, then you can very simply spend two or three minutes stepping towards being serene, living in bliss.

Repeated at intervals during the day this can become a simple routine and discipline. Doing so will build up your bodies' resistance to illness, prevent back and neck pains, and make you happier and more lively. If you do this regularly the huge bill for back and neck pain would be reduced dramatically. You'd be having a radical effect on the profit margins of major corporations. Hurray.

Those of you who are more advanced at relaxing know you don't have to be sitting or still to relax, you can do it whilst in motion. Marathon runners reach such a state, you can see it in the their faces and the motion of their limbs. When you are very good at it, you can even walk so relaxed that your feet don't leave an impression on sand.

Brian: 'I deliberately set myself the challenge of lying or sitting in a difficult and uncomfortable place. Once there, I consciously relax and settle into the position, I've got myself into some very interesting positions!'

3 Balancing and grounding

When you think of balance you can often think of inertia, things being still.

This is not balance, indeed it is the opposite.

Balance is about the constant movement of everything. You may be standing still right now, but the earth is moving at about 30,000 miles per hour around the sun, let alone how fast the universe is moving in space. You are moving, everything is in motion.

At a primary level of balance, we have opposites:

Black and White

Day and Night

Hard and Soft

When we bring them together they don't combine, they remain separate. This reflects a very primitive and unsophisticated understanding of the universe.

On a more sophisticated understanding there is the dance of opposites. When you combine two seemingly opposed states of being, the individuals are enhanced, not diminished, and the whole becomes more than it's component parts:

Female and Male become child
Light and Shadow become relief
Water and Fire become steam

More subtly, you can think of the state of balance as being a movement towards completion through transformation:
Each peak will inevitably become a trough
Everything that lives will die
Full will become empty
Within the first state lies the embryo of the second. Given time the first will become the second, the second will become the first, and so on.

Balance is about dancing between states of being, and seeing that there are two sides to every story. An example could be:

You may think capitalism is the only way of being that works, that people are innately selfish, peak oil is upon us, and disaster and chaos will surely ensue.

This doesn't have to be true. The opposite can happen.

You can be part of a movement that stimulates our ability to collaborate and help others, which believes in love and harmony. We can then use our technologies to feed the whole human race, use the alternatives to oil which already exist. Conflict and war can be eradicated.

They are opposites, but both are possible.

Exercise:
The choice is yours.
Neither of the alternatives above have happened yet, the future is in the balance.

Which future do you choose? If you choose the second, then do something about it.

The easiest place to start is with yourself, be kind, generous and loving to yourself. Don't continue to beat yourself up. Once you've started there you can externalise this. Start making friends with your neighbours, exchange goods and tools for free, smile at strangers!

Those of us who want the second alternative to happen need to start living as if it already exists (which it does) in order for it to come into being.

You can start by increasing the amount of exercise you do. This makes ecological sense for you and the whole of the planet. Sign up for an exercise class, practice yoga, go to a Zumba class, or go for a walk every day. They are all starting points for a positive future.

To be in balance in your body, you will need to be active and also passive. Too much of one of these states is not good for you. Unfortunately, we seem to do a lot more passive than active at the moment. The average person in the UK sits or lies down for between 12 and 14 hours per day. That is incredibly out of balance. We all need to challenge this. There are many actions you can take:

You could stand, walk or exercise whilst watching the TV. Try standing for the half hour of your favourite soap.

You could have a business meeting with someone in the park, and walk whilst talking.

You could watch a film whilst on the exercise bike. Remember to peddle!

There are many small ways you can change your present behaviour.

If you start taking regular exercise then you are listening to and honouring your body.

The main point is to do exercises that you enjoy. You are therefore more likely to continue.

Don't think of exercise as a drudge or a compunction. That isn't the way to success.

Start small and build it up, don't try to take on too much at the beginning, don't set yourself up to fail.

Often doing exercise in a group is more likely to be sustained than doing it on your own. The group dynamic makes it more enjoyable and keeps your interest longer.

Exercise:

According to the UK government only 37 per cent of men and 24 per cent of women take enough exercise to get any benefit from it. Their guidelines suggest:

* Adults should do a minimum of 30 minutes moderate-intensity physical activity, five days a week.
* You don't have to do the whole 30 minutes in one go. Your half-hour could be made up of three ten-minute bursts of activity spread through the day, if you prefer - it's the total that matters.
* The activity can be a 'lifestyle activity' (in other words, walking to the shops or taking the dog out) or structured exercise or sport, or a combination of these. But it does need to be of at least moderate intensity, measured by it making you slightly breathless or a little warm.
* People who are at specific risk from obesity, or who need to manage their weight because of a medical condition, need 45-60 minutes of exercise at least five times a week. For example, if you have diabetes, it will be much better controlled if you exercise like this.
* For bone health, activities that produce high physical stresses on the bones are necessary.

Balance for your body is essential, a balance between passive and active is very important. For the average person to lie or sit for 12 hours a day and only have to do 30 minutes exercise to balance it out seems like a good deal.

How do you ground yourself?

To understand the Core Values you need to think of yourself as a combination of three things - body, mind and consciousness:

Body- On the whole your body just gets on with things and functions without any input.

Mind- Your mind can race from the past to the present to the future, and can try to control your body's actions.

Consciousness- Consciousness mediates between the two, it is much more fluid and not fixed.

You can spend a lot of your life in the mind. Inhabiting your mind all the time isn't actually the way you were meant to live your life.

Whilst in this state your mind can often over-ride the messages your body is sending you:

'You're tired, take a rest'

'You've been sitting in this position for too long, change it'

These messages are mediated between your mind and your body by your consciousness. The consciousness interprets your bodies' needs and brings the messages to the attention of your mind. Your mind can either act on the information or ignore it.

If you spend 12 or 14 hours sitting on the sofa, and don't do any exercise, you will inevitably be spending too much time in the mind. You will be ignoring the messages from the body and allowing the mind to dictate to you. When you do this you are no longer in contact with the earth, the physical realm. Instead you are focused on the air, the intangible, the etheric, concepts not realities. You may focus on the past and future more than the present. Fear, apprehension, foreboding can constrict us; we give importance to things which don't exist. Whilst in this state you can become delusional:

What is happening in the soap opera on the television is important

    Celebrity is what I seek

    Watching TV all day is fine

    Just one more chocolates won't do any harm

    Not going outside for two days is fine

    Cigarettes are harmless

    I'll do it tomorrow

    I'll never be a success

    It's not worth trying

These are not the messages your body is sending you, they are all generated and created in the mind. In order to live a whole life, we need to bring a balance to bear within the three parts of ourselves; the body, the consciousness and the mind. We need to listen to all three.

Exercise:

A useful exercise is to 'ground' yourself every now and again throughout the day. It's not complex. You can do it now as you read this.

Place your feet, preferably without shoes and socks, on the ground. This can be anywhere, but it is enhanced if onto soil or natural materials.

Once comfortable and relaxed, bring your mind and consciousness to your feet. Your mind may resist (it's cold, wet, windy, I've got no shoes on, people are watching).

If you persist you can bring the whole focus of your being to the ground. There you can feel your body just being, this calms your mind, quietens it's messages, and then you can take some time to rest and become restored. Many people like to imagine fibrous roots growing out of the soles of their feet and spreading down into the ground, literally rooting themselves.

How do you re-align your body?

Following on from the last exercise where you root yourself, you can then use your consciousness to check into the whole body.

Exercise:

This can be done sitting or standing, it does however need some stillness and calm. Having grounded yourself as above, you bring your consciousness to your toes, to the soles of your feet, the arches of your feet, to the ankles, to the calves, to the knees...and so on up.

You name the body part, the more you name the better, you think of that part of you. Think about where it is, what it looks like, how it feels right now. Do this through the body all the way up to the head.

Spleen, bladder, kidneys, stomach, ribs, lungs, heart, spine, shoulders, neck, jaw, tongue, nose, etc.

Check into your body and all it's parts, relaxing any tension you might find in any of the places, letting go of stresses. If you work your way up from the feet through the whole of your body, you will ground the whole of your body.

Many people enhance this exercise by imagining a white flowing liquid welling up as they do it. A spring of light liquid coming up from the ground. By the end of the exercise you are literally filled with white sparkling light.

Depending on your own circumstances this exercise can take just ten minutes or you can take a lot longer, it is up to you.

It is well worth doing at least once a day. The conscious naming of the parts will distract the mind, enable your consciousness to go to those parts of your body, and relax and tone your body.

How do you put yourself into neutral?

By cultivating this healthier interaction between your body, mind and consciousness, you will be starting to spend more time in your body and not in your mind. As a simple guide for this:

If you are in the past or the future, you are in the mind.

If you are in the 'now', you are in the body.

If you just 'are', then you're in balance with your mind, consciousness and body.

It is simple to take time to breathe, relax, and ground yourself once a day. Doing so will improve your relationship between your mind and body. That is all very well and good, but these exercises mean very little if you are out of balance in your relationship to other people.

If you still react badly, violently, submissively, let others rule you, then you are not in balance. We will often have people in our lives who trigger us, and who seem to be able to upset us despite our best efforts.

In order to move towards having a balance relationship with other people you need to think about getting your mind into neutral. When your mind is in neutral, you can be in equilibrium.

There is a very simple statement, which enables us to remain in neutral.

'I don't like the way you are behaving, but I still love you as a person.'

This is one of the most liberating statements you can make, for yourself and the other person. In this mindset you can deal with the behaviour separately, compassionately, without damaging the individual. It is especially useful for parents in dealing with their children.

Exercise:

Take some time to breath deeply, bring your consciousness to your breath.

Once calm and assured, bring the following thoughts into your mind.

'I'm recognising there is difference between my behaviour and my true self.'

Take five deep breaths.

'I am able to change how I behave easily. I don't have to take things so personally any more.'

Take five deep breaths.

'I'm content to be who I am right here, right now.'

As ever, if you can find the courage to apply these message to yourself, you can then apply them to others.

Brian: 'I like to check at the end of each day as to how much left or right brained activity I've been doing. I ask myself was there sufficient play, imagination and creativity to balance out the time spent on the computer, working, or doing sensible things? If I've done too many sensible things I allow myself a half hour of being silly - dancing to songs on the radio, chasing the cat, playing with my children. Some days I realise that I've done an equal amount of left and right sided activity, and I take an extra half hour of play anyway'

4 Mind body connections

As explored in the last section on balance, we benefit from bringing the mind, consciousness and body into equilibrium. It is difficult to do this when the mind finds so many things to distract you with. The 'monkey mind' likes to remind you of your past indiscretions and failures, using them to frightening you about the perceived lack of abundance in the future.

By giving your power away to the mind you can allow it to believe it represents a solid-state entity - this particular mindset is permanent, there's nothing you can do to change it. The mind encourages you to become 'attached' to that particular set of beliefs. These messages can be very strong, very deeply entrenched:

'You will never have a decent relationship,' for example.

This isn't and can't be true for anyone.

No one thought, or state of being, is ever permanent. You are always in a state of flow, you are always capable of changing.

In order to grow as a human being you need to become conscious of these negative beliefs, examine them, and then move on. Yogic practices talk about the need to allow thoughts to arise, to be contemplated, and then scattered to the wind. This flow represents a flow that is essential for the development of an uncluttered mind.

Don't worry. Another set of beliefs will be along very shortly!

The key to this is if you actively participate in the thoughts as they occur, you can change them from negative to positive.

Exercise:

Find a relatively quiet place, and get comfortable.

Remember your posture and breath from the earlier exercises.

You can examine an example of a thought lots of people have whilst attempting to meditate. This is followed by a suggested pattern of responses that will allow the thought to flow, not remain the same. You don't need to say exactly these words, but you can use the meaning and sense of them.

Inwardly say this belief to yourself:

'I'm not doing this right, I'm not getting anywhere.'

Now examine the statement:

'This is a statement, it exists in my mind.'

Keep aware of your breathing, allow your breaths to be long and deep.

You are dancing between the opposites and finding balance.

Bring consciousness to the statement:

'It comes from my past, it is part of my background and upbringing.'

You can now move the statement on:

'Yes. This is an old pattern of mine. I give thanks to this belief. In this moment it doesn't serve me any more. I let it go.'

Keep breathing. Allow your breath to be long and deep.

Again, you are dancing between the opposites and finding balance.

Now you are going to replace the statement:

'I'm doing the best I can right now, I accept myself totally.'

Keep breathing. Allow your breath to be long and deep.

Your consciousness is transforming opposites into a state of wholeness.

By doing this with your thoughts you are moving from; 'I'm not doing this right' to 'I'm doing my best.'

You could address any number of beliefs and self sabotaging mechanisms this way. At all times move slowly, gracefully, don't try to make huge steps or jumps.

Allow yourself to flow.

How do you identify your internal messages?

Ingrained and fixed mindsets can become largely unconscious. You are so familiar with them you don't recognise them. They are self-imposed. When you imposed them on yourself you probably imposed them on others. Your parents and teachers will have passed many of their messages on to you. We gather such messages and beliefs, and we think they are universal. It is then easy to make sweeping statements, such as:

Everyone is afraid of the future

Nobody likes spiders

I'm really stupid and won't get anywhere

What's the point in helping other people?

I don't deserve to be loved

These particular messages and patterns are not universal (they are also untrue). You picked your beliefs because of your set of circumstances, not anyone else's. It is more than likely even your friends and families don't share exactly the same world-view as you.

The continuation of fixed and negative mindsets can cause you and those around you a lot of pain and trouble. Such mindsets can eventually have a very serious impact on the world. The following ones impact devastatingly on the individual and society as a whole, and have done for thousands of years:

All foreigners steal our jobs and scrounge money.
They're different to us because of the colour of their skin.

Mindsets and fixed beliefs are untrue. Your jobs is to change them and generate thoughts that serve a positive purpose for you and those around you. In order to do this you will need to look at yourself very openly and honestly.

Are some of your negative mindsets about people you haven't met?

Are some of them assumptions of guilt and blame for people you don't know?

If they are then you need to start loving yourself more. By hating or being prejudiced to others you are only ever mirroring the way you feel about yourself.

Exercise:
You are going to get in touch with your negative mindsets.

Take 5 minutes to think about the ones you believe about yourself. Think about them deeply, be honest. Write them down one at a time in a list. They could include:

I'm not clever

I'm fat
I can't sing
I'm a bad person
I don't deserve to be happy
I can't earn money

Now take 5 minutes to think about the negative thoughts you have about other people. Again, think about them deeply, be honest. Write these down for yourself again in a list. They could include:

My parents don't love me
My friend doesn't like me
My boyfriend is cheating on me
Most people are not trustworthy
The world is a dangerous place
I don't like foreigners

Now, take each of those lists and examine them closely. Read them intently. Then think about each statement, one at a time, and reverse it. For example:
'I'm not clever'.
Think about the times you have been clever. The times that you have shown intelligence. There will be plenty. Whilst thinking of those, write next to the original statement - 'I am clever'. Cross out the original statement.

Examine each statement, think of times when the opposite has been true, you will find them. Each negative statement can be contradicted, each negative mindset is not true, all the time. Everything you think negatively about yourself and the world can be turned around.
'I'm a bad person' is not true all the time, you have also been a good person - 'I'm a good person.' The world is not all black

and there is no absolute white, there are many shades of grey.

Do the same to the statements about other people. Building on this in the next exercise you are going to take some time creating good, healthy, positive thoughts about yourself and the world around you.

How do you replace 'negative' messages?

The negative patterns of your mind can be very difficult to overcome or to replace. If you battle, fight with them, you can often make them more powerful rather than less.

One of the most common ways of counteracting them is to use affirmations, as was illustrated above with in the meditation message. Affirmations can work if they are in the right tense. Some people start with the affirmation:

'I want to be thinner'

If repeated often this will continue the problem. The affirmation is in the future tense, it is saying I believe I will become thinner in the future, when that is, I don't know.

Affirmations need to be in the present.

'I am thinner'

You use them to affirm something which is already true, already exists, is possible. Relate that back to the previous exercise, 'I am clever.' If you focus on the times you've been clever, remind yourself, think it often enough, your can change your brain synapses. You see it is true, and you will start to change how you think about yourself.

Exercise:

A good time to practice affirmations is when you have just woken up, or you are just going to sleep. You are bridging the gap between the conscious and subconscious at those times.

Create a short, punchy, useful positive affirmation. Each time making it clear, succinct, to the point, it should not be woolly.

One example from the personal messages is:

'I am happy'

Breathe calmly and deeply, repeating your own affirmation ten times.

Now select one of the beliefs that you hold about others:

One example is:

'I am in a loving relationship'

Breathe calmly and deeply, repeating the affirmation ten times.

Exercise:

In the morning when you wake up connect with your breathing. Now send a wish of health and happiness to friends, family and the wider world.

This is a very helpful practice as it continues the intercourse between the mind and consciousness. You are telling your mind, there are people in the world who love you and you love them. The first thing you do in your day is to connect to them in a positive way. That's a powerful message for the mind.

How do you control the sound?

When you try to tune a radio there is a lot of background sound between stations. This is how your mind works, when left to it's own devices your mind will fill in space with background sound. The interference on the radio is the sound of your collective past, it comes from outer space and is a memory of past events. This is the same with your mind.

The background 'monkey mind' is just replaying events, thoughts and conclusions from your past. By consciously sending the mind positive messages you can tune in to a specific positive station on the radio. Here the message is clear, and you are transmitting it from a connection between the mind, consciousness and your body. From a positive place.

Exercise:
Use your breathing to calm your body and mind.

Decide to sit or stand comfortably.

Bring consciousness to your posture.

In this state bring some positive images into your mind's eye. This may be a favourite place in nature or a lovely desert island. Make this a place where you feel at home.

Whilst 'seeing' this image, breath deeper and relax your body.

Now, create a mantra, a short sentence which you believe in.

One example you may want to use is:

'I am safe, I am at peace, right here, right now.'

Repeat your mantra, whilst maintaining the image, the breath, and the relaxed posture. Do this for two or three minutes, and it will affect your whole day.

When you do this exercise you cut down on the background sounds. You are telling your mind that you want to be positive. Here in this slightly altered state, the message gets through.

It shouldn't be a struggle to maintain this state, just keep the image and the words flowing. If you want to do the exercise for longer, half an hour or an hour, make sure you do it at a time when you will be undisturbed. Whilst in this mindset you can be creative, imaginative, supportive, loving and collaborative. A lot of good and positive ideas will come up through you, you may be inspired. You will be 'in the flow,' there you can heal yourself, and you can be of great service to others.

Brian: 'I like nothing more than not thinking. I'm very good at it. Sometimes I go to stand by the river and I loose myself by looking deeply into the water as it tumbles, changes colour, murmurs it's way along. I like to stand and watch as the water passes and absorb myself completely in the wonderful tumbling journey down to the sea. Eventually I become part of the stream. I can stand like that for long periods.'

5 Growing

In our present culture we believe growth is exponential. We are told our economy needs to keep growing, our industries need to keep producing more and more. Output needs to increase in order for us to progress.

This is not true.

Growth actually happens in a different way, it is a two-way or cyclical process. It can occur in an expanding form, but it also occurs in a decreasing form as well. In fact, both are happening in relative terms all the time. Growth is a cycle rather than just a straight line.

Nothing in nature is only ever expanding; it is also simultaneously collapsing and diminishing. Science tells us the universe is expanding and it will also collapse. We seem to have forgotten that.

We have become obsessed by our ability to expand. In order to be whole human beings we need to be equally proficient at reducing. They are both forms of growth.

Exercise:

Find a relatively quiet place, and get comfortable.

Remember your posture and breath from the earlier exercises.

Consider the life cycle of a simple flower.

Imagine in your mind's eye a daisy or similar little flower.

Watch it like in time-lapse photography.

See it start life as a seed in the soil, and appreciate it takes a lot of bravery and strength to break up through the soil and out into the light. Once there, it draws strength from the sun, it moves in the cyclical motion of the sun, drawn upwards and around. As it increases in size it grows a bud and that turns into a flower. The flower opens and reaches upwards. The flower may be pollinated or not. Then it starts to wilt, it turns downwards, the body and leaves turn, they return to the ground from which it came. The whole of the flower then composts into the earth. There in the compost lies a new seed, ready and waiting.

In that cycle of growth and decline, there is no pause, there is no stopping. At all times the flower is a flower, no one part of the process is 'better' or more important than the next. The flower makes no judgement of its' life cycle.

Now, replace the flower with yourself!

See how you have grown.

See how you have reached up to the sky.

See how you have blossomed, bloomed in the warm sunshine.

See how your have decaying.

See how you have turned into rich soil,

See how you have become compost which is warm and restorative.

See how you are the seed lying in a bed of compost.

Remember you have taken this journey many times, you have grown, blossomed and composted many times.

You have done this over and over again.

You have taken this journey every day. You have grown and declined.

Every monthly cycle. You have blossomed and wilted.

Every year. You have had periods of quick growth and times of reflection.

Every life-time. You will pass through many cycles

You are constantly changing and growing. Even when you are getting older you are still growing. The ascent of youth is inevitably followed by the descent of maturity. There isn't an implicit judgment in this statement, one stage is not better than the other.

As a baby and a small child you know intuitively how to move your body, you move in a relaxed and comfortable way. As you grow up you are influenced by external circumstances. To the extent that if the way you grew up was stressful and harming, you will have adopted and created painful posture and movement patterns.

These become very familiar and often they reflect your self-image or lack of worth. This doesn't have to be an on-going and incremental process. You don't have to keep adding and inventing new and more painful postures, aches and pains, as you grow older.

There can be an arc of development. You can return to more intuitive and freer movement as you grow older. This return to flexible posture can be easily managed if you are down-sizing as you mature. Instead of accumulating more and more things as you age, you should be letting go and becoming more flexible again. As you age you can reconnect with your childish ability to be at ease with yourself, to be free of stress and fears. To have fun again after all that responsibility and seriousness.

Exercise:

Take some time to crawl on your hands and knees.

Just do it, don't think.

Move about in the room on your hands and knees, or feet.

See the world from this altered perspective. Some of you will find it awkward and difficult, don't push it too far, don't hurt yourself. Others will enjoy the freedom. See if you can speed up your motion, avoid crashing into things, or maybe not.

If you spend a few minutes every day on your hands and knees like this, you will connect to the joy of being a child again. If you do it often enough it is impossible not to enjoy it and have fun.

Who doesn't want that child-like energy in their life every day?

Why did you lose contact with this way of being? So you could become a 'grown-up?'

Get a life!

How do you listen to your body?

Your body is in conversation with you at all times, and your mind invests a lot of time and effort in ignoring or criticizing these messages. Your mind by seeking control most of the time can lie to you.

'It'll be fine if you smoke this cigarette, don't worry about it, it won't harm you.'

'It's not that awkward sitting here for hours on end.'

By not telling you the truth it can cause you to damage your body and other people.

This exposes the fundamental difference between the mind and the body; the body doesn't lie to you.

When she says she's tired, she really is tired.

It is the mind saying you're not.

If you can manage to listen to your body almost invariably the message is:

Be calm, avoid stress, live in the now.

Exercise:

Without thinking about it.

Start very slowly moving up and out of the chair you are presently sitting in, or the repose you're in.

Take your time.

Move slowly, very gently and steadily if possible, move into a standing position.

The longer this takes the better.

Once in the standing position, relax, and then bring your consciousness to examining just how complex, how intricate that manoeuvre was. Try to fully appreciate how complicated the act of standing up was. How many little shifts, changes, balancing acts the body has to undertake in order just to stand up.

Now, you can walk.

Walk slowly and gently in the room. Try to listen to your body whilst you are walking. Feel into any tensions, aches or cricks as you walk up and down the room. Make minute or major adjustments to alleviate any pains. As you walk try to listen to your body, s/he will more than likely be saying:

Be calm, avoid stress, live in the now.

How do you take your time?

The above is a rhetorical question. There will be activities you already do which enable you to slow time down. You may have a wide diversity of actions and exercises - a good long walk in nature, doing a physical and strenuous exercise or game, cycling, meditating, playing chess, any number of things.

These are the times when you lose yourself in the activity, time stops, because you are relaxed and actually looking after yourself. You all know how it feels to be in this state and you need to encourage your body and mind to use consciousness to create this feeling as often as possible in the day.

Almost invariably the constraints of the workplace and environment mean you do the opposite. You increase your stress and time speeds up.

Exercise:

It is very beneficial to create a little oasis of slow time; on your own, away from others in which you can walk or be in nature. This could be just for two minutes, ten or more is even better. During that time you will be reminding your mind and body of how good it feels to be relaxed. The best way to do this is to connect to nature, the natural world is always just round the corner, not far away.

The following are examples:

Go outside during lunch break and sit in the sun.

Look at and admire flowers, greenery, trees, bushes, etc. Indoors and out.

Notice the sky, watch cloud patterns.

Be outside in any weather and really 'see' the weather. It can be very restorative to be outside in a strong wind, or in the rain.

Look for and hear birds. See if you can identify them.

There is no place on earth where you can't connect to nature. Bringing consciousness to our connection to nature is a relaxing and restorative thing to do.

Exercise:

Once you are out in nature remember to say 'thank you'.

Thank you to yourself for taking the time out of your busy schedule.

Thank you to the natural world for always being present, always being there for us, without judgment, always supporting us.

Exercise:

Go for a weed walk. Spend time looking for and noticing the 'weeds'. The little and big plants who are growing, between the cracks, along the edges, in the dark places, in the nooks and crannies they weren't meant to be in. These weeds are always present, always pushing their way back into our lives.

Thank them for reminding you of your potential to grow under difficult circumstances.

Thank them for reminding you of how flexible you can be.

Thank them for bringing beauty, colour, diversity, non-conformity and vitality into your life.

How do you live in the 'now'?

Most of us believe we are living in the 'now', when else are we living?

When you think about it however, it is remarkable how much

of your mind's time isn't spent in the present moment. Your mind can pursue a wide range of distractions to avoid being in the present. For many reasons, time spent in the 'now' is very restorative. Whilst there:

You are not beating yourself up about past mistakes and failings.

You are not worrying about the possibilities of failures and a lack of abundance in the future.

You are not worrying about what other people think of you.

You are not thinking you're too fat/thin/ugly/spiteful /mean/selfish/lacking in worth/etc.

Exercise:

Next time you eat a meal or a snack, bring 'mindfulness' with you to the table.

Take your time to look at your food. Enjoy the diversity and richness of the colours.

See how complex and interesting the shape of the food is.

Take a moment before you eat it to thank all the people who produced it, who grew it, all the lives which have been affected by it's creation and the journey it has taken to be here with you.

Take a moment to thank the food before you eat it. For all the goodness it will bring you. For all the nutrition it will impart.

Then take a mouthful, savour it, chew it slowly.

Don't take great big chunks, don't wolf it down, take your time.

Be in the moment.

Taste the food, chew it a lot of times before swallowing. Notice the sensation of the food passing from your mouth into your neck, into your stomach.

Be present to the food, be present to the goodness which you are receiving.

The consequences of you bring such 'mindfulness' to eating

are you full quicker; you absorb more of the useful nutrients; and you eat less.

Job done!

How do you allow others to grow?

None of us live in complete isolation. All of us are connected to family, friends and relations. Within your individual complex mix of attachments, dependencies, love, hatred, indifference and commitment there are many different types of knots and ties. You can form any number of dependencies and relationships and these change and alter throughout your life. They can give you immense pleasure and can be incredibly painful, sometimes all at the same time. If you are committed to undertaking a personal development programme it will inevitably affect your relationships:

If you are doing the work positively such activities will help and enliven your relationship connections.

If you are doing the work negatively it will increase the complexity, dependency and pain.

Everything is connected.

In order to grow you can seek to decrease your dependencies and simplify your relationships as your self worth increases. The self-discipline you develop can be used to unravel and loosen the ties that were previously binding you. The more you value yourself the more you will value other people, and the more they will value you. What is on the inside is on the outside.

By having self-discipline and a personal development programme which makes you feel good, you are stepping away from neediness and control towards love, and then, eventually, unconditional love.

The paradox of this work is the more you are able to live without someone, the more you can see who they are and love them for their separateness from you.

You may well have been taught that to be in a relationship you need to fuel it with neediness and co-dependency. That is not the case.

Good relationships are built on mutual trust, honesty and love, not jealousy and mistrust. By role modelling your self-discipline, your increased self worth, you will encourage others to step into theirs. Always remember the only person you can ever change is you. Other people can change because you change.

Brian: 'I like to grow vegetables in the garden, I enjoy how it takes months for them to grow. I get a great deal of joy when the seeds turn to vegetables and then I get pleasure from eating them. Some of the seeds and plants are eaten by slugs. I don't curse the slugs, I know they are there for a reason, I think about how good the vegetables must have tasted for them as they ate them. I don't mind sharing.'

6 Self-discipline

If you turn over those large stones of self-doubt, called 'life's unfair' and 'what's the point', you will reveal the beautiful pebbles of 'self-discipline' and 'self worth'. Discipline can be a misunderstood word.

Self-discipline needs to come from love, not duty, it is fed by self worth.

It is important you enjoy the discipline, not feeling you must do it.

Self-discipline increases your joy, not your blame and shame.

Each of you can create your own unique discipline. It can apply to how you live, what you do, how you treat others, a whole range of different areas in your life.

Exercise:

A recent piece on the Internet gave some insights from a nurse who had worked in palliative care for many years. She asked her patients about regrets at the end of their lives, and these were the five most common:

1   I wish I'd had the courage to live a life true to myself, not the life others expected of me.
2   I wish I hadn't worked so hard.
3   I wish I'd had the courage to express my feelings.
4   I wish I had stayed in touch with my friends.
5   I wish I had let myself be happier.

Incorporating these principles into your life, using them as the starting blocks could create a very useful self-discipline. You can adapt and change the words, but the underlying principles remain the same:

I live my life as authentically as possible.
I work for passion and self worth.
I express my feelings.
I maintain my friendships.
I am happy.

That sounds like a very good mantra and affirmation.

What is self-discipline?

Your self-discipline could be to follow the Core Values and use them as a guide each day. You could use the five points from the palliative care nurse as a starting point, and live in such a way that you don't end your life having those regrets. You could combine the two. There are any number of alternatives. Select those that appeal, and don't be afraid to let go of routines or beliefs that no longer serve you. You will change, so be flexible.

In the past you may have gone to the gym immediately after Christmas. You may have resolved to eat less fatty food, or cut down on alcohol. Such acts of self-discipline are often undertaken for weeks or months, but mostly fail to be incorporated permanently into our daily routines. Why is that?

One of the reasons we may fail is because our lack of physical exercise or eating the wrong foods are not causes, they are symptoms. Beneath these habits lie the fundamental belief patterns that generate low self-esteem and affect self worth. They can come from very early childhood, or even before that.

Going to the gym doesn't often change all this deep-rooted trauma, it can be a temporary fix, but that isn't any good in the long run. You need to be aware of the bigger picture, look at yourself holistically, and use more balanced approaches.

Self-discipline is about not seeing yourself as a series of unconnected symptoms. If I got to the gym I'll be thin. There can be threads running through our lives that are complex and we need to look at ourselves in a holistic and caring manner.

1   If you are overweight there may be patterns of behaviour from childhood needing to be addressed.
2   You may need to look at where you are living.
3   Your close relationships may affect you.
4   Whether you are in the right job can be a problem.
5   Do you feel inspired or lethargic every morning?
6   You may have physical ailments, aches and pains, which you have had for years, and these may need to be addressed and altered through posture.
7   Diet may well play a part as well, you may need to look at intolerances as well as reducing portion sizes.
8   Friends and family may be supportive or keep you in the place of the overweight relative, the victim. Some people indirectly may want you to remain as you are, so they can

feel good about themselves, and you could be playing out a role for them.

9 There may be a history of abuse in your family, and you may eat to forget dark and personal stories.

10 There may be genetic reasons with your weight, you could come from a family of people with eating disorders.

These are just a few causes and symptoms, there could be any number of them.

There can be a multitude of subtle and not so subtle reasons for your present configuration as a human being.

Self-discipline attempts to look at this whole picture, or at least as much as is possible. You are a tangled mass of wires, leads, connections, painful stories, and trying to sort these out can often feel overwhelming. Just the thought of addressing all of them can lead us to despair, let alone knowing where to start, or what to deal with next. The paradox is that all these confusing and rapidly multiplying leads go to and come from one place. Self worth.

Self worth

Self worth is not given to us by others, it is generated from within ourselves.

You had a certain amount of self worth when you are born, and through life you are adding to it and taking away from it.

To have a lot of self worth doesn't mean you are egotistical or arrogant.

If you have a lot of self worth you will be content with yourself and the world.

If you have high self worth you don't need to damage or hurt others, you will only support others.

Anyone who harms or damages your self worth, is doing so from a place of low self worth.

Exercise:

It is best to do this now, as you read the text.

Sit in a comfortable supported pose.

Breath deeply, bring your consciousness to your breath.

Check your body for stresses and strains.

Let them go.

Now you are settled and at ease, envisage your body as being a pot, a glass jar.

Think of self worth as being honey. A liquid, flowing, sticky, sweet and very good for you. Without thinking about it, have a look at yourself and see how full or empty your jar is, right now.

Notice if there is a lot.

Is it spilling out?

Is the jar empty?

What colour is it?

What texture?

Some honeys are very fluid other honeys are very dense, what is yours?

Can you smell it? Does it smell sweet or maybe rancid?

Do all of this without thinking about it, without pre-judging.

Let that settle, keep breathing.

Now you can use your mind to analyse how much self worth you have, whether you need to add more?

If your jar is not overflowing then compile a list of the ways in which you could increase your self worth. Keep it light and simple, these are wishes or intents.

Here is an example of a list:

1 I can stop listening to my internal father, the critic, who is always saying I'm not good enough.
2 I can take more exercise.
3 I can spend more time with friends who make me feel happy, who care about me.

4   I can stop moaning about my boyfriend.
5   I can spend more time in nature.
6   I can buy those lovely shoes.

How do you enjoy self-discipline?

The human race is a long one. There is plenty of time. All too often we resolve to go to the gym and at the end of the first session we want to see results and are disappointed. Enjoy the journey, set yourself realistic goals, don't seek things too quickly. Having the imagination and creativity to seek to change is very powerful. Intent, as in the above exercise, is the first step towards change, action is the next.

Exercise:

Using the list of changes you created in the last exercise, go through them and set yourself a target for each one over the next week or so.

1   I can stop listening to my internal father, the critic, who is always saying I'm not good enough.
    Action: I say thank you, but enough is enough, to my internal father 10 times this week.
2   I can take more exercise.
    Action: I walk in the local park on Tuesday, come rain or shine.
3   I can spend more time with friends who make me feel happy, who care about me.
    Action: I phone one of them and arrange to meet.
4   I can stop moaning about my boyfriend.
    Action: I buy my boyfriend a small gift, or sent him a card.
5   I can spend more time in nature.
    Action: I walk in the local park on Tuesday, come rain or shine.
6   I can buy those lovely shoes.

Action: I buy those lovely shoes!

If we have self-discipline, we know our limitations. It is important you push the limits and boundaries of what you think you are capable of, but at the same time, loving yourself doesn't have to be hard work!

Self-discipline can be helpful: it can include taking time each day to meditate, stretch and exercise, being mindful of what you are eating.

It can also be indulgent: pampering ourselves, buying those shoes, being active in a favourite pastime, having fun, laughing, singing, dancing.

It is not being strict: not allowing yourself to eat anything, punishing yourself, being frugal and mean to yourself. Being critical when you fail.

Self-discipline actually comes from an understanding of what is important in your life, an understanding of your self worth. You can use self-discipline to prioritize what feeds you, rather than what you think is needed or feel obligated to do.

Most importantly, it is about increasing the amount of joy in your life. You use self-discipline to connect to joy, increase your self worth and remember how lucky you are. It allows you to join that dance class; which then enables you to meet new people who have positive attitudes towards life; who then encourage you to be brave and accept new challenges.

It is very worthwhile because as the saying goes; you are worth it!

Brian: 'I've developed my own self-discipline, it is mine and mine alone. I would never want to impose it on anyone else. It brings me joy and happiness to breathe deeply, to stretch my body, to do yoga, to go out in nature, every day. It is up to me when and where I do it. Some days I do my activities and then I just lie on the sofa and watch television and that can give me a lot of joy as well. I don't judge that part of the day as a missed opportunity. If I did it, I needed to do it. I ate a whole Mars bar the other day. I spent my time over it, I relished and enjoyed every piece of it. It tasted delicious. I didn't beat myself up because I ate it. That's discipline and self knowledge. Self-discipline increases happiness, not your sense of duty or the feeling that you are superior to others.'

7 Identifying the truth

Everything you hold to be true, when examined will reveal the opposite can be true as well:

'I'm happy.'	'I'm unhappy as well.'
'I enjoy my job.'	'Sometimes I don't like it.'
'We know each other well.'	'How can we know everything?'
'The world is a terrible place.'	'Oh, no it's not.'

The truth is difficult to find.

For example, within the restricted Western world-view we believe it is important people gain an education: that they are able to read and write. We hold this to be true, and in the majority of cases it is.

However, sometimes in receiving such an education individuals reject their cultural and ancestral roots, they look down their noses at their families and their primitive ways. As a consequence of their education, they disconnect themselves from their families, and move to urban conurbations. There they seek employment and the dream of being rich. When they don't find it, some become addicted to drugs, violence and abusive behaviour. The tragic consequences of such changes in people's lifestyle are seen on the edges of large cities all around the world. In the dissolute addicted behaviour of the disenfranchised.

They are no longer wanting or able to return to their roots, and failing to cash in on the promises of our materialistic dream.

In these cases, the education given these people could be seen as very damaging and disruptive, and is leading to the ever increasing numbers of disenfranchised, unsatisfied and unhappy people.

The truth is always far more complex than we think.

'The truth is out there' as the X-Files used to say. Truth has many different layers, and it is important we remind ourselves of that diversity every now and again.

'My truth.' There are certain things you, as an individual, think are true. These are different from:

'Your truth.' Other individuals have their own beliefs, and each one of us has a separate and unique interpretation of the world. Then there is:

'The truth.' This can only ever be a cultural reality. Individuals believe in a generic truth, which is inculcated and taught through the media, education system, family ties and values. For us this is the western world-view. We believe this is a solid state, it is not:

'The truth' is ever-changing, it doesn't ever remain fixed. What you thought was true about the world in 1990 is not the same now. The truth is different to:

'Their truth.' People from other cultures have different sets of values and beliefs, they do not necessarily agree with your cultural truth.

When we don't respect the fact that other people have their own truths, we can suppress and try to subjugate them by imposing our truth, our values and morals on them. This is one of the most damaging consequences of the last four hundred years. The loss of a diversity of cultural views of 'the truth', and the loss of respect for other points of view has made us all poorer and less intelligent.

How do you tell the truth?

Exercise:
Try this, it is quite challenging.

The next conversation you have, make a conscious effort to not use the words- you, we, they, them, etc - and replace all of them with an 'I'. It can be very revealing how such a discipline changes the meaning of the sentences being used:

'We are all feeling frightened' becomes 'I am feeling frightened.'

'We don't know what we are doing' becomes 'I don't know what I am doing.'

Statements about people or generalized situations, can change as well:

'The world is falling apart' becomes 'I am falling apart.'

'Nobody was feeling happy' becomes 'I wasn't feeling happy.'

Make a note for yourself about how this exercise went for you. It may lead you to interesting realisations about the beliefs you hold. The truth needs to be owned. If we own our truth then we are clear and concise in our communication. If we generalise we can often not express our truth and other people can misinterpret what we are saying.

How do you listen to others?
For those of you who work in groups or can bring a group together, you can use a very simple exercise to illustrate listening skills.

Exercise:
Sit in a circle.

The first person says a short maybe two-sentence statement about their life to their neighbour on their left.

The neighbour listens to the statement then repeats it back to the first person, as near to word-for-word as possible.

The second person then turn to their left, and says their own statement to the next neighbour who repeats it back, and so on, all round the circle.

Afterwards as a group you can have a discussion about what you noticed during the exercise.

It is amazing how difficult some people find this exercise. People often forget vital details, get dates or facts wrong, and stumble in the recollection. Obviously the pressure of undertaking the task in front of others will have a negative impact, but it is still remarkable how little you absorb.

When you are the listener you are focused and listening, but also filtering the information through you own background sound.

As ever, in order to improve our listening skills we need to be able to filter out the 'monkey mind', and pay as full attention to the other person as possible.

Really listening to someone is quite an art, and you need to practice it on a frequent basis.

How do you encourage others to tell the truth?

If you add the 'I-statements' and listening skills to your self-discipline you can make a difference to your relationships and you can improve your communication skills. If you do this on a regular basis you will become aware of how many presumptions there are in every day conversations:

'I'm feeling down.'
'Oh, I'm sorry you're feeling down. I know how that is.'

These two people are communicating and one of them may be

trying to be helpful. But, they are experiencing the world in very different ways. One person's truth for the words 'feeling down' can mean depressed, suicidal, or it can mean a bit off colour and it will pass in ten minutes. Does the second person really 'know how that is?'

Can we clarify and increase the depth of our conversations rather than keep them superficial and full of presumptions.

Exercise:

Next time someone says to you that they have a problem, don't fix it.

Try to avoid saving them or telling them your own similar story.

Just genuinely reflect their statements back to them. For example:

'I'm having a really hard time with my brother.'

'Oh, you're having a hard time with your brother.'

Now continue to give them genuine attention and see what they say. More than likely they will now further expand their understanding of the situation:

'He just doesn't listen to me, he doesn't respect me.'

'Your brother isn't listening to you, he doesn't respect you.'

Give the other person time to think about it. They will often come to a good conclusion:

'I think I need to be more assertive.'

'You think you should be more assertive.'

If you allow someone to find their own solutions they are more likely to act on them. Their problem hasn't been added to, it is actually diminished.

Brian: 'A relative of mine who lives in London said to me two months before the Olympics. "It's going to be a nightmare, the weather will be crap, the trains won't run, we won't win anything. The British are just useless at organising these things."

Two days after the closing ceremony that same relative said to me. "It was brilliant, I enjoyed every minute of it. I thought we British showed the world how good we are. It just goes to show all those doubting Thomas's who thought we couldn't organise it. I always knew it was going to be brilliant." The truth grows on shifting sand.'

8 Making it real

I have no attachment to your following these instructions or not. You may be encouraged and enthused by reading this last sections, and want to take up some or all of the exercises given. Good for you, please use whatever is useful, and ignore anything that doesn't suit.

Following and applying the simple exercises and instructions given above, can enable you to take care of yourself in a better, more holistic way, and by doing so you may well earn more money, or find the vocation you love rather than the dead-end job. Or not, who knows?

By committing to do something every day may help you form relationships, keep friends, and develop wider networks of interest and challenge.

Remember, the exercises are about improving the quality of your life, not about being a drudge or 'having to be done.'

They are all what you make of them.

Self service/selfless service

Any action you take can appear to be either in service of the self, or in service of others.

When you are developing your own personal or self-motivated plan you can seem to be focusing your attention inwards and selfishly. That is a judgement.

When you are serving others, putting other people's needs before yours, you can seem to be focusing your attention outwards, for the benefit of others. That is a judgement too.

As with all paradoxical (balanced) things, these two superficially separate and distinct actions are actually mutually supportive.

When you spend time developing yourself you are increasing your ability to help and serve others.

When you are being of service to others you are developing yourself.

Your life doesn't have to be one or the other.

What if you are struggling?

The key is consciousness. Bring the desired change to your attention, and seek opportunities to put it into practice. Don't beat yourself up. There is plenty of time. You are doing the best you can, at all times.

How do you document progress?

Whilst pursuing a busy lifestyle you don't seem to have much time for reflection. In order to live a more balanced life it is important to take time to reflect. This doesn't mean you lock yourself away in a cave for twenty years. It means you bring consciousness to your achievements and changes. You notice changes within and without.

The passing of the year, the dark days of winter, is a good time for reflection. In those months it can be quite shocking when you enumerate how much has changed over a twelve-month period. It is a good practice to list the changes, subtle, huge, vital, you have achieved in the preceding twelve months. You may keep a diary each day and this can be very useful to jog the memory as to what has actually changed.

In this reflection it is not so beneficial to then list all the changes you want to see happen in the forthcoming twelve months, as this may lead to disappointment and self-criticism.

Reflect on the positive changes you have achieved, not just work related, and then praise yourself. Reflection naturally leads to praise. It is very important that you praise yourself for the things you achieve. Give yourself a gift, honour yourself in small and big ways. It is amazing how infrequently you will do this.

The more often you praise yourself, the more frequently you are likely to praise other people. The reciprocity of 'gifting' is remarkable. The more often you praise others, the more they will praise you. That's not a bad habit to engender, not a bad muscle to keep exercising.

Exercise:
Make a list of recent positive changes you've made in your life in the last five years or so. They could include:

Starting a new relationship
Getting on better with relatives
Doing improvement work on house
Learning new skills at work
Gaining promotion

Then make a list of five things which have 'gone wrong' over the past ten years. They could include:

Breaking up with partner
Arguments with daughter
Moving and down-sizing house
Sticking in the same job
Being overlooked for promotion

See if there are links between the 'bad' and the 'good' events. More than likely there will be thin or very thick connections. Almost invariably, there will be benefits which have accrued from the, at first sight, negative events. Take your time to see the positive effects, the silver lining in the things that went 'wrong'.

Congratulate yourself, you've survived, you've turned things around.

How do you make ceremonies, rituals and rites of passage?

As part of the praise process you can create alternative ways of celebrating change that expand your consciousness. Ceremonies, rituals and rites of passage are symbolic and metaphoric markers, which humans have used for millions of years. They allow you to register change, to praise, love and honour, and mark the passage of time in a multi-layered way.

Exercise:

You can see on your calendar that Spring is starting, you can make a note of it in your diary.

Or you can go out into the countryside and observe for yourself how the snowdrops are now in flower, the daffodils are pressing up through the soil, the birds are starting to sing, the frogs have entered the pond.

Or you can create a ceremony that celebrates the symbolic coming of Spring with your friends. This may take the form of building a fire, creating an altar, singing some songs, having a dance. By doing these you are able to completely register and appreciate that Spring is coming.

You can feel and know it in your mind, consciousness and body. You 'know' things through your mind. Ceremonies and the like enable you to 'embody' them.

By creating symbolic events you are able to experience the world in a more holistic and diverse way. Such events also allow mystery and magic back into your life, they can deal with the impossible as well as the possible. Creating altars at home, or in nature, are a very simple way of remembering who you are. The ritual 'feeding' of them is a very beautiful and sustaining way of remembering what is important.

Exercise:

You can create a little altar to your family in your house by placing photos, objects, items on a neutral surface which will support them. Take your time arranging them, placing them in a way that pleases you.

It is best not to have this altar next to your bed. You want to honour your relatives, not have them in bed with you every night!

When you have an altar that pleases you, you can interact with it. You can say a little prayer to it every day. You can light a candle by it, burn some incense, whatever you feel is needed. The altar needs to be 'fed', and you will be in charge of what that means. You may need to change it, add things, take things away, as the unfolding story of your relationship with your family unfolds. A pleasing arrangement can often look untidy and messy six months later. You should clean it, dust it, refresh it, every now and again. A forgotten altar, covered in dust, is not working very well.

This subject is much larger than can be fitted easily into this section. Please know that whatever you do will be to the best of your ability.

How do you integrate all this information?

1   You can start by doing the first simple exercises on a regular and frequent basis each day:

Deepening the breath
Focusing on posture
Grounding and putting yourself into neutral
Allowing the internal messages to flow

None of these exercises in themselves are very time-consuming, you can do them simultaneously, and you can incorporate them into a ten-minute programme. If you repeat this two times a day then you are already starting to change.

Little steps lead the way to great changes.

2 You can then try to incorporate more complex exercises into your life, doing them maybe once a day:

Listening to the body
Owning and identifying the truth

You could use all of the above to create a personal self-discipline which you keep to each day. You could practice telling the truth and using I-statements for a while each day as well.

3 In order to progress the next two seem to be vital, they are essential for growth:

Spend 30 minutes per day for five days in moderate intensity physical activity.
Bring 'mindfulness' to the eating of one meal a day.

If you are doing all the previous and these two things each week, you will be changing. There will be a cumulative effect after just a couple of months. You will be starting to release your built up and old toxins. You will be positively affecting your body image and self worth. You be will increase your energy levels and overall health. Reducing dependencies and addictions.

4 Finally, you shouldn't forget to celebrate life and praise yourself:

Celebrate the coming of each season by arranging a dance, a meeting, or a ceremony four times in a year.

You could have a party once a year to celebrate who you are, and what you have achieved. All in all, these are not a huge commitment, but the benefits will be huge.

Brian: 'Stop worrying. Stop putting things off. The time is now. Become your full, whole, true, self. What else are you going to do? Right now. Right now.'

About the Author

Nick Clements runs a wide range of workshops, talks and one-to-one sessions for individuals, groups and companies all round the world. If you are interested in receiving information about his work, please contact: www.nick-clements.com

Roundfire Books put simply, publish great stories. Whether it's literary or popular, a gentle tale or a pulsating thriller, the connecting theme in all Roundfire fiction titles is that once you pick them up you won't want to put them down.